Reid—Vested Interest #4 by Melanie Moreland
Copyright © 2018 Moreland Books Inc.
Registration # 1150618
All rights reserved
ISBN: 1-988610-14-6

Edited by
D. Beck
Lisa Hollett, Silently Correcting Your Grammar

Cover design by
Melissa Ringuette, Monark Design Services

Interior Design & Formatting by
Christine Borgford, Type A Formatting

NEW YORK TIMES AND USA TODAY BESTSELLING AUTHOR
MELANIE MORELAND

DEDICATION

Family isn't always about blood. It's about love.
To my dear Mum-in-law, Valerie,
and my adopted sisters, Megan and Kay-
Thank you for being part of my life
and making me part of your family.
Your love and support mean so much.

And Matthew—always. Forever.

Eternal-E

CHAPTER 1

REID

I LIKED LISTS. I always had, even as a kid. They helped me focus. Even in the worst of places I lived, I could find a few scraps of paper and a pencil.

I would write out a list, then number what to do in priority. It gave me a sense of accomplishment when I could run a thick line through an item when it was completed. If I was lucky enough to have more paper, I could rewrite the list—smaller and more organized until I'd finished it.

Now, as an adult, I still liked lists. But with today's technology, I used my computer instead of paper, my keyboard instead of the stub of a pencil. With the click of my mouse, I could sort, organize, remove, and reprioritize my items.

I stared at my computer, looking over my latest list. I called it Project B.

Learn to talk to Becca like a man instead of a stuttering idiot

Get Becca to notice me as a man—not as the company IT boy

Finish the new program I developed for Becca so she falls in love with me

Ask Becca out on a date

Send Becca flowers

Buy Becca coffee

Kiss Becca

Lose my virginity to Becca

I pursed my lips and moved buying Becca coffee into second place. I wondered if I should send her flowers before or after the program installation. Once she saw what it could do for her, she might be the one sending *me* flowers. Perhaps she'd throw in a kiss or two. I was certain she'd say yes to a date.

I wasn't sure she'd go for the helping me lose my virginity thing. I probably had to work up to that idea.

I saved the file to my private drive, knowing I needed to concentrate on Bentley's latest request. I would return to my list once I had his requests done.

I tugged off my glasses and rubbed my tired eyes. I had pulled another all-nighter. Between all the ideas for Ridge Towers, the new programs I was working on for control freak Maddox, ensuring the security protocols were current for big-ass Aiden, and our systems were safe and impenetrable for overanxious Bentley, my days were full.

On top of that, I had to add in Becca detail. She sat less than twenty feet away from me, separated solely by a wall, yet it might as well have been twenty miles.

From the moment I had rushed into the boardroom, late and disheveled, planning simply to give my excuses and leave, I was entranced.

She sat in my usual spot at the boardroom table, a small intruder in my space. She gazed at me, her eyes wide with surprise. I knew I looked worse than usual and I should leave, but my feet carried me forward, and I sat across from her.

She was the prettiest woman I had ever seen—rich, dark brown hair, creamy skin, and brilliant blue eyes that captured my attention. She was dressed in a business suit, her hair perfect, understated makeup, and her small laptop open, a notebook and pen at the ready, a professional woman prepared to do business. Yet, there was a softness to her gaze, and her smile was warm, even a touch shy.

She was incredibly sexy.

So sexy, I almost missed my chair when I sat down. I was lucky Aiden saved me from that embarrassment. I was doing well enough on my own in that department. I couldn't tear my eyes away from her. More than once, I had to adjust myself discreetly under the table, grateful Bentley preferred wood to glass. My dick liked what he saw—more than liked.

That day, he decided she was what we had been waiting for all my life.

As I discovered, talking business with her was easy. She was intelligent, understood computers and the lingo. She asked smart questions, made notes she often referred to, listened carefully to my replies. But it was when business was done and she became Becca, the *girl*, I became Reid, the *loser*.

I had so much I wanted to say to her, but I found I couldn't say *anything*. There was this disconnect between my brain and my mouth. I could barely form a sentence in her presence.

I ran a hand over my face. My behavior hadn't changed much since she arrived. The only smooth interactions we had together were business-related. In meetings, we were on the same page. When she came to my office to ask a question, I could answer her without hesitation. Yesterday, she had told me about her dream report.

"One where I could have all the information about a campaign in the same place," she mused. "It would make my life so much easier."

My ears perked up. Anything to make her life easier was something I was interested in. I grabbed a piece of paper. "Tell me."

"I have to go to every site, and collect the click rates, follow-throughs, page views, etc. For print, I have to wait for the numbers to be sent and then download them. I would love something that took all that information and put it in one place. Then I could compare and analyze things so much faster."

I jotted down notes, my mind already working. "Can you send me examples?"

Her eyes glowed. "Really? You could do that?"

It was going to take a huge amount of work.

I met her gaze. "For you, yes."

Her smile was brilliant. I felt as if I had won the lottery.

But once the conversation was over, as usual, my throat dried up, and all I could do was to stare at her.

Wanting. Longing. Silent.

She smiled and left before the right words hit me. But it was too late.

I was always too fucking late.

I flipped open the cover of the thick file folder on my desk. I had been working on breaking down Bentley's notes, making my own list so I could ensure it all happened for him in the timeframe he wanted and the order he needed it done.

I clicked the icon for his list, scanning what I had typed earlier. Heavy footsteps made me glance toward the sound. Aiden stood in the doorway, his massive shoulders filling the space. He looked as if he was on the borderline of losing it. I stiffened at his words.

"Got a minute?"

Aiden was never that polite, not unless there was something wrong. "Yeah."

He entered and closed the door, ramping up my anxiety. He never shut the door.

He sat across from me, silent for a moment.

"What's up?"

He swallowed, meeting my eyes. "So Bentley asked me to come and talk to you."

"About?"

"You, ah, well . . ."

My stomach fell. "Are you firing me?"

"*No*. Absolutely not," he responded vehemently. "Not a chance."

I relaxed somewhat. "Okay, what's up?"

He lost it and bent forward, burying his face in his hands, his shoulders shaking with laughter.

I stared at him, unsure what the hell was so funny.

He leaned back, wiping his face. "Reid, dude. You need to get out of this office. Get some sleep. You were here all night again, weren't you?"

"Yeah. Why?"

He began to chuckle again. "Maddox and I were meeting with Bent. We all got a notice about a new checklist."

I glanced at my screen with a frown. "I wasn't finished with Bentley's file—I didn't send . . ." My voice trailed off as realization hit me. "Oh, holy fuck."

"As much as we appreciate being kept in the loop on your personal endeavors, Bent really doesn't want to know about your plans to have Becca punch your V-card."

I shut my eyes, actually embarrassed—which was a rare occurrence for me. Instead of saving my list privately, I had shared it on the drive with my bosses—all three of them.

"How angry is Bentley?" I asked, unable to look at Aiden.

Bentley's temper didn't explode often, but when it did, it was like a volcano erupting. You got out of the way as fast as possible.

"You know that sound he makes when he can't speak? The odd choking noise in his throat? The way his eye starts to twitch a little?"

I nodded, unable to speak myself.

"He did that. Twice."

"Fuck," I repeated.

"Well, obviously that's your end game, but Reid, dude . . . a list?"

"It's how I plan. I write shit out." I sucked in a big breath. "And get myself fired, it would seem."

Aiden chuckled. "Nah, you're good. We were all a little stunned, until Maddox started to laugh. I was so entertained, I fell out of my chair. Bentley saw the humor, and we all howled. However, he lectured me about your irresponsible behavior and sent me in here to 'sort you out,' even though he was still laughing when I left his office."

I exhaled hard. I had dodged a bullet there. I met Aiden's gaze. He was relaxed but serious.

"He was rather amused but also relieved you didn't save it on the company's shared drive. Our conversation would have been vastly different, and I would have had HR in here with me. He wants you to erase the list, immediately, and is requesting any further personal item lists like that be made in the privacy of your own home."

My heart stuttered at the thought that Becca would have seen it. Everyone would have seen it. My exhaustion was making me careless. And yes, irresponsible.

"Holy shit," I breathed out. "That would have been a disaster." I pulled my laptop close, my fingers a blur as I typed away. "Okay. It's in my private drive. I removed it from our shared one."

"Good."

"It won't happen again."

He smiled in understanding. "I know, Reid." He studied me. "If you're serious about Becca, you need to step it up."

"I'm trying."

"She's just a girl. Talk to her. Ask her for coffee."

I shook my head. "She's not *just* a girl, Aiden. I think she's the one."

His brow furrowed. "The one to be your first, or the one to be your last?"

"All of it."

He reclined in his chair, crossing his leg over his knee. "That's a pretty huge statement considering you can't talk to her unless it's work-related."

"She boggles my mind. It's as if I freeze."

"So, find common ground besides work. Drop into her office to say hi. Take her a coffee. Tell her how much you like her cookies. Offer to show her Toronto the way you wanted to when you found out she was moving here. Make a move."

"I know it sounds easy. It's only . . ."

"Only?" he prompted.

"I'm-I'm not sure I'm good enough for her."

"Because of your past?"

"I'm an ex-con. It makes life difficult. I have no family, nothing really to offer her except a great comic book collection and some vintage T-shirts. She deserves better."

He shook his head, his frustration evident. "Why don't you let her decide what she deserves? Let her get to know you, and you her. Stop looking at your endgame and take it a step at a time. You're putting unnecessary pressure on yourself. Live in the moment."

"Good advice."

"You're a great guy, Reid. As I've learned, your past is that. Past. You can't change it, but you can move forward. Don't make my mistake and let it define you."

I nodded, knowing he was talking about his recent marriage to Cami and the way she had changed him.

"And you do have family," he added, his voice low and serious. "You have us. You're a valuable part of our team, and you should be proud. You have fought your whole life and accomplished a lot. Don't forget that."

I blinked. Aiden rarely got personal, and his words meant a great deal to me.

He stood and went to the door, his hand on the knob, but he didn't turn it.

"And because we have to put our two cents in, we all agree. Buy her a coffee, have a conversation, ask her out, then send flowers. The rest will follow. Although, to be honest, Bent thinks flowers are always appropriate." He winked. "But don't go overboard."

I laughed. "Okay."

"I think you might find her as interested as you are, Reid. I'm just saying."

With a wink, he left, making me wonder what he knew that I didn't.

I looked at my computer, then glanced toward my door. I needed to talk to Becca and get both of us comfortable.

I knew only one way to accomplish it.

With a few swipes of my mouse, and some fast typing, I put my plan in motion.

I sat back and waited.

CHAPTER 2

REID

A SOFT KNOCK at my door made me glance up from my screen. Becca stood in the doorway, professional and polished. Her dark hair was up in a knot, her deep gray suit unwrinkled, the skirt hitting her knee modestly. My gaze was drawn to her heels. They were red and sleek, an unexpected sexy twist to her outfit. They made her legs look incredible.

I wondered how they would look wrapped around my waist.

She frowned, and I realized I had been staring. Again.

"Sorry. What's up?"

"I'm not sure. I was working, and my computer froze. I can't get to my document, and it won't allow me to reboot."

I hid my smile. "Odd." I held out my hand for her laptop. "Let me have a look."

She sat across from me. "I hope you can fix it. I was so busy, I hadn't saved the document."

"I have everyone's laptop set to autosave every two minutes," I assured her. "In fact, yours saves every sixty seconds. You'll never lose your work." I had made sure of that when I set up her computer. I added every safety feature and backup I could possibly cram into it.

She leaned on my desk, resting her hand on her chin. "You are so awesome."

My gaze flickered between her face and her chest. The way she sat pushed her breasts together. They were *right there*. Plump and inviting, the rounded orbs peeked out from between the silky folds of her blouse. Was she aware of what she was doing to me?

God, I wanted to touch them. Kiss them. See if her nipples were pink or rose-colored. If they became hard under my tongue, and if she shivered when I licked them.

I tore my gaze away, shaking my head at my dirty thoughts. It was as though I had a one-track mind when it came to Becca. I saw her, and all I wanted to do was touch her.

I tapped the keys, clearing the problem. With a smile, I handed her back the laptop. "All fixed."

"That fast?"

I shrugged. "Only a little glitch."

She shook her head. "I tried everything I knew of to fix it."

I winked at her. "It's why they pay me the big bucks."

She laughed, a soft and inviting sound. "I'm sure you're worth it."

She looked around my office. I followed her gaze, wondering what she saw. I had tried to tidy it lately. It was still messy, but better than it had been. At least, I had gotten rid of all the empty food containers.

"You're not a normal geek."

My eyebrows shot up. "Sorry?"

She grinned. "You don't have action figurines or a comic book collection lying around. No gaming posters or autographed memorabilia."

"They're all at home," I deadpanned. "All twelve of my collections. I keep them under glass. I don't want people touching my things."

She stared at me. Blinked. A flush started at her neck. It was fascinating to watch it spread, her cream-colored skin turning pink and warm. She looked mortified.

"I-I'm sorry," she stuttered. "I was teasing. I'm sure they're all very nice."

I leaped to my feet, hurrying around the desk. I kneeled beside her, horrified I had upset her. "Jesus, I'm an ass. I was the one teasing, Becca." I grabbed her hand and squeezed it, noticing how warm her skin was under mine. "I don't have any collections except some comic books—and I have those because I like to read them, and I never got one as a kid."

"Never?"

"No," I stated, hoping she didn't ask any more questions. "So, I have some now. And computers. I love taking them apart and rebuilding them."

She let out a long breath. "Oh. So, you aren't angry with me?"

I stared at her. Her eyes were so blue they reminded me of a picture I had seen of a sunlit ocean. But her gaze was worried, overcast like a cloud drifting across the water.

"No, Becca. I'm not angry." I leaned a little closer, unsure why I was doing so. "I could never be angry with you."

"Okay," she breathed out.

"I'm sorry I upset you."

She gripped my hand. I hadn't even realized I was still holding hers in mine. "It's all good. Right?"

"Right."

I glanced at her lips. She stared at mine. Her breath caught. I felt as if an invisible string was drawing me in. I pushed closer, wanting, needing something.

Her.

"Reid!" Aiden's voice boomed out from the hall. "What the hell is up with the six pizzas that arrived at the front desk? On my credit card, no less!"

Becca and I stood, backing away from each other, the moment broken. Our hands separated, and I felt the loss immediately. She smiled sadly. I hated her looking that way.

"Want some pizza?" I asked, wanting to make her smile.

"Did you really order pizza on his credit card?"

"He said he wanted some earlier. I only saved us time." I shrugged. "He'll eat most of it anyway. He always does."

Aiden appeared in my doorway, a huge slice held in one hand, a pizza box in the other one. He narrowed his eyes as he studied us, then grinned.

"Next time, it's on Maddox."

"Okay."

"I put the rest in the lunchroom. Help yourself."

"You're only taking one?" I asked sarcastically.

"Cami is limiting my carbs."

I snorted, and he grinned. "I gave you fair warning, Reid. Once I finish this one, all bets are off!"

He disappeared down the hall, laughing.

I indicated the door to Becca.

"You heard him. Go grab some."

"Are you coming?" she asked.

"I'll be right behind you. I need to close what I was working on."

She walked away, and I followed her movements with my eyes. I sat down heavily in the chair where she'd been sitting.

If Aiden hadn't interrupted, would I have had the balls to kiss her? Did she want me to?

I had no idea. Even worse, I had no clue how to figure it out.

⌒

MADDOX STROLLED INTO my office, Aiden on his heels. Maddox glanced around, his eyebrows rising as he took in the unusual neatness of my area. I had done a complete overhaul of my office after Becca had been there. Sandy had been shocked and delighted when she saw it that morning. She was even happier when I asked her to help me pick out some more new shirts and pants. It was easy to make the old broad smile.

The added touch was the framed Yoda poster I'd bought and

hung across from my desk, hoping to make Becca laugh the next time she came in. She hadn't seen it yet, but I knew she'd be around soon enough. Her glitch was set to go off in a couple of hours.

Maddox sat down, crossing his legs. "Turning over a new leaf, Reid?"

Aiden pushed my door shut and flopped into the other chair. The legs groaned in protest. "I think he's trying to impress a certain pretty marketing manager."

I rolled my eyes, though I knew my ears were turning red. "Whatever. I cleaned a little."

"How long did it take you?" Maddox asked with a grin.

"All night. I found my wallet I thought I had lost. It still had fifty bucks in it."

Aiden high-fived me.

"Great poster." He jerked his thumb toward Yoda. "I love the little green guy."

Maddox rolled his eyes. "Please don't do your imitation. It's scary."

"Whatever. Just jealous you are, mmm-hmm," Aiden quipped, his voice making my eyes widen.

"Dude, no," I groaned.

He shook his head. "Appreciation for my talent, you have not, mmm-hmm."

Maddox smacked his head. "No, you have no talent. You sound as though you're about to expectorate."

I chuckled watching them. They glared at each other, then joined my laughter.

I slouched in my chair. "So, what's up?" I glanced toward my screen. "I haven't sent the wrong shit out again, have I?"

Aiden chuckled, while Maddox shook his head. "No," he said. "I've been thinking about having you install the security program at another place."

"Oh yeah? Cool. I think I've got all the bugs worked out, but more feedback would be awesome. I want it perfect for Ridge Towers." I dug around and found a pen. "Where?"

"The apartment Becca is renting from me," Maddox stated.

My head snapped up, and I met his eyes. He was regarding me closely, his expression serious, but his eyes were amused. "We thought, perhaps, your time would be better spent using a direct approach, rather than fixing her computer every day." He arched a knowing eyebrow in my direction.

"Um . . ." I swallowed. She'd had to come see me many times last week. We hadn't had another moment the way we did the first day, but I kept hoping. The problem was I kept freezing and my brain couldn't come up with the words, and the silence became awkward.

"There have been a lot of glitches with the machine," I said, the words lame.

"*Glitches?*" Maddox laughed. "I work across the hall from the two of you. She is in here daily with a problem, or you're trotting down the hall to her office to help fix something. If the machine has that many problems, we should simply get a new one."

"No! I've got it handled."

Aiden stroked his chin. "Strangest thing too, I can't find a single ticket in the system about Becca's constant computer trouble."

"Oh yeah, well . . ." I rubbed the back of my neck. "It's easier to help her out, rather than crowd the system with tickets."

Aiden's head fell back, his laughter booming out in my office. "Crowd the system? Reid, since you came on board, we have no tickets. No downtime. No errors." He wiped his eyes. "Fess up, boy. What are you doing?"

I sighed. "I send little viruses to freeze her computer so she has to come see me. I wanted to take the time she's here to talk to her."

"And how's that working for you?"

I tossed my glasses onto my desk. "It's not."

Maddox leaned forward. "You are such a wimp."

"I know."

"You talk to Sandy. You talk to Liv. All the other females in the office. Why can't you talk to Becca?"

"I can talk to the rest of them because I'm not imagining their mouths wrapped around my dick every second of the conversation! I don't think about how I want to throw them on their desk and bury myself inside of them to see if it would be as fucking awesome as I dream it would be!" I burst out, slamming my hand on my desk.

They both gaped at me. Maddox glanced down, fighting his smile, but Aiden's grin was wide. "You are so fucked."

"Well, I want to be," I muttered.

"You got it bad."

"Tell me about it. My fucking hand is sore, and I keep running out of lotion."

"TMI," Maddox drawled.

Aiden hunched closer. "Okay. Listen up. Maddox is going to tell Becca he wants to install the system at her place. You're going to arrange a time suitable to her. You are going to show up and bring her a coffee. Smile at her. Chat as you're working, the way you chatted with Cami while you set up my place. Think with your big head, not the little one."

I met his eyes. "It's not little. Trust me."

He groaned. "Whatever."

Maddox snorted. "The point here is, be yourself. She likes you. You like her. Get to know her as a person. Let her see Reid outside the office."

"How do you know she likes me?"

Maddox rolled his eyes. "Why do I feel as if we're twelve and passing notes at school? She asked me about you once. I got the feeling she was interested. But she's a cautious young woman. So unless she thinks you feel the same way, she is not going to approach you." He stood. "Man up. I'll go let her know, and the rest is up to you."

He walked out of the office, leaving me with Aiden.

"He's right. Stop playing around. You want this girl? Go for it. I know this is all new to you, but the fact is, only you can do this, Reid."

"You're right. I've been an idiot."

"Yep." He walked to my door. "Now, go get your girl."

A FEW HOURS later, I stopped in the doorway of Becca's office. She was busy, her attention on her screen, her hand using the mouse to create some visual. Her brow was furrowed in concentration, and the tip of her tongue peeked out between her lips. I had to swallow, imagining how much I wanted her tongue in my mouth.

I studied her quietly, taking in her professional appearance. Not a hair out of place, her suit unwrinkled, her makeup light. Her office was organized, her desk precise. She even had a coaster under her cup of coffee. She wore a pair of reading glasses, the half-moon frames highlighting her bright blue eyes, making her even prettier.

Not to mention sexy. She was so sexy it made my heart race.

I glanced down at my black jeans and blue button-down. Self-consciously, I patted down my hair. I knew it was all over the place. Compared to her, I resembled an unmade bed, as Bentley often referred to me. Could she possibly be interested in someone like me?

I raised my hand to knock when she glanced up. Her eyes met mine, and for a moment, nothing existed but her and the hypnotic spell she had on me. She smiled, wide and sweet, the dimple in her chin clear.

"Hi."

I shook my head to clear it. "Um, yeah. Hi."

She leaned back, the movement causing her blouse to tighten across her chest. I tried not to stare at her breasts.

I failed.

She cleared her throat, and I snapped my gaze back to her face.

"So Maddox asked me to install the security system at your place?" I asked. I was shocked to hear how steady my voice sounded.

She nodded. "He told me you would be coming by."

I stepped in, edging my way to her desk. "Is that good for you?"

Let it be good for you, I pleaded silently.

"How long do you need?"

I shrugged. I could easily drag it out to a day or two. "I need to scope out the apartment first. Check the door and windows for the right layout. See what would work best. Map it all out and make sure I bring all the right equipment. The install is only a few hours, barring any complications."

I planned on there being lots of complications.

"Okay. So you need to drop by one night and do the install another day?"

"Yeah. How about tonight? I could swing by and get any info I need, and we'll go from there?" I faltered, remembering it was Friday. "Unless, of course, you have plans."

Please don't have plans.

Relief flooded through me when she shook her head. "Nope. Tonight is good."

"Great."

"You don't, ah, have a date?"

I wanted to snort. I hadn't had a date in a couple of years. The last one was such a disaster that I decided to stop trying.

"No."

"Okay, so tonight works. What day is best for the install?"

"Once I figure out what the best setup is for you, I have to get all the pieces ordered in. Next weekend should work. Saturday is best," I stated firmly. I could have her all to myself for the day if I played my cards right. "I like to come early in the morning."

Her eyes grew round.

Realizing what I had said, I grabbed the back of my hair, yanking on it in frustration. "I mean, I prefer to start early." I gripped my hair again. "In case there are any issues," I finished lamely.

I expected her to laugh. Or throw me out of her office. Instead, she smiled. "Saturday is fine."

"Okay, great." I began to leave her office. "I'll see you tonight."

"Reid." Her voice stopped me.

"Yeah?"

"Don't you need to know where I live?"

I wanted to laugh. I knew exactly where she lived. I might have been in the neighborhood a couple of times, hoping to bump into her.

Because I had turned into a Becca stalker. A fumbling, idiot of a stalker.

I smiled, offering her a half-truth. "Maddox gave me the address."

"All right. I'll see you tonight." She smirked. "If not before."

I couldn't resist. "It's a date."

I hurried away.

 ⌒

TIME DRAGGED ON until I could finally go to Becca's apartment. I was edgy at work all afternoon, and I didn't mess with her computer. I needed to play it cool. If that was possible.

She had dropped by my office to confirm the time, laughing in delight over my poster.

"Yoda is the best, he is," she quipped looking far cuter than Aiden while doing her imitation. She winked before leaving. "I think you got that just for me, Reid Matthews."

I didn't deny her words. I was too busy searching the internet looking for other Yoda merchandise to make her smile.

I gathered my stuff, shoving it into my messenger bag. I had changed my shirt, brushed my hair, yet when I looked in the mirror I was still a mess. I needed to ask Maddox how he always managed to look so . . . unwrinkled. However, I decided against it. He might try to take me shopping. Maybe I would ask Sandy—she loved looking after me, and she would be all over giving me advice.

I walked to Becca's, stopping to grab coffee on the way. The little corner shop next door to the coffee place had buckets of flowers outside. I gazed at them, wondering if Bentley was right about when to give flowers, or if I should listen to Aiden. A stooped, old woman wearing an apron, with her gray hair piled high on her head, shuffled outside and offered me a smile.

"You like?" she asked, her English fragmented.

"They are pretty."

"For your girlfriend?"

I sighed. "I wish. Just a friend, unfortunately."

She gave me a huge smile, the movement deepening the wrinkles in her face. Reaching up, she patted my cheek. "Give it time. You a good-looking boy."

I chuckled.

She bent and plucked a small bunch of daisies from a bucket. "Here. Bright. Pretty. Not too much, yes? To say have a nice day." She winked. "Soon, you bring her roses. I promise."

I laughed and handed her the five dollars the sign displayed for the flowers. I wasn't going to argue with her logic. I liked it. I didn't know if Becca liked roses, but I was willing to find out. I'd bring her any kind of flower she liked.

Have a nice day. That worked.

The intercom was full of static, but Becca knew who it was and buzzed me up to her apartment. When she opened the door, she looked so different from how she did at the office, and I tried not to gape. I certainly stared. Her hair was long and loose, cascading down her back like a ribbon of dark silk. She wore leggings and a T-shirt that hugged her curves. Her feet were bare, the toenails bright red.

Her eyes widened with delight when she saw the flowers. "For me?"

I couldn't resist teasing her. "No, I was gonna take them home— give the place some ambiance, you know?"

She blinked, her cheeks coloring, and the odd shyness I'd caught glimpses of appeared. I liked knowing I could bring that out in her. It made me braver than normal.

I thrust the small bouquet toward her. "Sorry, I was teasing again. Yes, for you."

"Why?"

I shrugged. "To make you smile."

"Reid," she breathed out. "How incredibly thoughtful. I love them!" She leaned up on her toes and brushed a kiss to my cheek. The gesture was sweet, and I enjoyed how her lips felt on me. I wanted to feel them all over me. She was close enough I could smell the scent of her skin—it was light and airy, reminding me of flowers and sun. I resisted sniffing her.

"Come in."

I followed her in, trying not to notice how the leggings clung to her perky ass and toned legs. It was impossible. It was a great ass. My cock agreed with me and I had to adjust myself before she turned around.

I set down my bag and took in her apartment. The kitchen was small but nice, the living area a good size. The kitchen was open, separated with a tall counter, and she had two stools tucked underneath. There was a small sofa in front of the window with a chair beside it. A little table sat in the corner, and she had a compact desk. Leaning against the wall were some shelves, the brackets on the floor. The rest of the room was empty.

"I'm still unpacking," she explained. "I left the things I dislike to the last."

"You dislike?"

"Putting up the shelves, hanging pictures. When I use a hammer, I seem to hit my thumb more often than the nail."

I grabbed the opportunity and indicated the shelves. "Do you need some help to put those up?"

Her eyes glowed, making her blue irises brilliant.

"Really?"

"Sure, I can do that." I glanced around. "Hang your pictures, hook up your electronics. That sort of thing." I met her gaze. "I'm your guy."

For everything, I added in my head.

She wrinkled her nose, which made her look adorable. "I don't have many electronics."

I gaped at her. "What?"

"It's so complicated. I rarely watch TV, so I don't have one yet." She tapped a component sitting on the counter. "I enjoy music. I use my Bose system a lot."

"What about streaming? Netflix?" I loved my computers, but nothing beat watching a movie or TV show on the big screen.

She grimaced, pulling open a cabinet and taking out a small vase. "I'm great with computers and software, but to be honest, electronics overwhelm me. If there is a show I enjoy, I stream it on my laptop." She filled the vase with water, adding the flowers. Smiling, she set them on the counter.

"I can't remember the last time someone gave me flowers. My dad, probably. These are so pretty!"

I felt about ten feet tall.

"I could hook it all to your TV once you buy one." I pointed to the empty space in her living room. "I could also set up a sweet system. You have lots of space."

"Oh, ah, I have something coming that will take up a lot of room."

"You do have some electronics?"

"Um, no. I gave up. If I wanted to watch a movie, I usually went to Richard and Katy's place."

"You're pretty close to them?"

"Yes. I miss them already."

I looked down as I spoke. "I'm glad you're here, though."

She covered my hand with hers, squeezing it. "Thank you. I'm glad too."

Our gazes met, holding in silence.

It was the perfect chance. I could ask her if she wanted me to take her around, show her Toronto. Spend some time getting to know me. But the words died before I could speak them. Then she glanced away, and the moment was gone.

Clearing my throat, I picked up a cup, took off the lid, and sipped at the coffee. "Okay, we can figure something out." I handed her the other cup. "Just tell me what you need."

"Thanks."

"Anytime."

I grabbed my messenger bag, a notebook, and a pen. "Can I take some measurements and look around?"

"Yes."

A buzzer went off, and for the first time, I noticed the aroma in the kitchen.

I inhaled deeply. "Do I smell peanut butter?"

Becca smiled and slid a tray from the oven. "Cookies for when you're done. To say thank you."

I eyed the tray, but she laughed, waving me away. "Too hot. Do your work, then you can eat them."

"Okay."

I RETURNED TO the living room. Becca was at the counter, tapping on her laptop. A plate of cookies sat beside her. I reached over, snagged one, and took a bite.

"Oh God, these are amazing. Peanut butter is my favorite."

"Good."

I pulled out the other stool. "May I?"

She laughed. "Of course."

She pushed a bottle of water my way. "Got everything you needed?"

"Yeah. I'll change the lock for the same kind we have in Ridge Towers. The camera is wireless. I'll need to add the software to your laptop and phone for you. You can control it, look to see who is at your door, unlock it remotely. It's a good lock too. You'll be safe."

"Is that all it does?"

"No, it has a lot of features. Maddox's connects to his concierge desk, and he can talk to them directly, have deliveries sent straight up, check out visitors. I'll set it up so you can use your phone to buzz people in from the front door."

She chuckled, reaching for a cookie. "I'll never get off the sofa."

I snagged another cookie. "Once we figure out what you want, I can set up a bunch of features for your electronics and your music.

Some wireless speakers would work well in here."

"That would be awesome, but I don't want to take advantage."

I wanted her to take advantage. Especially of me. In every way possible. I cleared my throat and shifted on the stool. "Nope. I offered, and I meant it."

"Thank you, Reid." She bit down on her cookie, a few crumbs sticking to her mouth. She swept her tongue over her bottom lip, and I had to bite back my groan.

I wanted to kiss her.

She tilted her head. "Are you okay?"

"Yeah, I'm fine." Desperate to change the subject, I waved toward the shelves. "Do I need to bring stuff over to hang those?"

"I have a little toolbox my dad insisted I should own. There's no drill though, and I'm not sure I have the things that hold them up."

"You mean anchors?"

"Yes."

"I can bring those and a drill. And we'll need a level. I have all that."

Or I would once I went to the hardware store.

"Are you sure?"

I bobbed my head in agreement. "Yep. When would you like me to hang them?"

"Oh, whenever you have time."

"I can swing by on the weekend. Tomorrow works, if you're free."

She frowned. "That's two of your Saturdays I would be taking. You must have plans . . . with your girlfriend . . . ?" She let the words trail off, not meeting my eyes.

"No. No girlfriend."

"Oh." That was all she said, but I noticed the way her mouth curled at the corners, as if she was fighting a smile.

"I-I won't be interfering with your, ah, significant other coming to visit?" I asked, my throat dry. "No. There isn't one."

We both smiled, our eyes locking. Her gaze skittered away, the light flush appearing on her cheeks once more. I had to stop myself from reaching over to feel if her skin was warm.

"So what do you have coming for this spot?" I asked, indicating the empty space behind me. "A dining room table or something?"

She bit her lip, leaning her chin on the palm of her hand. "No, I'm good with the counter. I don't do dinner parties."

"A new desk?"

"No," she repeated. "I use the space for exercise."

"Oh, like yoga?" I knew Cami, Emmy, and Dee had taken up yoga recently.

She tilted her head, studying me as I took a large mouthful of my water.

"No, I use a stripper pole."

My throat closed, mid-swallow.

Until that very moment, I had no idea how far I could spray water.

Apparently, it was really far.

CHAPTER 3

REID

I CHECKED THE contents of my bag, yanking the zipper shut. I had enough screws, nails, and anchors to hang the contents of a museum. My drill and level would be well used today. I glanced at my watch, wondering if eight a.m. was too early to show up at Becca's apartment.

After I had imitated a fountain the previous night, she had scrambled off the stool, grabbed a towel for me, and patted me on the back as I choked.

"I'm so sorry," she exclaimed. "I didn't mean to!"

I drew in some much-needed oxygen and mopped the counter in front of me. "No problem. I wasn't expecting the joke. My bad." I glanced at her. "Did I get you?"

She shook her head, eyes dancing. "No."

"Good."

She shrugged. "Even if you had, it's only water. What's a little spit between friends?"

Luckily, my bottle was only partway to my lips, or I would have choked again. I had to bite my tongue in order not to tell her I would like to trade spit

with her. Instead, I cleared my throat and swallowed the last of my water. I
slid off the stool, wiping my hand down my damp shirt.

"I'll see you tomorrow. What time is good?"

"I'm here all day, so whenever."

I left before I could embarrass myself further. Her unexpected remark caused a flurry of images to go through my head. The vision of Becca on a stripper pole became a constant loop in my mind. I knew she had no idea her teasing would result in a barrage of fantasies starring her, but I couldn't help it.

Deciding it was too early, I tidied my small apartment. It wasn't much, but it was close to the office, and when I rented it, it seemed like a palace. I had never had my own space before. Growing up in foster homes and ending up in prison pretty much guaranteed a lack of privacy.

It was a simple, basic setup—one room, with a kitchen at one end, and a futon I used as both a couch and a bed at the other end. The bathroom was by the entrance door, and it held a toilet, sink, and shower. All old and chipped, but serviceable. The walls were plain beige, with only a couple of posters hung to break the monotony of the space.

In the middle of the room, under the one window, was the desk I'd made from old cinder blocks I had dragged home and a heavy slab of wood. On either side were compact, heavy, steel shelves filled with computers and parts. My one extravagance, the TV, hung on the wall, and a nicer set of shelves held my comic books. I hadn't been joking when I told Becca I loved them. They were something I longed for as a child, and now I could buy them. I'd added some shelves to the cupboard at the front, and it served as a dresser and a place for my coat. I rarely had visitors. I lived simply, and until today, it never mattered. But as I studied the space, I knew I didn't want Becca to see it. She wouldn't judge me, but it was lifeless—a spot I used to sleep and change.

There was no doubt that I preferred my office at BAM. I was thrilled when I was given a chance with them. I had read about BAM in the paper, checked them out online, and one day, saw a listing on a jobsite for their IT department. I found the courage and took a resume to the office directly. Sandy had been at her desk, Aiden talking to her when I approached them. I waited until their conversation ceased, then asked politely if I could leave my resume with her.

Aiden frowned. "There's a website to file an application."

"I know. I did that as well. But I wanted to give you one in person."

He studied me. I knew who he was—I had seen his picture in the paper many times, and I'd followed the growth of their company while I was in prison. I held his gaze and was relieved when he extended his large hand.

"I'll take it."

"Thank you, Mr. Callaghan."

"You know my name?"

"Of course. I'm sure you'll check me out—I did the same so I would know who I'd be working for," I replied with a grin, faking the cocky assurance.

He chuckled. "Nice one, kid."

Sandy cursed as she tapped on her keyboard. "This is frozen again, Aiden. Every time I'm in this program, it happens."

He groaned. "I've done everything I can do. We'll get a new machine."

The words were out before I could stop them. "It's not the machine. Let me try."

I was sure he would refuse, but he stood back with a wave of his hand. I sat down, and in seconds, was into the system, scanning the files, and finding the problem. With a few strokes of the keys, I fixed it. Standing, I smiled. "Done. It should be fine now."

"What did you do?"

"There's a glitch I knew about. It's common and simply needs an override. You shouldn't have any more problems."

Aiden frowned. "My IT guys should have known that."

I shrugged. "It's something I picked up online."

"Thank you, young man." Sandy beamed at me.

"Reid," I said, extending my hand. "My name is Reid Matthews."

She shook my hand. "Well, Reid Matthews, I appreciate it. I'm Sandy, the real brains behind this operation." She winked. "Now, I suggest you head down the street and get a haircut. You need to look good for your interview."

I blinked. "My interview?"

She glanced at Aiden with a nod. "Tomorrow. Two o'clock. Right, Aiden?"

He grinned. "Right."

And that was how it all started. I was nervous about the interview and wore my best clothes, which, in retrospect were not great, but they were all I had. I cut my hair myself since I didn't have the money to have it done. I interviewed with Aiden, his questions direct and fast. I answered them all easily.

He sat back, tapping my resume. "You certainly seem qualified."

"I am. I would do an excellent job for you."

"You haven't worked much. The job you have is very limited for your obvious knowledge. It doesn't play to your strengths."

I wanted to laugh. A repair guy in a questionable computer shop was hardly even a job. I could barely make ends meet. I worked as a bartender to help fill the gap, but I hated both jobs.

"I know. I want to do more. If you give me the chance, I won't let you down."

"You took a lot of your courses online. Can I ask why?"

This was when every interview fell apart. I took in a deep breath. "Because I took them from prison."

He nodded, and I knew he had already discovered that information. He was simply checking to see if I was going to be honest. "What were you in prison for?"

I was sure he knew that too, but I answered. "I went to jail because, allegedly, I stole fifteen million dollars from a bank."

His eyebrow quirked. "Allegedly?"

"Look, Mr. Callaghan—"

He held up his hand. "Aiden. I told you to call me Aiden. We aren't formal at BAM."

It gave me hope that he hadn't stood and ended the interview. That was what usually happened.

"Okay, Aiden. I was young and stupid, and trying to prove myself. I spent a lot of time on the internet. I was checking out a problem for a friend, and I noticed something odd. After I did some checking and a bunch of tests, I went to the bank and told them about a hole I found in their online program and the fact that I had the solution. They laughed at me, which really wasn't surprising since I was a kid. They refused to listen."

Aiden leaned forward, interested. "What did you do?"

"I hacked in to their system and sucked fifteen million from them and put it in an account elsewhere—I never planned to keep it. I sat back and waited for them to come to me so I could show them how it happened and what they needed to do to stop it happening again. I planned to give the money back. As I said, I was young and stupid. I thought they would be thrilled at my ingenuity and offer me a job."

Aiden began to laugh. "That's not what happened, I'm guessing."

"Nope. I was arrested on a bunch of cyber-based crime charges. They threw the book at me to set an example, and I spent four years in prison, finally getting out with good behavior."

"Did you return the money?"

"Yes."

"That didn't help?"

"No." I met his eyes. "I did my time. I learned my lesson. But no one will touch me." I sucked in a long breath. "This is the first time I've made it past 'I was in prison,' to be honest."

Before he could say anything, I leaned forward, my hands locked in fists on the table. "I'm a hard worker, Aiden. I can overhaul your systems, make them tighter than Fort Knox. No one can out hack me. I was, am, one of the best, even if part of the terms of my release prevents me from active hacking. Plus, I can do anything with computers. Write any program you want. Rebuild and maintain the machines. Add all sorts of improvements and features. Keep you up to date and running faster than you ever dreamed. Anything to do with a computer, I'm your guy. I have tons of talent, and I just need a chance. Someone to give me one chance to prove myself."

I slumped back with a shake of my head. "That's all I'm asking for. A chance."

He studied me, his fingers tapping the wooden table.

"I'd do a good job for you. You wouldn't be sorry."

"I need to think about it."

I nodded, defeated. At least he'd listened to me. That was more than I usually received. I stood and shook his hand. "Thanks."

At the door, I paused when he called my name. "Reid."

I looked back.

"Come back tomorrow. One o'clock. I'm not promising anything, but I want you to meet Maddox."

It was all I could do not to launch myself at him and hug him. But I resisted.

"One. I'll be here."

I shook my head over my musings and glanced at the clock. It was a few minutes before nine. I almost sent Becca a text asking if she was ready for me, then cringed at my words and changed it to asking if it was a good time. Her reply was prompt.

Can we make it ten?

I replied with a fast yes.

I poured another cup of coffee and returned to memory lane.

Maddox Riley was quiet, observant, and somehow scarier than Aiden. His eyes saw everything; right down to the cheap pants I had purchased last night in order to look the part. I had persuaded the woman who ran the rooming house to let me use her iron, and I was at least wrinkle-free, but the shirt and pants I wore probably cost less than Maddox's socks.

Still, he was professional, kind, and surprisingly nonjudgmental, even though he made me nervous. I relaxed after a few minutes as he went over my resume the way Aiden had done. He rested his chin on his hand.

"Aiden told me of your prison record."

"Yes. I don't put it on my resume, but I don't hide it either."

He nodded. "Aiden runs intense security checks. Best to be honest." He sat back. "Why'd you do it?"

I shrugged. "Young, stupid, and arrogant. I thought if they saw the problem with their own eyes, they would be impressed." I laughed abruptly. "I didn't consider the fact that they might think I was actually stealing their money. I left a trail so plain even an idiot could've followed it. I only wanted their attention."

"And you got it. But not in the way you hoped."

I nodded, unsure what to add.

"How did you take courses in jail? I would have thought you'd be banned from computers."

"I was for the first while. But surprisingly, one of the bankers disagreed with the decision and came to my defense. He helped my lawyer get that removed as part of my rehabilitation. I was able to take courses and use the computer with supervision. He was fascinated by what I had done."

"Did you have ways to get around the supervision?"

"Yes," I replied honestly.

"And did you?"

"At times."

He tapped his cheek as he stared over my shoulder.

"Why aren't you working for him now?"

I stroked the edge of the table, my voice quiet. "He died of a heart attack."

"Have you been involved in illegal activities since going to prison?"

"No."

"Would you if given the opportunity?" Maddox's gaze was intense.

"Since I highly doubt BAM is involved in illegal shit, the answer is no," I huffed. "I made a mistake, and I paid for it." I leaned forward, suddenly pissed off with his question. "I was a kid. I fucked up. I paid the price. All I want is a chance to move on and put all that shit behind me. For one person to believe in me." I tapped the table with my finger in fast jabs. "If you or Aiden needed me to do something, I would follow orders. If it were for the good of the company, I would do whatever I had to do. Would I do something to benefit myself? No. It was never about that. It was simply a bad decision."

Our eyes locked. Maddox's gaze was shrewd, but not unkind.

"What did you do with the money, Reid?" he asked quietly.

"I gave it back."

One eyebrow rose in disbelief. "You had it for over six months. Fifteen million yields a lot of interest in that time frame."

"They got it back with interest. The same rate they were making when I 'borrowed' it."

"And you expect me to believe someone as smart as you had it in a safe place making minimal interest?" He ran a finger along his chin. "Especially once you were arrested and were facing jail time?"

I was about to tell him to fuck off. He was a numbers man and smart. He had already figured it out. I knew I had lost my shot at the job, so I had nothing left to lose. I glared at him, furious he had gotten to me. Furious that I had allowed my hopes to grow when I knew better. He would never give me a chance to work at BAM.

Crappy jobs and an equally shitty life were all I had, and all I would ever have because of my past.

"I put it in bitcoin. I paid them back every penny they were due. The rest of the interest I kept and it's still in either bitcoin, or various long-term plans. Every month, someone receives a donation to help feed their kids. Buy them new clothes. Get out of an abusive relationship—whatever they need it for. They never know where it comes from, and they never will. I got nothing then. I get nothing now. I wanted nothing. But once the fuckers decided to make an example out of me, I made sure someone got something good out of it." I stood, pushing back my chair, the bitterness almost choking me. "Thanks for your time. I won't take up any more of it."

I made it to the elevator, pushing the button repeatedly. I had to get out of there before I broke down. I didn't even stop to say goodbye to the nice woman, Sandy. I had liked her and looked forward to knowing her more. I had wanted to get to know them all more. I couldn't believe how badly I had wanted the job. The disappointment was crushing.

"Reid!" Aiden grabbed my arm before I could step into the elevator. "Hold up."

I shook off his grip. "What?"

He grinned, shaking his head. "A bit of a hothead, aren't you?"

"What you do want, Mr. Callaghan?"

"For you to come back into the boardroom and finish the interview."

I ran a weary hand over my face. "I thought I was finished."

"Nope. We have a couple more questions, and you'll have to meet with

HR and sign some papers."

I grabbed the side of the elevator, my knees threatening to buckle. "What did you say?"

He pulled me out of the elevator, leading me down the hall. "You're in, kid. I like you. You're exactly what I need, and even Maddox likes you, despite your temper. He wants to know more about bitcoin and how you got so smart about investing. Numbers fascinate him. Bentley might be unhappy, but he'll come around."

"Are you shitting me?"

He stopped at the boardroom door. "No. You want a chance? I'm gonna give it to you. Maddox and I are putting ourselves on the line for you, Reid. Do you understand?"

"I won't let you down."

"I know."

"Why are you doing this?"

Aiden paused, his hand on the door. "I checked you out, Reid. You've had a shit life. I get that." He tilted his head toward the boardroom. "We both get that. We believe in second chances, because we both got one." He eyed me sternly. "You are gonna have stipulations and guidelines."

"I can work within your boundaries."

"You are gonna work hard."

"Not an issue."

"I will be all over you if I suspect anything but your best."

"Noted."

"And here's a tip—all the cursing isn't the best interview technique. But we're cool."

Unabashed, I grinned. "Sorry, my mouth runs faster than my brain sometimes."

"I can't wait to see you in action." He clapped me on the shoulder. "Let's go, kid."

I followed him, knowing that my life was about to change.

I loved my job. I threw myself into it wholeheartedly. I worked mostly with Aiden, but Maddox was often part of my meetings, Bentley joining in on rare occasions. I was one of four IT people, all of us answering to Aiden since the head of the department had recently left.

After a week of working nonstop, I went to Aiden, showing him some huge gaps in their system and ways to improve the performance and firewalls. He put me in charge of the project, and a month later, gave me the job as lead guy in IT.

With the pay increase, I found my little apartment and was able to begin to enjoy life. When Bentley's girlfriend, Emmy, was kidnapped, Aiden came to me, asking for my help.

"Whatever you need to do, Reid . . . I know you're banned from hacking, but forget it. Break any law—I will cover you. Do you understand? I need her home and safe."

Once that happened, again, my life changed. Bentley's gratitude knew no bounds. A corner office, a new title, and access to all the equipment and software I could dream of. Those alone made me happy.

The massive wage increase was the icing on the cake. But the best thing of all was the sense of finally finding my place. I was one of them. Not on a wealth scale, but as their friend. A trusted ally. It was their trust I valued the most. Their faith in me. They had my back as much as I had theirs. When Maddox needed my help, I was glad to be able to return the favor of his trust. We had gotten closer during my time with BAM, but it cemented our relationship. I felt as if I was no longer alone in the world. I had three brothers, whom I would do anything for, and I knew they felt the same in return.

Life was good.

I glanced at my watch, picked up the heavy bag, and slung it over my shoulder. It was time to go to Becca's.

Now, if I could take my brothers' advice and man up, life would be great.

CHAPTER 4

REID

ON MY WAY to Becca's, I stopped to pick up coffee again. The old woman was outside puttering around her pails of flowers. When she saw me, her face creased into a deep smile.

"Your girl, she like the daisies?"

"Very much."

"You see her today?"

"Yes."

She plucked a single lily from a pail. "You give her this. Beautiful."

I took the single stalk. It was heavy with blossoms, the deep pink and white color majestic. I dug into my pocket, but she held up her hand.

"No. Not today. I give to you, you give to her."

With a grin, I leaned down and kissed her cheek. She patted my face with a smile so wide, her eyes disappeared.

"Good boy," she muttered. "Go see your girl."

I grinned and made my way to Becca's. She opened her door, gasping in delight when I presented her the flower with a flourish.

"Milady."

This time, I got the kiss on the cheek. Her lips were soft, and they lingered on my skin. I had to resist turning my head to feel her mouth on mine.

I followed her down the hall, once again admiring her pert ass. She had a towel flung over her shoulder, and I noticed the dampness on her skin. I thought she had just come out of the shower until I walked into the open area of her apartment and saw the pole.

Holy shit.

Becca had a stripper pole. A real, actual stripper pole. And she had been using it this morning.

"Oh God," I uttered. "You weren't joking."

She slid the lily into a tall, slender vase. "No. It's great for core workouts." She indicated her laptop on the counter. "I take online classes. I ordered a new pole and it arrived yesterday, so I set it up last night after you left." She laughed lightly. "I'm a bit out of practice."

"Oh," I croaked, trying desperately to stop the barrage of images floating through my head. Becca on the pole, graceful and sensuous, her body fluid and supple. Becca dancing for me. Me grabbing Becca off the pole and pulling down her leggings. Becca under me writhing and moaning.

Shaking my head to clear it, I had to turn away as my cock decided he liked the images far too much.

"I-I hope I didn't interrupt."

"Nope. All done."

I cleared my throat and handed her a coffee, grateful the counter was separating us. I pointed to the pole. "Is it, ah, safe?"

"Oh yes. I can't do every movement since it's not anchored the same way as in a studio, but I use it more for the exercise than the extreme moves, you know?"

"Uh-huh," I muttered.

"It's not like anyone sees me, and I'm certainly not planning a career as a stripper." She paused with a wink. "Unless, of course, my job at BAM doesn't work out."

I gaped at her, then realized she was teasing. I chuckled. "Well, let's hope it goes well."

She leaned on the counter, the damp cotton of her T-shirt sticking to her body, and her position mashing her breasts together. I swallowed, trying not to stare at the perfection of her tits.

"Would you come see me, Reid? If I did?" she asked, her voice pitched low.

"If you did?" I asked stupidly.

"If I had to pole dance for a living?"

The thought of her on a pole in front of other people—men—ogling her, made me stiffen with jealous rage. Nobody was seeing her on that pole except me.

"I'd buy every dance," I said through gritted teeth. "Every night."

She stood, lifting her cup to her mouth. A smile played on her lips. "Okay, then."

I nodded. "Okay, then."

"Shall we put up the shelves?"

I drained my coffee. "Yeah."

BECCA

REID MATTHEWS WAS a complete mystery to me. I had never met anyone like him. The day he stumbled into the boardroom, he had captured my attention. His wild hair, ragged T-shirt, and jeans were so out of place in the business setting, but I soon forgot about that when he began to speak. He had a low, deep voice that was hypnotic. He used his hands as he spoke, drawing attention to his long fingers and wide palms. He yanked off his glasses when making a point, his hazel eyes swirling blue and green under the lights. He was well-spoken and smart, and his knowledge of computer components, operating systems, and how everything worked together evident. When asked a question pertaining to anything business-related, he was brilliant.

But when it became personal, he changed, drawing into himself. His smile was tentative, his words chosen carefully, and his demeanor guarded. I wanted to know why.

Often, I caught him staring at me during meetings, but his gaze would skitter away. Before I arrived in Toronto, he had been in constant contact, calling and texting me daily about the oddest things to do with my computer needs and things for my office. I found it endearing and always tried to extend our chats, but once I became personal, he shut down.

He was the first person I saw the day I walked into BAM to begin my job as a liaison for The Gavin Group. He was standing in his office doorway, his intense gaze focused on the door when I entered. The expression on his face when he saw me made my heart stutter. It was open and welcoming. He showed me around the office, excitedly presenting the incredible system he had set up for me, pointing out all the different features of the monitors and programs he had installed. He stood behind my chair, leaning over me as he tapped on the keyboard.

"It's amazing, Reid," I exclaimed. "Thank you for doing all this for me."

Our eyes met and held. He was close enough I could smell his scent. It was clean and masculine. Fresh-cut cedar and pine. It suited him. The thick, dark glasses he wore emphasized his heavy brows and the beautiful color of his irises. His jaw was sharp, covered in scruff, and his bottom lip fuller than the top one. I wondered if it would be soft if I ran my tongue over it.

My breathing hitched at the thought, and I inched closer, stretching my face toward him.

Reid's eyes widened and he stood, running a hand over the back of his neck in a nervous gesture. "Okay, I'll let you get on with things. I've bothered you long enough."

Without a thought, I laid my hand on his arm. "You haven't bothered me at all, Reid."

His gaze jumped from my hand to my face and back again. He stepped away.

"If you need me, I'm down the hall. Next door. Right there." He pointed *to the right, then turned in the opposite direction and hurried away.*

His reaction had mystified me, and I realized I had probably crossed a line. Since that day, I had only become more confused. He was hot and cold. Some days, I was certain he was as interested in me as I was in him, and others, I was sure I had only imagined the spark between us. There were moments I swore he was going to grab me and kiss me.

And I wanted him to. So much. But he never did.

I saw him a lot. My computer seemed to have a lot of glitches that only he could fix. If I had a question or anything I needed, he was the first to help me, always seeming to be close by. But that was it. He never took my hints at dinner together or even lunch. My attempts to draw him out personally failed every time. I resorted to accidentally jamming my printer, freezing my computer, and loosening the connections on the fancy monitors he had installed on my desk.

Still, we went nowhere—until Maddox informed me, he wanted the apartment to have the security system and programs installed that Reid was working on for Ridge Towers. When Reid had come to see me about it, I was certain he was as excited as I was. He had shown up last night with flowers and coffee. We had talked and laughed, and his reaction to my stripper pole comment was hilarious—although he had left not long after it occurred.

His retort to my question this morning was surprising and telling. His eyes had narrowed, his expression intense. His fingers curled around the paper cup, holding it tightly as he informed me in a voice that made me shiver, he would buy every dance. It sounded possessive.

I liked it.

I watched him move around my apartment, eyeing the right spot for the shelves. He reached into the pocket of his duffel bag for a pencil. I tried not to ogle his ass, but it was impossible. It was a great ass. His entire body was great—tall, lean, yet muscular. I had felt his strength when he hugged me once.

I wanted to feel it again.

I knew he worked out with Aiden. I heard them joking in the

hall about their routines and Aiden whooping his ass. Once I had seen him coming upstairs from a workout, a towel draped around his neck. His wife-beater was soaked with sweat, his skin damp. I could see the effects his sessions with Aiden were having on his body. His chest was broader, the muscles in his arms defined and thick. His body was toned and hard. His hair was a mess, and his shorts hung low on his hips and showed off his powerful legs. He was sexy and relaxed, and the grin he had thrown my way before he disappeared into his office for a shower made me want to follow him and help him in that shower. And by help, I meant rip off his shorts and swallow his cock until he screamed my name.

"Becca?"

I shook my head to clear my lust-induced fog. "Sorry?"

Reid tilted his head, his hair falling over his brow. "Are you okay? You're looking at me funny."

"Oh, sorry. I was thinking about, ah, something that I'd like to do."

"Do you need me to come back another time?"

"What? No. No, I'll get to it later. What were you asking?"

"Do you want all four shelves here?"

"Um, no. Two over my desk and two on that wall."

He brushed his hair off his forehead. It fell right back into the same spot and I chuckled.

"I think you need a haircut."

"I know. Sandy keeps badgering me to get one. I get busy and forget."

"She's sort of a den mother, isn't she?"

He laughed, drawing a faint line with the level. "She's the closest thing I have ever had to a mother."

"Oh?" I asked.

He stopped and looked over his shoulder. "I was in foster care all of my life, Becca. I'd never had a real home or a family until I found BAM."

His words hit me in the chest. The pain evident in his quiet voice told me more than a scream ever could.

"Reid, I'm sorry. I didn't know."

"Of course, you wouldn't. It's fine, really."

I hated the ache I heard in his words and tried to find a lighter note. "I could cut your hair."

The level wobbled and he turned. "What?"

"I could cut your hair. I always cut my dad's. I trim mine."

"You cut your dad's hair?"

"Yeah. My mom always did it for him, but after she died, I took over."

He edged closer and grabbed my hand. "Your mom died?"

"When I was ten. She had a brain aneurysm. She was fine one day and gone the next."

He squeezed my hand. "I'm sorry."

"It was only my dad and me after that. I tried to fill in, you know. I learned how to cook and helped him with the house stuff . . ." My voice trailed off, and I shrugged.

"And cut his hair."

"Yeah. So, I could cut yours, if you wanted," I added, unsure about the look on his face. "To say thanks for the shelves."

He stared at me, squeezed my hand again, and a grin broke out on his face. "Yeah, I want."

"Okay."

He turned back to the wall and picked up his drill. "Okay, let's get this done."

⌒

MY GAZE SWEPT the room. "Reid, it looks great!"

The shelves were up, perfect and level. He had hung my pictures patiently, never once complaining when I changed my mind or asked him to try a different spot. He carried in the two boxes I had of books and knickknacks from the storage closet and helped me unwrap them. One by one, he handed me each piece, as I placed and moved them until they were in the right spot. After we were done, he broke down the boxes and took them to the recycle bin without question.

He was relaxed and wore a warm smile, and we had talked constantly. I made sure not to delve into anything else personal. We chatted about the office, the Ridge Towers project, and Bentley's wedding that was happening soon. He told me some funny stories of the mischief Aiden liked to cause, making me chuckle. It was a good morning.

"I'm glad I could help," he responded.

"Are you ready for lunch?"

"You didn't have to do that, but it smells awesome."

"Do you cook?"

"No. I do a lot of takeout, so a home-cooked meal is a treat."

"Good. We can eat, and I'll cut your hair."

"That sounds perfect."

He sat at the counter, and I piled his plate high with the casserole I had made. He dug in, his low moans and muttered praises letting me know he enjoyed it. He ate two platefuls before he laid down his fork.

"That was incredible."

"Good."

He drained his glass of water, pouring himself another. "Are you finding your way around the city okay?"

I pursed my lips. "It's a bit overwhelming. It's so much bigger and busier than Victoria. I walk to work, and I found a few stores, but I need to venture out more. Get to know the subway system. Find more shops and explore the galleries and museums. There is so much here to discover." I leaned a little closer. "I have to admit, I'm directionally challenged. I get lost easily, so I take it slow and get to know the area before wandering too far."

He glanced down at his plate, pushing his fork toward the middle. "I don't want you to get lost. I-I could show you around, if you wanted. I've lived here all my life." He looked up, nervous. "I know it pretty well. If y-you wanted," he added again.

I laid my hand on his arm. "Yeah, I want." I echoed his words from earlier.

He stared down at my hand, then lifted his, covering it. We gazed at each other, and our breathing picked up. He held my hand tighter, pressing it into his skin.

"Reid," I whispered.

He tilted his head. "What?" he whispered back.

"Are you ever going to kiss me?"

He inched closer, and I leaned toward him. "Do you want me to?"

"Yes."

Like magnets, we came together. His lips hovered over mine, his breath lightly fanning my face. "I've wanted to kiss you since the moment I saw you."

"I wanted you to," I replied. "So stop talking."

His lips pressed, light and fleeting. Then again, lingering longer. A third time, they touched, moving and teasing. Still light and soft. I moaned, sliding my hand up his neck to his hair, twisting the strands.

"More," I breathed against his lips.

His hand cupped the back of my head, and he molded his mouth to mine. Our lips moved, and his tongue slid along my bottom lip in a silent plea. His groan when our tongues met was low and rough. He slid his arm around my waist, yanking me close. Still, his mouth was tender, adoring, and sweet. With gentle sweeps of his tongue along mine, he held me captive with his lips. He never pushed or groped. I felt his adoration and the way he was holding himself back. He tugged again, pulling me tight to his torso, and I gripped his leg to steady myself, brushing his erection. He jerked, pulling back. His glasses were askew and smudged, his breathing erratic.

"Sorry," I murmured.

"I think I should be the one saying I'm sorry."

I dared to run my fingers over him again, feeling the hard length of him. "Don't be sorry."

He covered my hand, swallowing hard. "You-you can't do that."

"We're both adults."

He shook his head. "Not yet."

I kissed him. "Okay."

He sighed and pressed his fingers to his mouth. "It's not that I don't want to, but . . ."

I cupped his face. "It's okay, Reid. I'm not in any rush. Can I at least kiss you again?"

He yanked me back to his chest. "Fuck yes."

I NEED TO cut your hair."

He smiled against my head. We had moved to the sofa and kissed for what seemed an eternity. We explored each other's mouth, learning what the other liked. So far, it was everything. After, we simply cuddled. I couldn't remember the last time a man had been happy to cuddle on my sofa.

"Okay, cut my hair."

"I have to get up." I was curled into his side, his arm wrapped securely around me.

He dropped a kiss to my forehead and stood. I tried not to stare at the ample bulge in his pants and failed. I lifted my head, meeting his eyes, rubbing my hands up his thighs. "Are you sure I can't . . ."

"No. Once we know each other."

I let him pull me up, and I told him to go and get his hair wet in the bathroom. I moved the dishes from the counter and found my scissors. He came back from the bathroom, his hair wet, and the towel draped over his shoulders. I tried not to be disappointed he hadn't removed his shirt. He sat in the chair I had brought from the bedroom, and I briskly toweled his hair. We were quiet as I combed and snipped. I tapped his knees so he would open his legs, and I stepped between them, concentrating on his long bangs. He slid his hands along my thighs, settling them on my hips.

"So are you and your dad close?" he asked.

"Yes. He had to become both Mom and Dad, you know. He gave up a job he loved to be there for me."

"His job?"

"We lived in Vancouver. He was a street cop, and he worked a lot of shifts."

Reid's hands tightened on my hips. "Your dad's a cop?"

"Retired now."

He seemed tense, so I stopped cutting and lifted his chin. "You okay?"

He nodded, not saying anything. I bent and dropped a kiss to his lips. "I won't cut you, and I won't make you look funny." Smiling, he dropped his face, but I noticed the smile didn't reach his eyes.

"What did you mean he gave it up?" he asked.

"I was too young for him to be gone so much with shifts. He transferred to Victoria and took a job as desk sergeant. He did straight days so he would be home with me at night and on weekends. Where we lived was quiet, and there wasn't really much crime." I paused as I measured his hair, making sure I was cutting straight. "He hated it. He never said a word to me about it, but I knew it. He was bored and he missed being on the street. But he did it for me. So I didn't have to worry about losing him as well."

Reid's voice was edgy. "He sounds like a great guy."

"He is. Gruff and hard-nosed, but he's my dad," I chuckled. "Growing up, he was strict with me. He had rules I had to follow, and he watched over me carefully. He wouldn't allow me to date until I was sixteen, and even then, I didn't date much. My dad scared them away, I think."

Reid made a funny noise in his throat. His hands slipped off my hips, and I moved to the back, trimming the bottom of his hair. "I didn't really mind. I was busy with school and I hung with my girlfriends. I was on the swim team, and I loved to run. Boys weren't a big thing. He was looking out for me and, really, his rules were easy to follow."

He grunted.

"He did so much for me," I continued. "I wanted to make him proud. He had a stroke a few years ago and could no longer live on his own. He's in an assisted living place—he has a small apartment and is doing well. There's a dining room where he goes for his meals, and he has a tiny area where he makes snacks, coffee, that sort of thing. He has a lot of friends in the same place, and he is happy and settled. He stays busy, and his health is good. I don't have to worry he is alone, you know?"

"Was it hard to leave him?"

"Yes. He was insistent I go. He knew how much I wanted to spread my wings, and he said it was time. I know Richard and Katy check on him. They take the girls to see him on occasion too. And I plan to fly home every couple of months." I toweled his hair and combed it through one last time. "I talk to him every few days. He makes sure I am behaving myself. Following his guidelines."

"Guidelines?"

I stood in front of him, brushing off his shoulders. "Yep. The same rules as when I was young and he talked to me about dating and how I should be treated. 'They disrespect you in any fashion, you walk. They give you trouble, you call me. If you're afraid, find a safe place and I will come get you.'" I smiled at him with a shrug. "Dads. I guess they are a protective lot."

"Your dad was right. You should be treated well. Like a queen."

I fluffed his hair. I had a feeling Reid would treat me better than well, and my dad would have no complaints.

"As I got older, he added another line. 'No druggies, boozers, or cons, Becca. They can't be trusted. A leopard never changes his spots.'"

Reid stiffened. "Cons?"

"Convicts," I explained. "My dad saw too many bad ones, I guess. Repeat offenders. He begged me never to date one, not that I was interested. I prefer law-abiding citizens."

Reid didn't say anything else.

I finished his hair quickly, running my hands through the strands. A tremor went through his body, and his shoulders slumped.

I rubbed his arm, his shoulders damp from the water. "Are you cold?"

"No."

"What's the matter?"

His voice was dull. "Nothing." He stood abruptly. "Are you done?"

"Um, yes. Did you want to take a look?"

"No, it's fine."

I reached out to flick a strand of hair off his cheek, and he jerked back, my hand hanging in the air between us.

"I just remembered I have someplace I have to be," he said, looking over my shoulder.

I blinked. "O-kay?"

He grabbed his bag, heading for the door. "Thanks for the haircut, Becca. And lunch."

I hurried after him. "Reid? What is it?"

"Nothing. I'm fine." He shook his head, looking anything but fine. "I'm late. I'll see you on Monday."

He left, rushing out so fast he forgot to shut the door.

What the hell had just happened?

CHAPTER 5

BECCA

AFTER REID TORE out of the apartment, I cleaned the hair from the floor and sat down with a cup of coffee. I was confused and worried.

I traced the edge of the lily closest to me, the velvet texture of the flower soft under my touch. It had been such a fun morning. Reid had been relaxed, patient, and open. I loved hearing him talk. He was intelligent and funny. He was also a great listener and asked a lot of questions, which showed he was paying attention—a rare combination.

Then, he kissed me. The sweetest, hottest kiss I had ever experienced. He was tentative, gentle, and warm. I felt his adoration in the kiss. I also felt the way he reacted. His cock pressed between us left me no doubt of his desire. His quiet insistence we weren't ready had only increased how much I liked him. The kisses we shared on the sofa, and his reaction to me, made me certain of his attraction. It was mutual.

But he had shut down. I went through our conversation and dropped my head into my hands. I had gone on about my dad. Reid had no parents, and undoubtedly, I made him uncomfortable and upset him the way I blathered on about how close we were. It must have struck a chord within him.

I would apologize on Monday.

I looked around the room, smiling at everything Reid had helped me accomplish. It felt like home now. We had hung my pictures, and the few knickknacks I took everywhere were now displayed. My books were on the shelves, my pole fully set up. Reid had even planned where a TV could go when I was ready. He assured me with wireless technology he could hide the electronic items so it would have a clean look.

The way he kept glancing at the pole made me smile. It fascinated him. I wondered if he, like many other men, found it a turn-on. I wanted to find out.

I finished my coffee and set the empty cup in the sink, once more looking at my flowers. Daisies yesterday, lilies today.

I sighed.

Would there be any others, or had I ruined that chance?

MONDAY MORNING, REID sat across the room from me at the usual, start of the week staff meeting. He was quiet, volunteering nothing until Aiden called on him, and his answers were short. Normally, one of the three BAM men would be telling him to wrap up the technical jargon and move along. There was always a great deal of laughter and teasing during those meetings. Today, it was as if everyone felt the odd vibe in the room. I noticed Aiden looked between Reid and me more than once, but he remained silent. After the meeting, Reid went to his office immediately and pushed the door shut behind him. I got the hint and didn't bother him. I did my work, talked to other coworkers, and tried to ignore his closed door.

I barely slept that night.

When I arrived at work on Tuesday, Reid's door was open, but he wasn't at his desk. When I casually asked Sandy, she told me there was a problem in the server room and he'd been in there all morning. I didn't hear his voice all day.

For the first time since I arrived, my computer appeared to be in perfect working order. Not a glitch in sight.

Wednesday, out of desperation, I jammed the printer and deleted a file I needed on purpose. Picking up the phone, I called Reid.

"Becca," he answered in a flat voice. "What can I do for you?"

I ignored his bland greeting. "Reid, I've lost a file. I can't find it anywhere. I was wondering if you could help me."

"Send me the name, and I'll look in the system and find it. You probably put it in the wrong drive."

"No, wait!" I gasped, knowing he was going to hang up.

"Yes?"

"My printer isn't working."

I heard his low sigh. "Fine, I'll be in shortly."

Typically, he appeared right away. This time, I waited almost thirty minutes until he walked into my office, looking as if he would rather be anywhere else.

"You didn't send me the file name."

"Hello to you too, Reid. I hope the rest of your weekend went well?"

He looked shocked. "Sorry, I have a lot on my mind."

"I see. So that's your excuse for being rude?"

"I'm not being rude. I'm busy."

I crossed my arms. "I've been here for weeks. Every day, you say hello. Every Monday you sit beside me at the staff meeting. Every day you talk to me, even if it is all about BAM. This weekend, you kiss me, and now you can't say hello or come close? Did I do that bad a job on your hair I deserve the silent treatment? Or am I that bad a kisser?"

He gawked, his mouth hanging open. He shook his head wildly. "No."

"No to what? The hair or the kiss?"

He sat down, defeated. Bending forward, his hands clutched between his knees, he lowered his head.

I waited, resisting the urge to drum my fingers on my desk. Finally, he lifted his head.

"My hair looks great. Even Bentley told me it was an improvement. Usually, he only says something when he hates it. So for the cut, I'm grateful."

"And?" I prompted.

He glanced behind me, not meeting my eyes. "Kissing you was the best thing that's happened to me in a very long time. But it can't happen again. I think we need to be friends."

I held my temper and resisted telling him I didn't appreciate him making the decision for both of us. "I thought we were friends."

He smiled, but it seemed strained. His eyes looked tormented. "We are, and in order to stay that way, we need to be *only* friends."

I had to stop myself from reaching out to him. "Whatever I said to upset you, I'm sorry."

"You said nothing. I realized, though, that if we attempt anything else and it doesn't work, it would be too uncomfortable for us working in the same office. So before we make that mistake, we have to stop." He blew out a big breath. "Friends."

I studied him, wondering if he knew what a shitty liar he was. One of his hands clenched and unclenched. The other tugged on the hem of his hoodie. His gaze was everywhere but on me. He gnawed at the inside of his mouth. He played with his hair. His tells screamed much louder than his words. He wanted to be only friends no more than I did. But I smiled at him and tilted my chin.

"If that works better for you, I understand."

Disappointment and devastation crossed his face before he schooled his features. "Thank you for understanding."

"That's what friends do."

He held out his hand. "I'll look for that file for you."

I waved him off. "I found it just before you came in."

"The printer?"

"The cable was loose. I don't need you anymore. It's fine."

His shoulders sagged, and he turned to leave.

He paused at the door, but I kept my head down. It wasn't

over—not by a long shot.

After he left, I shut my door and called Katy, Richard's wife. She was my closest friend in BC, and I needed her advice.

After hearing about Gracie and Heather's latest news, and how much Richard missed me in the office and she missed me in general, Katy cleared her throat.

"Okay, kiddo—what's up? I can tell something is wrong. If you hate it there, say the word and Richard will have you back here in a second."

"No, I like it here, it's just . . ."

"Just?" she prompted.

I told her about Reid. Our little dance in the office. Kissing on the sofa and his sudden retreat. His odd behavior all week.

"I think I talked too much about my dad. I didn't think about how it would make him feel since he doesn't have parents."

"I think there is more to it than talking about your dad. I think you hit a nerve, but I don't know him, so what it was, I can't say."

"I was wondering about talking to Aiden for advice. Reid is close to him."

She laughed. "Who would you talk to if you were here and needed some advice in the office? Who would know more than anyone?"

I answered without hesitation. "Laura." She was Graham's wife and his partner at The Gavin Group. She knew everything that went on in that office.

"Exactly. I think you need to talk to Sandy. From what Richard has said, she runs them all, the same way Laura does. She's the eyes and ears of the place. She would have more insight than anyone."

"Good advice."

I heard the telltale cry of a baby in the background.

"I have to go. Heather woke up, and that means my twenty-minute reprieve from both of them is over. Once the baby wakes up, Gracie is done with her nap." She sighed, but I knew she wouldn't trade it for anything. "Just like her father. Opens her eyes, and she's raring to go."

I chuckled. "Kiss them both for me."

"I will. Let me know how it goes."

"You'll be the first one."

Thursday, I brought in cookies—oatmeal raisin. I left some in the lunchroom, then sought out Sandy. She was in the boardroom, preparing it for a meeting with the partners. I handed her the small container. "For you."

She peered inside with a delighted smile. "Oh, my favorite! Thank you."

"I was thinking of going to Remi's for lunch. Any chance you'd like to join me?"

"As if I would turn down lunch at Remi's—what time?"

"One?"

"Excellent."

I appeared by her desk five minutes early and swallowed to clear my dry throat when I saw Reid there. He looked tired and despondent, talking quietly to Sandy. I straightened my shoulders.

"Hey, Sandy, are you ready?"

She stood, gathering her purse.

"Hi, Becca," Reid mumbled.

I smiled brightly. "Hey, Reid. All okay with the server room?"

"Yeah, it's fine."

"Good. That's good."

"I heard there were cookies today."

"Yep. Oatmeal raisin."

"I didn't get one before they were all gone."

Sandy looked between us, ducking her head. "Becca brought me my own container. Wasn't that kind?"

"I usually get one too," Reid muttered.

I laughed, hooking arms with Sandy. "I didn't know if you liked oatmeal raisin. You'll have to be quicker next time. Or, you know, *tell me* what you're thinking."

We headed to the elevator, Reid staring after us.

Once we were inside, Sandy pressed the button.

"Well, this should be interesting."

SANDY LISTENED TO me talk, not saying anything until I was done. She finished her chicken piccata, laying down her fork and knife and patting her lips with her napkin.

"So, Reid spent the day, kissed you, you cut his hair, you two talked about your pasts, and he walked out?"

I pushed my eggplant parmesan around my plate, my appetite nonexistent. "Yes."

"Well, you did a good job on his hair. He looks tidy for a change."

I half smiled and set down my fork. "I think I upset him talking about my dad. It was insensitive of me to talk about how close we were when Reid has no family."

She raised her eyebrows. "He told you that?"

"Yes."

"What else did he tell you?"

"Not much. I think his past makes him uncomfortable."

She pursed her lips and sipped her mineral water. "Tell me exactly what you said."

I repeated the conversation as best I could remember.

Sandy nodded her head. "It's not that you're close with your father. It's your father's advice."

I grimaced. "Not to let men take advantage?"

Sandy sighed and patted my hand. "You are a lovely girl, Becca. Incredibly intelligent. I think you'd make a good match for my Reid. That boy is lost and needs someone to ground him."

"Thank you . . . ?" I had a feeling she had more to say.

"But as intelligent as you are, you're missing the big picture."

"Which is?"

"I cannot betray Reid's confidence, but I will say this—think about what your father said to you. Carefully."

I mulled over the words, my eyes growing round.

"Reid. Oh my God, is he a recovering alcoholic?"

She shook her head imperceptibly.

"It's not drugs. I've heard his views on drugs."

Her head barely moved.

My mouth formed an O.

"Reid's been in jail?"

"You would have to ask him that question." She bent close, tapping the table. "And if you choose to ask him, I expect you to have already decided to listen to what he has to say and realize people move on from their mistakes. If not, I suggest you do exactly what Reid has requested and remain friends."

My heart beat hard in my chest. I thought of Reid. How he treated everyone around him, including me. With respect and kindness. The pain on his face the past week. How much I missed talking to him. The way I felt when he kissed me. How incredibly sad I would be if that never happened again.

I couldn't wrap my head around the idea Reid had been to prison. Whatever had landed him in jail must have been huge. Sandy was right, though. He had moved on. His coworkers at BAM clearly liked him and held him in high regard. Obviously, the partners knew his story. I needed to show him enough trust to confide in me as well.

I lifted my chin. "I can listen."

"Good. I thought you would."

"I like him," I admitted. "A lot. I don't want to hurt him."

"Then don't. It's simple. If he chooses to tell you his story, and you can't accept it, walk away. If you opt to stay with him, know you will have to support him fully." She raised her eyebrows. "Even against your father. You decide how much this affects you. Nobody else."

She was right.

I squeezed her hand. "Thanks, Sandy."

"Don't make me regret being so gossipy."

I laughed. She'd scarcely said a word, instead allowing me to work it out myself.

"I won't."

"You need to make sure Reid comes to your place Saturday."

"You think he might not?"

She exhaled, her expression sad. "Regardless of what Reid tells you, I will say this; he is vulnerable in ways my other boys are not. His life experience is limited. You need to remember that. If he is feeling at risk, he might send someone else."

"Shit."

She crossed her legs and signaled for the check. "You're a smart young lady. I'm sure you can ensure it's Reid who shows up for the install." She pushed my hand out of the way when I reached for the bill.

"Ensure it?"

"He's a bit dense, but he is a man." She winked. "All men are territorial. Even dense ones."

"Ah."

She snapped the billfold closed and stood. "See? I knew you were intelligent."

Laughing, I followed her out of the restaurant.

I MADE MORE cookies on Friday and dropped by the IT department, making sure they got some. I chatted with Craig and Dean longer than necessary, feeling Reid's eyes on me as he worked on something in the server room. Later that afternoon, I locked myself out of my computer on purpose and called Reid for help.

He was still uneasy and quiet as he worked, resetting my password. He pushed my laptop toward me. "You've never had problems remembering your passwords before now, Becca."

I shrugged. "I changed some earlier as per your protocols. I guess I forgot to write this one down."

"Okay. It's all set." He stood and strode toward the door.

"Oh, Reid."

He turned at the door, not speaking, his face showing his emotions despite his attempts otherwise.

"You haven't mentioned it, but do you still plan to come by tomorrow, or will you send one of the other techs to do the install?

Craig is great, if that works better for you. He makes me laugh."

I knew he had seen me talking with Craig earlier. Reid's hand tightened on the doorframe, and his voice was dark. "*No*. I said I'd do it. I'll be there."

I shrugged, acting nonchalant. "Whatever."

He looked furious. "*Craig* doesn't have the experience. It's my system. My responsibility. I'll be there."

I knew very well that Craig had done some installs. I looked down to hide my grin. "Okay."

"Ten?"

"Actually, I have plans for later, so can you come at nine thirty?"

"Sure." He paused. "Are you sure tomorrow still works?"

"Sure. You said it wouldn't take long. It's good."

"Okay. I'll see you tomorrow."

"Okay."

He left in a huff, and I covered my mouth as I chuckled.

Sandy was right. Even the dense ones were territorial.

CHAPTER 6

REID

I TOSSED MY phone on my desk with a low growl and threw myself into my chair so hard it slammed into the wall.

I wanted to scream. Throw something hard. Storm back into Becca's office and drag her from her chair, then kiss her the way I wanted to on Saturday. Hard, without restraint. Tell her I didn't care what her father told her. That he was wrong.

Convict or not, I was the right person for her.

Craig makes me laugh.

Not fucking happening.

I dropped my head into my hands.

I fucking made her laugh too. I wanted to be the only one who made her laugh the way she did when she was with me. I wanted to be the only one she did a lot of things with outside of work.

There was no way in hell I was sending Craig to her apartment. No one was going near her on the weekend except me.

I lifted my head, glancing around my office, desperate for something, anything, to take my mind off Becca and her words.

For the first time in my life since I had discovered computers, nothing distracted me.

With a low curse, I pushed off my chair, grabbed some workout gear, and headed down the hall to Aiden's office. He looked up as I walked in.

"Feel like sparring?"

He studied me briefly, then stood. "You're on, kid."

"I'm so taking you down, old man."

He chuckled, reaching for his bag. "Oh, it's like that, is it?"

"Exactly like that."

"Then let's go."

⟀

AIDEN SHOOK HIS head, a smirk on his face. "Come on, kid. Where's all your smack talk now?"

I groaned, sweat running down my neck. My shirt was damp, and I had to wipe my forehead repeatedly. He was kicking my ass, barely breaking a sweat, and enjoying himself.

"You are such an ass," I huffed.

"And you need to talk. What the hell is going on with you?"

"Nothing."

In a second, he had my legs swept out and my body pinned to the floor. He grinned down at me. "We can keep going and I will work your ass until you collapse, or you can talk. Your choice. You've been sulking all week, Reid. Man up and get it off your chest."

"I haven't been sulking."

He lifted one eyebrow, still holding me on the mat.

I pushed on his hold and rolled away, flipping him off.

He stood and grabbed a couple of waters, tossing me a bottle. "Talk."

I gave in and told him everything that happened on the weekend. Including what Becca said about her father and his thoughts on convicts.

Aiden drained his water and shrugged his shoulders. "Good advice to his daughter. But you're missing the point here, Reid."

"Which point? Where Becca doesn't like cons, or the fact that I am one?"

"The fact that, while her father is correct, you aren't the usual leopard, Reid, so your spots *can* change . . . You haven't made crime your career, which is what many of them do. You did something incredibly stupid, but you learned your lesson."

He crossed his legs with ease, his arms wrapped around his knees. "I mean, it's hardly a shock that a cop would warn his kid about dating anyone with a shady past—drugs, alcohol, or jail time. But Becca isn't a kid anymore, and you're not a convict."

I didn't say anything.

"You need to talk to her. Be honest, and go from there."

I grunted, staring at my worn sneakers. I picked at the loose trim, thinking I needed to buy a new pair.

"So what got you all riled up and needing a beatdown?"

"She told me I could send Craig tomorrow to do the install—as if I'd send that fucker to her place."

He laughed, falling back on the mat.

I glared at him. "Glad I amuse you."

He sat up and wiped his eyes. "Not you, kid. Becca. She's good."

"What are you talking about?"

He stood and extended his hand. I let him yank me to my feet, and he slapped my shoulder. "You're new at this relationship game. I get that. I know it seems a huge thing, but trust me—talk to Becca. She wants this as much as you do. Both of you have been driving me nuts all week."

"What do you mean?"

"You're all emo and snippy. She looks as though someone kicked her puppy and she is going to cry any second."

Becca looked as though she was going to cry? I thought she looked as though she didn't care.

"Was she trying to make me jealous with the Craig thing?"

He chuckled. "Ding-ding. The boy finally gets it. She *is* interested. Now go get cleaned up. Tomorrow, grow a pair and talk to her. Be honest."

"How honest?"

He met my eyes, his expression serious. "Tell her your story. If she's interested, she needs to know it anyway. If she decides you have too much baggage, you're better off knowing now. Or else, if you don't want to risk it, you stay friends. It's A or B. Your choice."

He was right.

There were two possible scenarios that made me cringe, but if Becca chose to hear me out, it would be worth it.

I kept telling myself that all night.

⁓

I ARRIVED THE next morning at nine thirty as Becca requested. I didn't stop for coffee, and I had no flowers for her. I avoided both places this morning, unsure if either was appropriate.

Music thumped from behind Becca's door. Confused, I lifted my hand and knocked—then again, when she didn't answer. The volume lessened, and Becca pulled open her door. Her face was glowing, the skin glistening with moisture. She had her hair pulled away from her face, showing off her elegant neck. Her shoulders were bare, the neckline of the shirt torn and ragged. She was breathing heavily, the rapid action drawing my eyes to her chest. She was braless, her nipples straining against the tight shirt. Her black leggings clung to her like a second skin. There was a towel flung over her shoulder, and she wiped her face.

"Oh hey, Reid. Come in. I'm running late."

Disappointed at her casual greeting, I followed her down the hall. Her ass looked especially pert and full today. I wanted to cup it. To grab her and kiss her, and grind my erection into her so she knew what she was doing to me. To prove that I was feeling was anything but casual.

Instead, I set down my bag, trying to appear nonchalant. "Am I interrupting?"

"No, I'm taking my class. Do you need in this area?" She indicated the empty space behind her.

"No, um, I can start anywhere."

She lifted a bottle of water, taking a long swallow. The action caused her throat to work, and I was fascinated watching the pull of her muscles. When a small river of water escaped the bottle, racing down her skin and disappearing into her neckline, I was certain I whimpered. Her expression never changed.

"How about I start at the door?"

"Sure. I'll be here." She pointed behind me. "I poured you water. I know you like ice."

"Thanks."

I opened my bag on the counter, making sure I had everything I needed. I carried the control panel to the door, along with the contact and other items I would need. The music started up again, and I glanced down the hall, freezing. My eyes widened when I realized what class she was taking. One, until this moment, I didn't know existed.

Not yoga or one of the jazzer-whatever classes.

Pole dancing.

Becca was fucking pole dancing in front of me.

I stared as she went through some moves, seemingly forgetting I was even in the area. I knew my mouth hung open. I knew my dick lengthened.

I knew I was fucked.

She was elegant and graceful, a blur of movement as she twirled and arched.

Wicked and tempting as she wrapped her legs around the pole and bent backward. The bow of her back was mesmerizing as she hung upside down with only the strength of her legs holding her in position.

I had to turn away, fumbling with the items in my hands. I shut my eyes, counted to ten, and reached for the drill. I needed to concentrate.

Except my gaze drifted back to her and I stared for endless moments, caught up in her actions. She hung on the pole using only her hands, her legs split and wide, balancing. She transitioned into a spin and moved onto yet another seductive move.

I dropped the control unit, annihilating it when the drill landed on top. Cursing, I picked it up; grateful I always carried a spare. In the kitchen, I dug the other one from my bag, then desperate to cool off, grabbed the glass of water she had for me and drank it. I leaned against the back counter, watching Becca's mesmerizing form.

She did a series of moves, ending with a one-legged spin, her arms controlling the motion. When she was done, she bent low, one leg around the pole, her arm locked in position. Her hair dragged on the floor, her other arm stretched back, highlighting her curves. Her face tilted in my direction, and our eyes locked across the room. Her chest heaved, mine matching her breathing without thought. A slow, sexy smirk split her mouth.

"You like that, Reid?" she asked, her voice a throaty purr.

The entire week crashed down on me. The worry, disappointment, and frustration made me react. I didn't care about her father's views, her ideas of convicts. I didn't care we needed to talk. It didn't matter. All that mattered was touching her. She knew what seeing her would do to me. She did this deliberately to provoke me.

It was my turn. The only thing standing in my way was the counter.

I was going over it.

I saw it all in my mind: vaulting the counter, grabbing her in my arms, and kissing her until she begged me to take her. Then, losing my virginity to the only woman I had ever wanted that way.

Reality was slightly different.

I cleared the counter easily, my height and frame giving me the advantage. Her eyes widened at the sight of me hurtling toward her. She twisted so her feet hit the floor, but she clutched the pole with her hands, watching me advance. My foot caught my bag, though, sending tools and screws everywhere. Instead of lunging and grabbing her in my arms, I stumbled on the contents, crashing into her. I gripped at her arms, yanking her up, somehow wrapping her hair around the pole instead of my fist, making her gasp in pain. She slid from the pole to the floor with me on top of her, hitting her squarely in the chest, driving the air from her lungs in a painful-sounding whoosh. Her leg jerked, kneeing me in the groin, causing an agonizing groan to escape my mouth.

"My hair," she gasped.

"My dick," I squeaked.

We started laughing. The sound drowned out the loud, thumping music. Carefully, I untangled her hair, reached for the remote, and turned down the volume. I brushed back the damp tendrils from her face and lifted myself off her, hovering over her torso.

"Better?" I asked.

"Yes."

She wrapped her leg around me, pulling me into the cradle of her body. "Okay?"

The heat of her shot through me. "Oh God, yes."

Our eyes locked. She licked her lips. I gazed at the plump flesh, then met her gaze again.

"I want to kiss you."

"You do?"

"You're so fucking sexy." I tilted my hips. "That show was for me, right?"

"Yes."

"You want me to kiss you again? Like last week?"

"Please, Reid."

"I need you to know something."

"What now?" she demanded. "For someone who wants to kiss me, you talk a lot." She pushed against me, her mouth so close I could almost taste her. "You need to shut up."

God, I wanted to taste her. She was my obsession. But I had to tell her.

My mouth hovered over hers, desperate to connect. "We should talk."

"Kiss first, talk later."

"I'm serious."

Her arm snaked around my neck, pulling me close. "So am I."

I tightened my grip on her, frantically trying to control myself. "I'm a virgin, Becca."

She froze. "What?" she breathed out. Her hand gripped my ass, her body pressed tight to mine. The feel of her launched me into another orbit like a rocket and scrambled my already addled brain.

"I'm a virgin, and I want you to punch me," I burst out.

"Punch you?"

She looked startled, and I realized what I said. "My card. I want you to punch my V-card."

Her eyes became round and huge in her face. "Reid . . ."

"You. I want it to be you."

I crashed my mouth to hers. As I slid my tongue along her bottom lip, she opened for me. She tasted salty, sweet, and all Becca.

Kissing her felt like coming home, to the only home I wanted.

I only hoped she felt the same.

CHAPTER 7

REID

I HAD NO idea how long we stayed on the floor. Our mouths never separated, our bodies tightly melded. She was warm, supple, and wrapped around me. Her mouth was heaven. I would never know how I had existed before kissing Becca. Going forward, I only knew it was going to happen daily, multiple times.

She was pure opium, and I was hooked.

She slipped her hands under my shirt, skimming along my back, and under the waistband of my sweats. I bucked into her with a groan, shifting, sliding as our bodies moved across the floor. Her answering groan was different from the other noise she had been making—the low, passion-filled whimpers that turned me on. This was more guttural, almost painful. Somehow, in my lust-filled haze, I realized her hands were no longer tugging me closer, but pushing on my shoulders.

I lifted my head, my breathing hard. "Becca?" I pleaded.

Don't ask me to stop, please don't say it.

"I think-I think you're screwing me."

I chuckled, dragging my mouth along her cheek. "I don't know much, but I do know we haven't gotten there yet, baby."

"No, Reid. I think I'm lying on one of your screwdrivers. It hurts."

I sat up, pulling her with me. Sure enough, not only was she lying on a screwdriver, there was an assortment of anchors and screws under her. I rubbed her back in contrition.

"I'm sorry. I guess we got carried away."

She snuggled into me, wrapping her arms around my waist. "I don't mind getting carried away with you."

"Are you okay?"

She tilted her head, meeting my eyes. "Yeah, I'm fine." She traced my lips with her finger. "More than fine."

I captured her hand, kissing her fingertips. "Me too."

"Are you really?" she whispered.

"Really what?"

"A virgin."

"I am." I sucked in a deep breath. "I guess we actually need to talk."

"We should," she agreed.

"I would rather keep kissing you."

She smiled, pushing my hair off my forehead. "Why don't I have a shower while you work on the system? After, we can talk and figure out the rest of the day."

"The kissing sounds so much better."

She leaned forward, brushing her lips to mine. "We will kiss more."

"Yeah?"

"Promise."

"But you have plans. You told me you were going out."

She lowered her eyes and shrugged. "I may have fibbed a little."

I recalled Aiden's words. *She's good.*

"You were setting me up?"

She met my gaze. "I didn't know what else to do."

"Did you fake the password thing yesterday too?"

"Yes."

I gripped her hips tight. "Did you really want Craig here?"

"No. I wanted you. But you were so distant." She lifted her hand, running a finger over my jaw. "I . . . ah, I know, Reid."

"Know what?"

"That you've been to prison."

I jerked as if she had slapped me. "You know that, and you still want to kiss me?"

"Yes."

"Did Aiden . . . ?" I found it difficult to believe he would have said anything.

"No one actually. I had lunch with Sandy. But she said nothing. She didn't break your confidence."

"Oh. She did one of her obvious, say-nothing-but-lead-you-in-the-right-direction moves . . . The slight bobbing or shaking of the head?"

"Yes."

"She's good at that. An expert, really. She could patent it, I swear."

"Are you angry?"

I sighed, tucking a stray piece of hair behind her ear. "No. I'm partially relieved, to be honest. Shocked you let me kiss you, though."

She inched forward, so our bodies were tight together. "I know how much they all respect you at the office. I also know you wouldn't be where you are if they didn't trust you. That says a lot about the person you are now. I don't know what happened in your past, but if you want to tell me, I will listen."

"I have to tell you. You deserve to know, regardless of your decision." I swallowed hard, feeling my nerves kicking in. "You should know about me."

"Okay. Let me grab a shower."

BECCA

WE SAT ON the sofa, facing each other, our legs crossed. Reid looked nervous, his gaze flitting around the room. Unsure how to help him, I scooted nearer so our knees touched. Reid looked down at our position and offered me a small smile. I slipped my hand into his and squeezed.

"Whatever you want to tell me, I'll listen."

He gazed over my shoulder absently as he gathered his thoughts.

"I was found in a bus station when I was about two weeks old. It was around the holidays, and the station was crazy with travelers and package pickups. A woman found me in the washroom with a note pinned to my blanket reading, 'Please take care of me because my mother can't.'"

I held his hand a little harder. "Oh, Reid."

"The cops were called, and I was taken to the hospital. They tried to locate my mother, but they never found her. She could have boarded a bus or purposely come to the station to drop me off or brought me from somewhere else. It was too hectic, and no one noticed." He lifted one shoulder. "Nowadays, there are cameras everywhere tracking people—twenty-five years ago, not so much. My mother picked the perfect spot to desert me. It was crowded and busy, and she was a faceless woman in a sea of people. Even carrying a baby, she didn't stand out." He sighed heavily. "I suppose I should be grateful she left me where I would be discovered easily."

"What happened?"

"I was placed in foster care."

"Babies are usually adopted, aren't they?"

He nodded. "Unless they have what had been described as the 'worst case of colic ever known.' Apparently, I exhausted many prospective parents. All I did was cry and scream. I was too much for anyone long term, I guess. They passed me from place to place, and eventually, they gave up and I ended up back in the system in an orphanage. No one wanted me."

My heart broke at his words. I couldn't imagine a small child being passed around, never having a home or someone to love him. Unbidden, a tear ran down my cheek and, startled, Reid leaned over, wiping it from my skin. He stared at the wetness on his finger as if mystified by my emotion.

"Tell me more," I whispered.

"I finally got over the colic, but I was still sickly and hard to deal with. I was sort of lost in the cracks. I went from place to place but never found the right fit since I required so much work. As I got older, I never seemed to connect to anyone. They described me as being dissociated. But no one had ever shown me how to love, so I had no idea how to show it back."

"Of course not," I murmured.

"When I was seven, I got into a foster home. The woman who took me in was Ellie Reid. She was older and kind. Like a grandmother, I think. There were six of us and it was crowded, but she tried hard. It was the first time I ever felt as if someone cared. She wasn't rich, in fact, she could barely scrape by, but she did her best. We shared a room with bunk beds, my clothes were hand-me-downs, but she was patient, made sure we had food and a place to sleep. She walked us to school every day, and she helped me with my homework. I was there for three years." He ran a shaky hand over his face. "It was the closest thing to a home I ever knew."

"What happened?" I asked, already dreading the answer.

"She died. She didn't show at school one day, and I walked home with the other kids. I wasn't the youngest anymore, so I made sure they came with me. When we arrived, there was an ambulance at the house and police. I was taken away and put back into the system." Reid stood and walked around restlessly, picking up things then setting them down. He stared out the window for a while, his throat working constantly. I knew he was trying to control his emotions.

I held out my hand, grateful when he took it. I tugged him down to the sofa. "Do you want to stop?"

"No. It's always hard to talk about her. The rest—" he shrugged "—is simply history."

"Okay."

He turned to face me, moving until our knees touched again. I leaned forward and pressed a gentle kiss to his mouth. He wrapped his hand around the nape of my neck, keeping our lips joined. Neither of us deepened the kiss—it was a simple show of support, one I felt he needed.

He drew back, running his fingers over his mouth, pressing them into the flesh. I had noticed him do it every time we kissed. I wondered if it was a nervous habit, but I decided to ask him another time.

"What happened to you next?"

"I went back into the system. I was ten, and not a lot of people are looking to adopt a ten-year-old. They sent me to a group home. After that, there was a disastrous attempt with a foster family, then back to the group home, and finally, I ended up with another woman who took in foster kids." Reid's facial expression indicated disgust. "But unlike Ellie Reid, she was only in it for the money. There were nine of us, all between ten and fourteen, crowded into her basement. It was a fend-for-yourself type of place."

"Did you tell anyone? Complain?"

He shook his head with a sad smile. "So I could return to the group home, Becca? That place was worse than hell. I spent all my time trying not to get beat up, forced into a gang, or worse. At least at Mrs. Keen's place, she ignored me most of the time. There was one meal a day. If you were lucky enough to be around when the food went on the table, you grabbed what you could. If not, you waited until next time. I forgot what it was like to have decent clothes and sleep in a bed. Usually, I slept on the floor. Everyone ignored me there and overlooked me at school. I was basically invisible."

My chest ached at his words. The way his voice shook at times, trying to conceal his emotions as he spoke. I wanted to erase his pain, but I knew it was impossible. All I could do was hold his hand and listen.

"One day, I was so hungry I wandered into the neighbor's garden. It was overgrown and full of weeds, but things were still growing. There was a long row of carrots. I dug some out and ate them." He chuckled without humor at the memory. "I hardly wiped the dirt off of them. Then I found some potatoes and ate those too, before the neighbor found me in his yard."

"Oh no! What did he do?"

"Rodney Matthews was his name. He was a gruff old man. Huge. Used two canes to walk. He yelled at me about trespassing, asked me where I lived. When I pointed out the Keen place, he sort of growled under his breath about her. He told me rather than get me in trouble with the old cow that he was going to let me work off the food."

"How?"

"I had to weed the garden. He sat and watched me, yelling if I tried to pull the wrong thing. I think he would have scared most people, but I found his yelling almost comforting—because he saw me. He watched me. I wasn't invisible. It took me all day, but I got it done. He had me pick more vegetables, and I had to carry them inside for him." A glimmer of a smile crossed his face. "That was the day my life changed."

I rubbed my thumb back and forth on his hand.

"He lived alone—his wife had died over twenty years prior. His house was small, but compared to where I lived it was a palace. He had his entire living room filled with computers. Working ones, dead ones, parts, pieces—and he had a massive table that he called his workstation. I had never seen anything like it."

"Is that what he did? Fix computers?"

He shot me grin. "That was his hobby. He was captivated by them. He knew everything there was to know about computers—how to build them, run them, and anything else to do with them. He did online work for computer companies, like a help desk. That was his day job anyway. His other job was much more interesting."

"He was a hacker?"

"Yes, he was."

I pursed my lips. "I see."

Reid chuckled. "That gruff, cantankerous old man became the reason I am where I am today. For some reason, he liked me. He let me hang around. He'd feed me. He showed me his computers. I was interested, so he let me mess around with some of his spare parts, and I built myself my first computer." He laughed lightly. "It was shit, but I did it."

"How?" I asked.

"He had lots of books, and he let me read them. My teachers never thought much of me, but I loved to learn. They overlooked me a lot, so I read and taught myself—and I absorbed. Rodney's books fascinated me. What he *did* fascinated me. I watched and learned. The next computer I built was better. So was the one after. He started to teach me how to use them." Reid sighed. "I was in love. All I thought about was computers. I couldn't get enough. I spent so much time at his place you would think I lived there."

"Your foster place didn't question it?"

He laughed again, a bitter sound. "Not even once. It was one less mouth to feed, one less kid to take up room. As long as I was around on inspection day, she didn't care. I made sure I was present, said exactly what the caseworker wanted to hear, then I was gone."

He grew quiet for a minute. "Rodney's health was failing. I started doing more of his work—taking over things. He started paying me for my jobs. I stopped showing up for inspection day. I stopped going to school. He spent hours teaching me, showing me everything he knew." Reid shook his head. "I'll never forget the day he looked at me and said I had surpassed him. There was nothing more he could teach me."

"How old were you?"

"Seventeen." He lifted his shoulders and rolled his eyes. "A very cocky seventeen. I thought I knew everything. Rodney yelled at me all the time to watch my attitude."

I could picture him—young, brash, with a chip on his shoulder.

"Mrs. Keen kicked me out. I was old enough I didn't need social services, and I was on my own. I stayed with Rodney, sleeping on the couch, doing his errands, and helping him. His one rule was that I had to finish school. I was so far ahead of my class, it was easy, and I did it online." He exhaled. "That was when it started."

"When you got into trouble, you mean?"

"Yeah. I was looking for a job, but with no experience, plus my age, I wasn't finding much. Fast food places, that sort of thing. I thought I was better than that. Rodney told me to get an attitude adjustment and it would teach me some humility flipping burgers. But with his health issues, he convinced his employer to hire me, so I worked with him. He wanted me to get some experience and find a job in the real world. He warned me often enough not to fall into the trap of becoming a hermit like him."

He was quiet as he stared past my shoulder out the window, a frown on his face.

"What happened, Reid?"

"It started simple enough. Rodney was having trouble with his bank. Online banking was becoming mainstream, and he used it since he had so much trouble getting around. But every month, it seemed there were issues. I decided to check into it, and I hacked into their system."

"That's illegal."

He swung his legs over the sofa, stood and began to pace again. "I know. I hacked in to everything I could, Becca. I never did anything. I liked to see if I could do it—it was a never-ending challenge to me. Usually, the answer was yes. Then I would leave. I didn't steal or try to change things. I was just"—he shrugged—"arrogant and stupid."

"I see."

"But what I saw in the banking system that Rodney used was scary. Their security was lax. I found the issue that caused Rodney's problem in three days of digging. I spent weeks writing the proper code to fix it and make sure it never happened again. During that time, Rodney became very ill. Ill enough he had to go into the hospital." Reid swallowed and shut his eyes. "He died."

"Reid," I murmured, "I'm so sorry."

He wiped his face, turning away from me. "He had a daughter, but they were estranged and had been since before his wife died. His daughter had nothing to do with him. He told me there was bad blood between them, and she refused to mend fences. She never came to see him and every letter he sent her, she returned unopened. But once he died, she was there." He clenched his fists. "She kicked me out of his house, tossed all of his stuff into the garbage, and put his house up for sale. I watched it happen. I had been there for months and months, his only friend, and I had no say. All she wanted was the money. She had no interest in the man or what he did for me. She called me a user and a squatter, then had the cops remove me from the house."

His voice was pain-filled. I could feel his intense sorrow for the loss of the one man who had cared enough to help him. He cleared his throat and kept talking.

"I found a little room. It wasn't much, but it had a door with a lock and a place I could sleep. I had the money I had been earning and some Rodney had given me for his, ah, other work. The night I saw the dumpster delivered, I went back to Rodney's and broke in through the back door. I spent all night taking his books and notes. I made sure I had his favorite computer and tools. The stupid picture we had taken one day of us working together on a computer. Things that meant something to him—I stole them. I'm not proud of it, but I couldn't let her trash things I knew he loved, things that meant something to us both."

"It wasn't stealing," I soothed. "I'm sure he would have wanted you to have them."

He shrugged and was silent. He tugged a hand through his hair and wiped at his face again. I wanted to reach out and hug him, but I could tell he didn't want that right now. He had been in denial when he said the rest of his story was only history. It had shaped and affected him more than he realized. He started speaking again.

"Without Rodney, I was alone all the time, and I made some bad decisions. I tried the right channels. I went to the bank and spoke with the manager about their online system and the problems I found. He laughed at me. I mean, I don't blame him, really. I was a punk kid with an attitude, telling him his banking security system was flawed. He told me to go back to chasing girls, and doing whatever else kids my age did, and not to worry about the glitches—the experts would solve them. He even refused to look at what I brought with me to show him for proof. I was angry and pissed at the world. He made me feel about two inches tall." Reid's voice dropped, becoming angry yet saturated in sadness.

"It hit me that I didn't matter, that I would *never* matter. The only person who cared about me was dead, and I wasn't even allowed to say goodbye. His daughter didn't have a funeral for him. She didn't stay around long enough to bother. He was cremated, his ashes buried, and I never found out where until later. I fumed and stewed for days, then I decided I was going to show the people at the bank I knew more than they did."

He walked around the room, his steps fast. "I hacked in to their system again, and I took fifteen million dollars. I hid it in another account elsewhere."

I gaped at him. "You stole fifteen million dollars?"

"No, I borrowed it. I didn't intend to keep it. I simply wanted to show them how flawed their system was. I was stupid and arrogant enough to think that once they saw what I could do, they would want to meet me and would finally listen. Once they heard what I had to say, they would give me a job—a real, respectable job."

"That's not what happened, though."

He laughed, the sound loud and bitter. "No. I left a huge trail behind. I didn't try to hide what I did because I wanted them to come to me. They did—with handcuffs and a warrant. My public defender was useless, they refused to listen, and in the end, I went to jail."

I couldn't take the distance between us anymore. I stood and wrapped my arms around him, pressing my chest to his back. He started at my touch, then his body sagged in relief. He wrapped his hands around mine, and spoke quietly.

"When BAM gave me my first bonus, I had a headstone made for Rodney and had it placed on his grave. He deserved a permanent marker for his life. I go and sit there a lot and talk to him."

I squeezed his hands. "I'm sure he hears you."

He shrugged then inhaled deeply, slowly letting out the air in a long sigh.

"I made a lot of mistakes, Becca. But I'm not a bad person."

"No, you're not."

"Rodney would have kicked my ass for pulling that stunt. He was a hacker too, but companies hired him to lock down people like me. I should have listened to him. I should have done things differently."

"I think you paid the price."

He ran his fingers along the top of my hands, and he spoke quietly. "Will I continue to pay, Becca? Does my past mean you can't be part of my future?"

I heard the edge to his voice, the one that expected me to tell him to leave. But I couldn't. Reid Matthews had more than paid for his error in judgment. His entire life, people had cast him aside and looked down on him.

I wasn't going to be one of them.

I tightened my arms. "No, Reid. I want to be part of your future."

He said nothing. I felt the long tremor that ran down his spine, the splash of a tear that fell on my hands.

I pressed my forehead onto his back. "I'm here, Reid."

He turned, wrapping his arms around me. I knew he was about to snap. I tightened my grip on him, letting him know I was right there and ready to catch him.

REID

BECCA WENT TO the kitchen to make us something to eat. I was sure she was allowing me some time to collect myself, which I appreciated. I had never broken down in front of another person the way I did with Becca. She made me feel safe enough to allow it to happen. I had never divulged the details of my story to anyone the way I had to her.

Aiden, Maddox, and Bentley knew most of it, but I had told them in bits and pieces as we got to know each other. They had become my family, allowing me to be part of their brotherhood. They trusted me the same way I trusted them—with an unwavering conviction. They teased and called me kid, but it was done in a way I didn't find offensive. It was how they worked as a unit, using laughter to show they cared. Aiden had a nickname for everyone he cared for, so it cemented my bond with them.

I passed a weary hand over my face and stood. I began to gather all the pieces of equipment that went flying when I vaulted over the counter to get to Becca. I heard her laughter and glanced up. She was sliding a plate across the counter.

"You know you could have gone around the corner and saved yourself all that work."

I shook my head with a grin. "That would have taken too long. I needed to get to you."

"Mission accomplished." She winked. "Come and eat."

I sat on a stool, waiting until she joined me. We munched on the sandwiches, sitting so close our thighs pressed together.

"Is it a coincidence your name is Reid Matthews?" she asked.

"No. I changed it legally when I got out of prison. They called me Johnny Dee my whole life—a spin on John Doe since they had no idea what my mother might have named me, if anything. I hated it. I wanted a name that meant something. So I took the name of the only two people who ever tried to make a difference in my life—who made me less than invisible. I was determined to make them proud."

She leaned closer. "I know they would be. That was a lovely tribute to them."

"I try to live up to it every day."

"Do you have a birth certificate?"

"One was issued by the province. They gave me a birthdate of the first of December. I had it all changed—" I winked at her "—legally."

"Really?"

I chuckled as I took a bite, chewing then swallowing. "It was very complex, and I won't get into all the details, but yes, it is legal."

"Did you ever try to find your mother?"

"Rodney and I did, yes. The parameters were massive, though. I didn't even have a birth date to go on or a province to start with. Even checking all baby boys born in all of Canada around the date they guessed I was born was overwhelming. Their date was only a guess. I could have been three weeks old or ten days. They had no idea." I wiped my mouth. "In the end, I decided it wasn't worth it. She abandoned me. It was more a passing interest than a need to know. I decided to leave it in the past where it belonged."

She sipped her iced tea with a sad smile, but she didn't push it.

She asked about the money. I told her the same thing I told Maddox, explaining how I sent money every month to someone who needed it.

"How do you find them?"

I looked at her, my eyebrows raised. "I use my skills."

"Oh."

She worried her lip. "How did you meet Aiden and get hired with BAM?"

"I took a lot of courses while I was in prison. I read everything I could, including the daily newspapers. Anything to keep my mind active and up to date. There was a picture one day of the three of them—Bentley, Aiden, and Maddox—and I read the article about their friendship and company. It—they—intrigued me. I wondered what it would be like to have that sort of connection. I started following them online, reading different articles about them. One day I saw an ad for an IT job at the company, and I went for it." I finished my sandwich and pushed her plate toward her. "Eat up."

As she ate, I told her my story of meeting Aiden and Maddox and my temper. She listened with wide eyes as I confided in her the story of Emmy's kidnapping, the stalking incident with Cami, and Maddox's hit-and-run.

"You helped with all of that?"

"Yes." I tilted my head. "I only hack and use my talent when asked, Becca. And only for good. I learned my lesson, and I follow Rodney's legacy. I promise you, you have nothing to worry about in regard to my career or being in trouble with the law."

"I believe you." She went into the kitchen and returned with coffee and a plate of her peanut butter cookies. I ate two in rapid succession, groaning with enjoyment.

"You make the best cookies ever."

She smiled. "Maddox might have told me peanut butter was your favorite."

"They are."

"Could I ask you, ah, something?"

"You can ask me anything."

She drew in a deep breath and blew it out. "You were in prison for how long?"

"Four years."

She played with a plate in front of her, turning it around several times. "Were you, ah, safe?"

I covered her hand. "It wasn't a fun place, Becca. But it wasn't a maximum-security prison. My cellmate was an old guy who had been there off and on for years. One of the career criminals your dad warned you about. But he was decent, and he protected me, I guess you could say. He said I reminded him of his kid. So, if you're asking what I think you are, no, I was never raped. I was okay."

"Oh, good," she breathed out. "Okay."

"Prison wasn't fun, and I saw a lot of things I wish I had never had witnessed. I was scared for four years," I admitted. "I will never forget those feelings, or everything I witnessed. No matter the level of security, I was still in prison. It was a long four years paying for my crime. I had no family or friends, no one to come see me on visitor day. I never made a call unless it was to my public defender asking about something or checking on my next opportunity for early release. The same with mail. I never had a card or letter unless it was related to my case." I stroked the edge of the counter with my finger, repeatedly tracing a trail on the granite. "I was lonely."

I let my thoughts settle, then continued. "When I got out, I had to figure out how to live in the real world, what to do, and how to find my place. It took me a while to find a job, and though I hated it, it was honest. I lived in a tiny room again, but at least I was free and I could sleep." I heaved a sigh. "I never really slept that entire four years. I was always on guard, listening, waiting, tense. The first thing I bought with my first paycheck was two deadbolts, and I installed them on the door. I think that was the first decent night's sleep I had in years."

I glanced at her, shocked at the tears coursing down her face. "Hey," I murmured, brushing at the wetness in wonder. No one had ever cried for me until today. "It's okay, Becca. It's all behind me."

She sniffled and wiped away the tears. More gathered in her eyes. I decided to stop talking about my time in jail and move forward.

"Getting the job with BAM was a game changer. The guys opened up a whole new world to me. I owe them everything. My loyalty, my gratitude, my life. I have a job I love, a place to live, people I call friends and care about like family. Who care about *me* the same way." I hesitated, then wrapped my hand around hers. "The only thing missing is someone to share it with. I was really hoping you might be willing to take a chance on me, the way they did."

"I want to."

"You're still concerned about my past?"

She dashed away more tears. "No. I'm amazed at what you've overcome. How you pushed yourself and became the person you are."

I drew my finger under her eye with a frown. "Why are you crying, Becca?"

"It hurts me to hear what you went through, and how lonely you were, Reid. Not only in prison, but your whole life. I-I can't stand to think about it."

I turned fully in my seat, edging closer to her. She shifted so our knees pressed together. I ran my hands up and down her arms in a comforting gesture. "I'm not lonely now. I never feel lonely when you're close."

"How do you feel?"

I smiled, tracing her cheek. "Hopeful."

"Hopeful?"

"Hopeful that maybe I finally found someone who can accept me for Reid, mistakes and all."

"I don't see mistakes when I look at you."

"What do you see?"

She tilted her head and studied me. "A strong, caring man, who instead of becoming bitter and twisted, found a different path and is more than his past."

I slid my knee between hers, pushing closer.

"Could I be *more* for you, Becca?"

Her breath washed over me. "Is that what you want?"

"Yes. I know I'm terrible at showing it, but I want more with you."

She lifted her hand, clasped the back of my neck, and played with the ends of my hair. Her touch made me shiver and brought a sense of relief that coursed through my body.

"Why do you say that?"

"Every time I'm around you, I get flustered. I have so much to say, but I forget how to say it. I stumble around a lot and stutter."

She slid her hand into my hair, caressing my scalp. I wanted to bury my head into her chest and let her keep doing that for the rest of the day. Her touch felt so right.

"You do stare at me a lot." She cleared her throat, her voice teasing. "Especially at certain areas."

Guilty, I lifted my gaze. I had been staring at her breasts again. Between her mouth and tits, I was fascinated.

I cleared my throat. "Parts of you are pretty spectacular."

She raised her eyebrows and laughed. "Parts?"

"W-Well," I sputtered, "all of you is . . . But some parts, yeah, extra spectacular."

Her dimple appeared. "I see."

"You make me stupid. I can't concentrate."

"You're getting better. Practice makes perfect."

"Can I practice with you?" I grinned.

She closed the distance between us, her mouth touching mine. "Yeah, Reid, you can practice."

Then she kissed me.

⌢

WE MOVED TO the sofa, both of us more at ease. We kissed again, her mouth far too tempting to resist—especially when she seemed to feel the same about mine. Her taste and the way her tongue felt pressed to mine was heaven. I loved the way she tangled her hands in my hair and the light tugs as our mouths moved together. I pulled her onto my lap, the feel of her curves pressed to mine increasing my desire. Not used to being touched, I found it an odd sensation. Becca was the exception to the rule. I was certain she was the exception to every rule for me.

No one had shown me any affection unless Mrs. Reid gave me a fast hug or Rodney punched my arm in one of his offhand gestures. Aiden, Maddox, and Bentley were big into fist bumps and high fives as their displays of acceptance. Sandy knew my boundaries and accepted them, although I didn't mind her pats on my cheek and motherly hugs on occasion.

But with Becca, I craved her closeness. The way her hands felt on my skin, her body against mine. Whenever she was in the room with me, I wanted to be close.

The way we were now, with my chest touching hers. Mouth to mouth, sharing oxygen. Our tongues sliding, tasting, and exploring. She made a sound, low in her throat—a cross between a whimper and moan—and it cranked me up, making me want to hear it again. Discover what other sounds she made.

She eased back, dropping her head to my chest, breathing hard. I kissed her hair, the silken strands tickling my lips.

"Too much, BB?"

She lifted her face, a lazy smile curving her lips. They were swollen and pink, wet from my tongue. Her cheeks flushed, and her eyes glazed over. I ran my finger over her cheek. "Another spectacular look."

She rolled her eyes. "BB?"

"I think of you as Becca Baby. If I think it too often, it's going to come out at work. So I shortened it."

"I see."

"You hate it?"

"No. I've never had a nickname."

"Not even when you were little? Your dad didn't have a nickname for you?"

"No, my dad was, *is*, a no-nonsense guy. My name is Rebecca, and that's what he called me. He still does. He didn't like it when I shortened my name."

I tucked a piece of hair behind her ear. "Why do I have a feeling your dad and I will never get along?"

She looked thoughtful. "There is that chance. But then again, he might surprise me. He disliked Richard intensely when he met him, and now they get along fine."

"Why did he dislike Richard? I mean, he's your boss."

She sighed, laying her head on my shoulder. It fit there as if it was made for her. I leaned my head on hers as she spoke.

"My dad sees things as black and white. He grew up in a different era, and he forgets things have changed and evolved, I think. At times, he is inflexible. He, ah, accused Richard of having inappropriate thoughts about me."

I lifted my head, gaping at her. "What?"

"I know. It was ridiculous. Anyone who has ever met Richard and has seen him with his wife would know how stupid that sounded. He adores Katy. Worships her, in fact. I spent a lot of time with Richard at work, and I talked about him. My dad assumed there had to be more than a work relationship. In his mind, why else was Richard bothering with me?"

I felt a ripple of anger flow through me. "That's rather insulting. To both of you, but especially you. You're his daughter. Surely, he knows you better than that?"

She smiled at me. "I love that you immediately jump to my defense."

I shrugged. "I know you well enough to know that."

"I was embarrassed and upset. It caused a rift between us. Richard was furious and went straight to my father, with Katy in tow, and told him off. They both did. Richard told him he should be proud of me, not casting aspersions on my character—or his. He said my father had insulted him and his wife, and that they were both very fond of me. He said his expectations of me were business-related and nothing else." She lifted one shoulder. "He told my dad to get his head out of his ass, apologize, and figure out what year it was. He made him apologize to Katy."

"What about you?"

"My dad waited a few days, called me, and I went to see him. He did apologize to me." She sighed. "He's a hard man at times, but he is my dad."

"What if he hates me and tells you to dump me?"

She was silent for a moment. "I hope that doesn't happen, Reid," she admitted. "But I'm a grown-up. I decide who will be in my life, not my dad."

"It would still be difficult." I ran my fingers through her hair. "I don't want to complicate your life. But at the same time, I want to be in it."

She smiled, cupped my cheek, and pressed her mouth to mine. "We'll figure that out when it happens, okay? Right now, I'm happy to be here with you."

I tugged her closer. "Me too."

A while later, she shifted and met my gaze, her expression curious. We hadn't moved, curled together on the sofa, talking, kissing, and holding hands. I hadn't gotten any of the things done I had planned, but I refused to move. I liked being near to her.

"Reid, I need to know . . . why-why are you still a virgin?"

I lifted one shoulder, trying not to grin at her hesitance in asking. "How I grew up wasn't exactly conducive to having a girlfriend, Becca. I mean, I kissed a few girls when I was a teenager, and I dated a couple of women when I got out of prison, but somehow, to me, I wanted it to be special. No one ever made me feel as if I wanted to share that part of me. It was one thing I had that was mine."

"I'm not a virgin," she stated, worried.

"I would hardly expect you to be. I think if I hadn't gone to prison, I wouldn't be one right now either. But that's the way life turned out. I'm not ashamed of it, even though I know it's highly unusual."

She looked toward the counter, tracing her finger around the edge of her coffee mug. A smile played on the corner of her lips as she remembered how I vaulted over it earlier. The thought made me smile as well.

"Is it wrong I find that kind of hot?" she asked under her breath.

Her gaze flew to mine. "The virgin thing—not that you've been in prison."

I chuckled. "I figured that. But, seriously, Becca, will you be able to move past the prison thing? And the fact that I have no family, no clue who I am, really?"

She frowned. "I'm sorry you were in prison. I hate what you went through your entire life. But you do know who you are. You chose that person. You're Reid Matthews."

"And Reid Matthews is . . ." I left the sentence hanging, wanting her to finish.

She smiled. "Reid is someone I want to spend a lot of time with. I want to know him—all of him."

"I'm rather new to the whole dating thing. I'll probably screw it up."

"I don't think you give yourself enough credit. We'll take our time and learn together."

"Does time include more kissing?"

"Definitely."

"And, ah, other things?"

"When you're ready. You've waited so long, Reid. Don't rush." Before I could reply, she said the words I was desperate to hear.

"I'm not going anywhere."

WE SPENT THE entire day together. I worked on the system, with Becca acting as my assistant. More than once, she rose up on her toes for a kiss. More than once, I had her pressed to the wall, devouring her mouth. It was the best install I had ever done.

"You are such a good kisser," she murmured against my mouth. "How can a virgin be so good at kissing?"

Pleased she was enjoying my caresses, I grinned. "I have kissed girls and women, but, as I said, I haven't gone beyond that." I cupped her face, dragging my lips across her cheek to her sensitive earlobe.

"I was waiting for the right person."

"And I'm that person?"

"Yes," I stated with conviction, dropping another kiss to her mouth. "You are." I ran my fingers over my lips, then grabbed my drill.

"Why do you do that?"

"Do what?"

"You press your fingers on your mouth every time we kiss."

"Oh, ah . . ." I stalled, looking over her shoulder. I felt heat prickle my neck.

"Tell me," she insisted. "I want to know."

"I like how it feels when you kiss me. I guess I'm sort of sealing you into me. Keeping your taste locked into my mouth."

She stared at me, blinking and silent.

"Is that weird? It's weird. I'm sorry."

I wasn't prepared when she launched herself at me. The drill flew one way; we hit the wall behind me, a mass of entangled arms and legs, her mouth on mine, hard and passionate. I slid down the wall to the floor, taking her with me. She was ferocious in her intensity, her kisses deep and possessive.

"You say the most erotic words," she groaned. "Sealing my taste into you?"

"So, not weird?" I moaned as she kissed her way down my neck.

"No, not weird." She hovered over me, her dark hair falling like a waterfall around us. "You turn me on like no man has ever done, Reid. Ever." She kissed me again.

I was good with that.

Eventually, we got off the floor, finished the install, and I explained how everything worked. Since her apartment was smaller and older, she had no use for many of the features, but I liked knowing her place was more secure. She loved the little camera so she could see who was at the door and the fact that she didn't have to have keys since she admitted to losing them a lot.

I pushed her laptop toward her. "Okay, you need to input your password. Make it something you can remember, but it needs a capital letter, a number and a special character."

She frowned in concentration.

"I can always override it, if you forget," I offered.

She tapped the keys with a grin.

"Enter it again."

She did, her grin getting wider. I looked at my screen. "Okay. You're done."

"You want to know what it is?"

"Um, you want me to know? I can unlock your door, then."

She sidled close, sliding her arm around my waist. Tucked in tight to my side, she grinned at me.

"Reidskiss#1"

I chuckled. "Really?"

"Yes."

I wondered if she knew how her words made me feel. She liked my kisses. She liked me. I mattered to her. I felt ten feet tall.

"Can I take you out to dinner?"

"Really?"

"Yes. I want to take you on a date." I looked down at my casual jeans and shirt. "I guess not a proper date, but I'll make up for it next time."

"You don't have to be in a suit for it to be a proper date, Reid. I like casual. I have to be dressed up all week for work, so it's nice to relax on the weekends."

"What's your favorite food?"

"Hmm. Chinese or Italian. I love them both."

"There is a great place a couple of blocks from here. Awesome Chinese. Small and casual. After, we could take a walk and get ice cream. For some reason, I always want ice cream after Chinese food."

Her eyes glowed. "Me too!"

I held out my hand. "Okay, BB. Let's go."

BECCA STUDIED THE menu on the wall, her nose scrunched in thought. She looked adorable, and I kissed the end of her nose. "Make up your mind."

"I never know what to get, so I get the usual, then I wish I had tried something different." She nibbled on her lip in frustration.

"Get a triple scoop."

"I can't eat that much ice cream!"

"I can. I'll get a triple, you get a double, and we'll share. Five flavors." I nudged her forward. "Now pick."

Ten minutes later, we were strolling down the street, hands clasped, eating ice cream. My huge cone contained chocolate peanut butter, marshmallow fudge, and moose tracks. Becca had banana fudge and black cherry. All of them were awesome. I ate faster than Becca, and she kept slapping my hand away from grabbing her cone. Laughing, I yanked her into my arms and kissed her in the middle of the street, not caring who might be watching. She tasted of ice cream, happiness, and life. Simply being with her made me happy. I had never known a feeling like it in my life. She clung to me as if she felt it too. When I lifted my head, I gazed down at her, mischievousness making her eyes dance with delight. Ice cream dripped down my hand, and with a sexy smirk, she licked it off my skin, her tongue lingering on my fingers. I groaned and shook my head.

"Tease."

She shook her head slowly. "No, it's a promise."

I rested my forehead on hers. "You can't say things like that to me."

"I think I just did."

"I want you so much," I pleaded to her skin.

"I told you there's no rush. I'm not going anywhere."

I laughed and stood back, trading cones with her. "Unless I explode."

She giggled, the sound teasing but still seductive. "I won't let you explode"—she slid her hand into my back pocket and squeezed my ass—"unless it's in the very best way. I promise."

As we walked, I licked the cone, needing to stop the ice cream from cascading down the sides. She watched me intently.

"I can hardly wait to see what you do with that tongue on me."

I almost swallowed said tongue. Choking, I mock-glared at her. "What did I say about not saying stuff like that to me?"

She snickered, trading cones once more. "I love seeing your reactions, but I'll stop if you want."

I studied her. She was happy and laughing. I felt lighter, more at home with myself than I had my entire life. I liked how her hand felt resting against my ass. I enjoyed how she felt nestled into my side. I loved tasting the ice cream her tongue had licked.

I caressed her hip. "Nope. Keep it up, BB. I'll pay you back one day."

She winked. "I'm looking forward to it."

We stopped to listen to a street musician playing his violin on the corner. His bow flashed as he wrung out notes I didn't know a violin could play—he was wickedly talented. I finished the last of my ice cream, then polished off Becca's. As the music continued, I stood behind her, linking my arms around her waist, tugging her close. I rested my chin on her head, letting the spirited music drift over me. Becca's fingers tapped out the beat on my arm, and I tightened my grip. It felt right standing with her, and I enjoyed the feel of her warmth. After the music faded, I reached into my pocket and tossed a couple of bills into his open violin case.

"Awesome, man."

He grinned. "Thanks."

We strolled away, getting closer to Becca's place. At the corner where the coffee shop and corner store were located, the old woman was outside, fussing with her buckets, lifting them to carry inside for the night. I hurried forward, lifted the last two buckets, and followed her inside.

She beamed at me, her face a crisscross of wrinkles, like that of a well-worn map, a lifetime of smiles etched into her skin.

"Your girl?" she asked, tilting her head to the door.

I glanced at Becca who was watching, curious. She had a small smile on her face, observing me talking to the flower lady.

"Yes," I confirmed. "My girl."

She bent and searched the buckets with fingers knotted with arthritis, pulling out a rose in a deep red. The petals were full and lush, a perfect specimen of the flower.

"You give. One is romantic."

"She will love it."

In an odd gesture, she reached up and patted my face. "I think you good boy. You deserve."

"Can I help you with anything else?"

"No. Flowers are inside. I close now."

I stepped outside, hearing the door lock in place behind me. I handed Becca the rose. Delight spread across her face, and she burrowed her nose in the blossom, inhaling deeply.

"Thank you."

"You're welcome."

She stepped closer, gazing up at me. "For someone who claims he has little experience, you are very good at this dating thing."

"Yeah?"

She slid her arm around my waist, tipping up her head. "Yeah."

"I think it might have something to do with the person I'm with," I replied. "You make it easy, Becca." I ran my fingers down her cheek. "It's all you, BB."

She pressed her mouth to mine.

"I'm good with that."

I was as well.

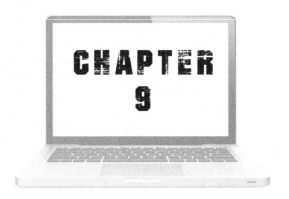

CHAPTER 9

REID

IT WAS DIFFICULT to leave Becca. But I knew if I stayed, things were going to progress and fast. She was right when she said there was no rush, but still, being alone in her apartment and close to her was too much of a temptation.

"What are you doing tomorrow?" I asked and picked up my bag, stalling for a few more minutes of her company.

"Laundry, some grocery shopping. Then I'm meeting Cami and Emmy for coffee in the afternoon. They're going to show me a couple of places to shop." She smiled. "You?"

"A few errands and I'll probably go into the office." I lifted the bag to my shoulder with a shrug. "I have lots of stuff I can work on, and I wasn't there today. In fact, I'll probably do some work when I go home. I like to work at night."

"You work a lot. Do you go in every weekend?"

"Typically. I'm a night owl. I don't need much sleep."

"Usually, I go to bed early. I need a good eight hours. I always have." She chuckled. "I think I was the most boring student at university. Everyone was partying or up late watching TV, and I was asleep."

"I don't think you could ever be boring."

"I'll remind you of that when you're playing video games to keep yourself entertained while I nap."

I didn't know how to tell her that idea pleased me. With her curled up next to me as I played games or worked on code. I liked the idea, a lot.

"Sounds good." I flashed her a grin.

"I don't want to keep you from your work, Reid."

"Don't worry about it. One reason I worked so much was that I had nothing else to occupy my time. I'm sort of hoping that's changed."

"It has, but I don't want you to fall behind."

I laughed. "That won't happen. Plus, Aiden and Maddox will be thrilled. They've been telling me to get out and live."

Her brow furrowed. "What, ah, what are we going to do about the office?"

"Whatever you're comfortable with. I know you're a private person, Becca. I won't embarrass you at work."

She captured my hand. "You could never embarrass me. But I think we need to keep our relationship between us. At least for a while."

"So, you don't want me to say anything to the guys?" I asked, brushing my hair off my forehead. "They know me pretty well and have been sort of helping to push me in your direction. I don't think I can lie that well."

"No, I know they're your friends and you confide in them. I meant no PDA in the office or preferential treatment."

"Too late. They already told me they know you're my priority at work. They tease me about it all the time."

She chuckled. "Okay, then. Maybe watch you don't go overboard." She bit her lip. "Maybe no, ah, really *personal* stories?"

I had to laugh at her request. "I won't say or do anything to humiliate you or us." I lifted one eyebrow, teasing. "At least, I'll try. Aiden says I am the king of overshare." At her look of worry, I pressed a kiss to her forehead. "My relationship with them isn't conventional, Becca. They're my bosses, but also my friends. The closest thing to family I have. I do promise anything I tell them is between us, and I can be discreet when it comes to you." I sighed heavily, my breath moving the tendrils of hair that fell over her brow. "You mean too much for me to be flippant or careless with our relationship. Trust me when I say that."

She grinned. "I do. No doubt Cami and Emmy will pump me for information about you, and they'll share with Aiden and Bentley."

I laughed. "Bentley won't comment, but Aiden will. And he'll fill in Maddox. They'll probably be in my office waiting to pounce on Monday wanting deets."

"This is unconventional."

I looked down at her. "Is it too much?"

She studied me, then cupped my cheek. "No, Reid. Not too much. We'll figure it out, together."

I liked that word.

"Yeah." I grinned. "Together."

⌒

WHEN I WAS in prison, time had no meaning. My days were an endless loop of repetition. Wake up, eat, study, read, eat, do assigned chores, eat, study more, sleep. I didn't think, I didn't plan, and I didn't hope.

When I became part of BAM, some things changed, while others remained the same. My life was still on a loop, but it was one that I chose. I slept and worked, but the additions of Bentley, Aiden, and Maddox gave my life meaning. The work I did mattered. I mattered. Still, time had no meaning. The days flowed into each other, time flying by as the days and nights blended.

Until Becca came along. Time took on a completely new relevance.

Normally, a Sunday flew by like every other day—filled with computers, words, codes, and graphics. Monday would arrive, another workweek ahead, broken up by moments of laughter and friendship.

However, this Sunday dragged. I couldn't concentrate on work. I prowled my small apartment, then headed to the office, hoping for distraction. It never came. Instead, all I did was think of Becca. How her mouth felt on mine. The way her body fit to me when we were close. The way she listened to my every word. Her tears because she felt my pain. Her laughter because I made her happy.

Everything about her.

I tried to resist contacting her. I told myself to chill and be cool. I would see her in the morning. It was not a big deal. But my mind kept wandering. Finally, I gave up, deciding I wasn't at all cool, and Becca was well aware of that fact.

I dialed her number, smiling at her breathless greeting. From the sounds behind her, I knew she was outside. I wished I were with her.

"Reid, is that you?" She giggled. "It's your number, so it has to be—hi!"

I relaxed, hearing her enthusiasm. "Hey, BB."

"Everything okay?"

I reclined in my chair, tucked my phone between my shoulder and ear, and stretched my arms upward, shutting my eyes. "It is now."

"Now? It wasn't before?"

"I wanted to hear your voice, and I didn't know if I would look needy calling you, so I tried to resist." I sighed with a laugh. "But I'm not cool, and I decided you already knew that, so I'm calling to say hello and see how your day is going. Make sure you're okay."

There was a muffled sound, and the noise in the background dimmed. Her voice was soft. "You wanted to hear my voice?"

"Yeah."

"And check on me?"

"Yeah," I repeated. "I'm lame, I guess."

"No," she murmured. "You are anything but lame. I think you're wonderful."

I grinned so wide, my eyes shut again. "Yeah?"

Apparently, I could only say one specific word to her right now.

"Yeah," she responded. "To answer your question, my day is good. Not as good as yesterday, but still nice."

I sat straighter, holding the phone close to my mouth. "Yesterday was better?"

"Yesterday was awesome," she breathed out.

"Even the part where I tried to give you a concussion with your stripper pole, and then screwed you in the totally wrong manner on the floor?"

"Ahem."

My eyes flew open, meeting Aiden's amused gaze. He was standing in the doorway, his arms folded over his massive chest. I felt the heat of my embarrassment stain my cheeks.

Becca giggled, bringing my attention back to the phone. "Well, part of that was good. But what happened after was even better."

"I agree."

"Are you okay?" she asked. "Are you at the office?"

"Yes, I am. Aiden just arrived in my office, in fact."

"Oh." Her breath hitched. "Just now?"

"A few minutes ago, I think."

"Oh. *Oh.*"

I was back to my one-word answers. "Yeah."

She laughed. "Well, I'll let you go explain that to him. I'll join Cami and Emmy. Would you-would you call me later?"

"If it's okay."

"Reid, you can call me anytime. I like to hear your voice too, okay?"

"Okay."

"Have fun."

I hung up as Aiden walked in and flung himself into the chair across from my desk. He leaned back, crossed his arms behind his head, and stared at me.

"Mission accomplished?"

"Which one?"

"Project B?"

I smirked—you'd think we were planning a strategic mission. "Stage one is complete."

"Sounded to me like it went further than that from where I was standing."

Knowing it was Aiden, and he'd find out from Cami anyway, I told him. I gave him the short version, but it was enough to send him into gales of laughter. I described vaulting over the counter and what happened after I grabbed Becca. He leaned forward, his shoulders shaking as he guffawed. My lips twitched and I had to laugh. Listening to myself as I retold it, I also found it amusing.

I slouched in my chair with a sigh. "It worked out. We talked and cleared the air. I told her my story."

He frowned. "All of it?"

"Yes. I told her my history. What I did, why, and the consequences. She knows I was in jail and how I came to work here."

"She's okay with it?"

"As okay as she can be. I'm not sure her father will agree. He sounds like a black-and-white sort of guy. I was in jail, therefore I'm bad news." I rubbed my face. "But we'll cross that bridge when we come to it. Meanwhile, I get Becca in my life. I'll worry about him later."

"So, she's your girlfriend now?"

I grinned. "Yeah, she is."

He held up his hand for a high five. "Finally."

I WAS IN the server room on Monday morning when Becca arrived at work. I heard her voice as I made my way down the hall. She was speaking to Sandy, laughing at something she said. I rounded the corner in anticipation of seeing her and stopped cold. She wasn't alone at Sandy's desk. Colin, Sandy's grandson, was there, leaning on the tall granite counter that surrounded Sandy. He was smiling and chuckling at whatever Becca was telling him. He stood too close to her, and I didn't like the intent expression on his face as he talked to her. I watched as he scribbled something on a piece of paper and handed it to Becca. My hands became fists, and I had to take a couple of deep, calming breaths as I approached the desk.

"Morning."

Three sets of eyes shifted to me. I only cared about one, and the intensity of Becca's bright blue gaze made me smile.

"Hi," she breathed out.

I smiled back, but that was all I could do, once again tongue-tied when it came to her.

"Hey, Reid," Colin greeted me, extending his hand. "Just the man I need to see."

I tore my gaze from Becca's and shook his hand. "Oh?"

"Could I see you in private?"

"Sure."

He pushed off the counter, stopping to kiss Sandy. "Later, Nan."

"Behave."

"Always."

She snorted. "Right. Come to dinner on the weekend."

"I will."

He smiled at Becca. "Great to meet you. I hope to see you again soon."

She smiled in return. "You too."

"Be sure to use the number I gave you."

"I will."

I headed to my office, muttering under my breath. The only place he was going to be seeing Becca was beside *me*. He could stop smiling at her that way and giving her his number. She wasn't available.

In my office, I tossed my phone on my desk and sat down. Colin followed at a leisurely pace, sitting down and crossing his legs. I studied him with narrowed eyes. He was good-looking and confident. Sandy was proud of him and all he had accomplished. He was an ER doctor, and until this very moment, I had always liked him. Now, he was annoying the hell out of me by simply breathing. Because he was breathing the same air as Becca and I didn't like the way he looked at her.

She was mine.

"What's got you all hot and bothered?" he asked.

"Nothing."

He chuckled. "Right." He relaxed in the chair. "Becca is a pretty girl. Nan is very fond of her."

"She won't be using the number you gave her."

One eyebrow rose. "Oh? And you know this because . . . ?"

"She isn't available," I spat.

His head fell back, and he laughed. "Nan didn't say it was you."

"What are you talking about? Something amusing you?"

"You are, Reid. You need to chill, my man." He chuckled again. "I wasn't giving her my number. Becca asked me if I knew of any doctors accepting patients. I gave her my *girlfriend's* number since she is about to open her own GP practice and will be accepting new patients." He snorted. "I never thought of you as the jealous type. I only said she was pretty."

"I'm plenty chill," I retorted, his explanation taking the wind out of my sails. "She *is* pretty," I added.

"Nan mentioned in general conversation that she thought Becca was seeing someone. I know who that someone is now."

I shifted in my chair. "We're sort of new."

"Good for you, man."

"Sorry about the misunderstanding."

He shook his head. "I get it. No worries. But given the way she was looking at you, the girl isn't interested in anyone's number but yours."

I grinned, my humor restored. I had always liked Colin.

"Good to know. Now, what's up?"

His expression changed to serious. "A case came in last night. Third time she's been in the ER in six months."

"Domestic violence?"

"Yes." He nodded. "She talked—finally—and wants out, but she has nowhere to go and no money to try. We kept her in. She had her daughter with her, and the cops arrested her husband." He met my eyes. "I don't think she'll survive a fourth visit."

"I'll make the arrangements. The fund will set her up."

Colin knew about my underground fund. With my permission, Sandy had told him. On occasion, he brought a case to me, and I let the people I trusted help them. The woman and her child would find a safe haven with a shelter and financial help to start a new life.

"Can she leave the hospital today?"

"Yeah, she's okay to leave, but I told her we had to keep her another night in case you could help."

"She wants this?"

"Yes."

"I'll make the arrangements, and they'll take her in today."

He slid a piece of paper my way. "That's her info. The head nurse knows."

"Okay." That was how it worked. Colin needed someone he trusted to make sure the right people got to the woman before her husband did. She would disappear along with her child and be safe before he got out of jail. My people would help her get free.

He stood. "I'll go back to the hospital and tell her." He shook my hand. "Thanks, Reid." He stopped at my doorway. "Remember what I said. Chill. You have nothing to worry about."

I waved him off. "Yeah. Thanks."

I heard his chuckles all the way down the hall.

Reaching into my drawer, I pulled out my personal computer. It was time to do some good.

THERE WAS A knock on my door.

Glancing at my watch, I was shocked to see it was almost two. I looked up, smiling when I saw it was Becca. "Hi."

She entered and took a seat in front of my desk. "Hey."

"What's up?"

She frowned. "I haven't seen you all morning. You didn't come to the staff meeting."

"Oh. Yeah. Something came up."

"You're not avoiding me? You seemed out of sorts earlier."

I ran a hand through my hair and pushed my glasses up my nose. No matter how often I had them adjusted, they slipped down. It might have something to do with the way I tore them off my face several times a day and tossed them onto my desk.

Maybe.

"No, I'm good. Could we maybe talk about it over a late lunch? If you haven't eaten yet?"

A smile played on her lips. "I haven't. Are you asking me out, Mr. Matthews?"

"Would you say yes if I was?"

"Try me."

"Would you have lunch with me, Becca?"

She leaned closer. "Yes, I would. On one condition."

"Anything."

"The lunch should be somewhere you can kiss me."

I swallowed. "I can arrange that."

"Okay." She stood, crossing her arms. "I'm waiting."

"Oh." I jumped up from my chair. "You mean now."

She chuckled. "If it's a good time."

"Yes." I wanted to be alone with her. "Definitely a good time."

WE WALKED TO a small place off the main road. It looked like a grocery store out front, but in the back, behind the deli and hot plate counter, was an unoccupied, small, covered patio with a few tables. "You grab a table, and I'll get lunch. The pasta is homemade and awesome."

"Okay."

As she sidled past me, I slipped my arm around her waist and tugged her close. I pressed my mouth to hers, moaning when she opened for me right away and flung her arms around my neck. It was a kiss of hello and I missed you. One still full of new feelings and discovery.

She smiled as I drew back before I got carried away. The thick bushes behind us suddenly looked inviting. As if she knew what I was thinking, she grinned and sat down.

I gazed at her, mesmerized by her natural beauty. Her dark hair was in a braid today, off to one side. Her face glowed, and her eyes sparkled with happiness. She wore a deep teal-colored dress that set off her skin tone. She met my gaze with one of her own.

"You stare at me a lot."

"I like what I see. It makes me happy." I paused. "You make me happy, Becca Holden. It's a rare feeling for me."

Her smile was one of her shy ones. Probably my favorite. It was different from the businesslike smile she used in the office and the confidence she exuded. It said I pleased her, and it showed her softer side. One I knew few people saw.

"There you go, saying the perfect thing again."

I bent low, kissing her again, hard and deep. "You make it easy."

Leaving her gaping and flustered, I went to get us lunch.

⁓

"SO YOU ARRANGED to help this woman?" Becca asked, her eyes wide with surprise. "You make a call and it gets done?"

I had explained why Colin wanted to see me and why I hadn't been at the meeting. I knew I could trust her. Aiden had known and made sure I knew what had occurred and what items I needed to follow up on. Luckily, there wasn't much. My department was too well organized.

I finished a mouthful of pasta and shook my head. "No calls. I have a computer I only use for that purpose. It's untraceable and unhackable. I have contacts in different organizations. I get in touch, arrange the money, then I'm out of it. The person who benefits has no idea where the money comes from."

"Do the people you contact know where it comes from?"

I shook my head. "It took me a long time to set it all up. All they know is the money is clean and they can help those in need with it. Sometimes, I distribute the money myself. Other times I use these people. But it isn't traceable back to me. I'm not putting Bentley at risk or his company. He knows what I do. They all do. They know the precautions I take and why I do it. I have their full support."

"You're like Robin Hood."

I laughed and finished my pasta. I pushed her bowl toward her. "You need to eat while I talk. You never finish your food."

She chuckled self-consciously. "I get so caught up in listening to you, I forget."

"I'm not Robin Hood, Becca. It's part of my amends toward my past. Some would argue the money isn't clean. It's tainted."

She chewed, looking thoughtful. Patting her mouth with her napkin, she met my gaze. "Like my father, you mean?"

I shrugged. "Others as well, I'm sure."

"I disagree. You went to jail. You did your penance. You paid them back the money plus the interest they lost. You owe them nothing, and they took four years of your life." Her voice shook.

I was shocked to see the glimmer of tears in her eyes. I reached for her hand and squeezed it. Her emotions got me every time. "It's okay, Becca. It's in the past."

A tear ran down her cheek. "I feel as if you were the one robbed."

I wiped the moisture from her skin. "I like to think it happened for a reason. Because of being in jail, I worked hard to learn everything I could. I got a job with an amazing company. I get to help people who need it. People, who, like me years ago, get overlooked." I wrapped my hand around hers, stilling her fidgeting fingers. "I got to meet you."

I met her gaze. "I'd do it all over again if it meant I got to meet you."

She sniffled, offering me a watery smile. "You say the best things."

I winked then indicated her half-eaten bowl of ziti. "Are you going to finish that?"

She pushed it my way. "No."

I polished it off in about five minutes. I had gained a new appreciation for food when I got out of prison after four years of bland. The textures and spices. The smells and nuances of different cultures. I loved trying new dishes. Becca enjoyed experimenting as well, and Toronto was a melting pot of ethnicity. I looked forward to discovering lots of new places with her.

"So, can I ask you something?"

I swallowed the last mouthful. "You can ask anything."

"What is the deal with Colin?"

My hand holding my glass of water froze partway to my mouth. "Excuse me?"

She began to laugh and reached across the table, patting my arm. "I should have phrased that better." She lifted one eyebrow in a gesture I was too familiar with after working with Sandy.

It said: Busted.

"You were a little abrupt with him this morning."

"We worked it out."

"You weren't actually jealous, were you?"

I looked down at the table and shrugged. "This is all new for me, BB. All I saw was a handsome guy handing you what I thought was his number. I realize it was stupid and my reaction was over the top." I met her gaze. "But I also realized I have no claim on you. You are free to date anyone you want." I swallowed the bitterness I felt.

She studied me for a moment then smiled. "No one has ever been jealous regarding me before. You were kinda cute." She sat back. "Even if it was, as you say, over the top."

"I apologize."

"I would never date someone else while I was with you, Reid. If you don't understand that, let me reassure you right now."

"Me, either. You're it for me, Becca. Done and dusted."

Her eyes grew round.

"I mean . . ." I scrubbed my face in frustration, realizing how that sounded. "I mean I don't want to date anyone else."

"Okay."

I sighed. "So much for saying the right thing."

She chuckled. "You did fine."

"So what did you want to know about Colin?"

"Oh. How on earth is he Sandy's grandson? He must be thirty. She told me she turns fifty-five next month. Is he adopted?"

I leaned back. "Ah, no. Sandy was a bit of a wild child. When she was eighteen, she married a man who was forty and had a son her age already. His son—Aaron—got married and had Colin when he was twenty-four, and a daughter, Jennifer, a couple of years later. She was a very young grandmother."

"Wow!"

"I know."

"Is she still married?"

"Yes. Her husband, Max, was a doctor. He retired years ago, and his health isn't great. But they are still together. She looks after him with some home care help. He still adores her and she him."

"And she got on well with his son?"

"Yep. They are great friends, and Sandy loves Colin to bits. He gets a kick out of telling people she's his grandmother—they never believe him. He teases her about it a lot."

"You've spent a lot of time with them?"

I drained my water. "Yes. When I joined the company, Sandy took pity on me and fed me a few times. Max is great, and I enjoy talking to him. I've only met Aaron a couple of times, but he seems like a nice guy. He lives in Ottawa but comes for visits to see Colin, Max, and Sandy often. Aaron's daughter, Jennifer, lives in Europe, so Sandy doesn't see her granddaughter very often. I haven't even met her."

"Sandy never had kids?"

"No."

"Sandy would have been a great mom."

"I think that's why she is so close to Colin."

"Makes sense."

"Anyway, I rigged a bunch of things at their house to make it easier for them. Colin sees them a lot, so we became friendly. I heard him telling Sandy one day about a patient he was worried about, and I told him what I did. Since then, on occasion, he asks for help."

"Wow. That must be quite a story—Sandy, I mean."

"I don't know everything, but she told me some history. It caused a huge scandal, I guess—the age difference and him having a son her age. She knew Aaron first, and they were friends. She met Max at some social function, and she said it was love at first sight for them both. They went through a lot, but they made it."

We walked back to the office, our fingers entwined. In the elevator, Becca turned to me. "Thanks for lunch."

"Anytime."

"Can I repay you with dinner tomorrow?"

I didn't hesitate. "Yep."

She pressed a kiss to my mouth before the doors opened and our hands separated. I followed her down the hall, pausing in my doorway when she spoke my name softly.

"Reid?"

I turned. "Yeah, BB?"

She glanced around quickly, then kissed me again.

"You do have a claim. I wanted you to know that," she declared, then hurried away.

The grin never left my face the rest of the afternoon.

CHAPTER 10

REID

I STARED AT the computer screen—for the first time in my life, I didn't understand the images in front of me. I restarted the video, slowing it down, trying to memorize the instructions. I was failing big-time. I glanced at my phone, checking the time. It was after seven, and the office was empty. I studied the screen again, thinking of Becca's offhand remarks over lunch at my desk earlier that day.

"Bentley's wedding is in two weeks—how exciting!"

I nodded, noncommittal.

"What's the matter? Are you an I-hate-weddings kind of guy?"

I chuckled, looking at her sandwich, wondering if she was going to eat the other half. She'd been working on the first half for a solid ten minutes. My entire sandwich was gone in five. "I have no idea. I've never been to one."

She gasped. "Really? I love weddings!"

"Nope." I tugged on her plate. "You gonna eat that, BB?"

With a laugh, she pushed the plate my way. "You're hanging around Aiden far too much. You're beginning to eat like him."

I picked up the sandwich with a grin. "I'm still a growing boy. So why do you love weddings so much?"

She leaned her elbow on my desk, propping her chin in her hand as she gazed past me out the window. *"I don't know. The beautiful dresses, the words of love, the flowers, and everyone smiling."* She shrugged. *"It's really nice. The speeches are usually long, but I imagine since it's Aiden and Maddox speaking, they'll be pretty entertaining. Later, we can dance!"*

I almost choked. *"Dance?"* I managed to get out.

She bobbed her head enthusiastically. *"I know we're not announcing we're a couple, but you'll dance with me, right?"* She moved her index finger around the desk in small circles. *"If you'd rather not, I can ask Craig or someone else."* A little grin tugged on her lips. *"I think I heard Sandy say Colin was bringing her. I'm sure he'd dance with me."*

I narrowed my eyes. *"I don't think so. You want to dance? Then we'll dance, Ms. Holden. I'm claiming all of them. Now."*

She stood, brushing off her skirt, fighting a smile. *"If you insist."*

"I do."

"Yep. That's part of the wedding! Look at you getting into the spirit!" She picked up her phone and left.

It was only after she'd walked out that I realized she'd played me. Damn, she was good.

Really, though, I was fine with it since I didn't want anyone else dancing with her.

Except, I had no idea how to dance. I had never attended a dance growing up, two-stepped with a woman in a country bar, or even swayed with someone in a drunken haze.

More virgin territory.

That was why, on a Friday night, I was studying dance videos and websites. Surely, it couldn't be that difficult? Lots of people did it. I had seen Becca dance. She was graceful and fluid. I just needed to make sure I didn't stomp on her toes. I looked back at the screen and realized watching wasn't going to cut it. I needed to practice.

I checked the hallway, glancing up and down. It was deserted. Satisfied, I returned to my desk and turned on my wall of monitors. I studied the movements for several minutes, then pushed off my desk.

I recalled the instructional tutorial from earlier.

Relax.

Keep your head up and back straight.

Listen to the music.

Let your body feel the rhythm.

I rolled my shoulders, already confused. How was I supposed to relax but keep my back straight and my head up? I decided to go with relax.

I hung my head and listened to the music. It had a nice tempo. Self-conscious, I tapped my foot to the beat and attempted to follow the steps on the screen. I was awkward and stiff. I kept going the wrong way instead of the way they instructed. I stumbled and had to right myself.

It was much harder than it looked.

I tried again, cursing loudly when I slammed into the corner of my desk. I kicked at the edge, wondering how bad it would really be if Becca danced with Colin. He had a girlfriend, after all.

The flash of jealousy that hit me at the thought of her in his arms instead of mine made me try again. This time, I tripped over a chair.

I stood up, brushing off my pants as I heard the sound of clapping. Startled, I spun around to see Aiden in the doorway, his expression amused. He indicated the monitors behind me.

"What the hell are you doing?"

I hit the end button. "Nothing."

He walked in, his shoulders shaking from laughter. "I think you were attempting to dance, but at first, I wasn't sure if you were having a seizure or drunk."

"It wasn't that bad."

He met my gaze. "Yeah, kid, it was."

I sighed, dropping my head to my chest. "Becca wants to dance at Bent's wedding."

"And?"

"It's another punch card, Aiden. I don't know how to dance. I have never danced in my life!"

He frowned. "Not even when you're alone in your boxers making a sandwich and a good song comes on the radio? You don't start busting a move?"

"First off, thanks for the visual, and second, no. Never. And I don't think 'busting a move' is what Becca wants. She wants slow and romantic—" I jerked my thumb in the direction of the wall "—like they're doing."

He rubbed his chin and shook his head. "I think that's a little out-of-date for Becca. She wants you to dance, not waltz."

"Dammit, I wasted a couple of hours."

He snorted. "Boy, if that was after a couple of hours, I wouldn't want to see what you looked like to start." He shrugged off his jacket and rolled up his sleeves. "Okay, let's get at it."

"What?"

He grinned. "You wanna learn how to dance? I'm gonna show you."

⌒

"SERIOUSLY, COULD YOU step on my foot again? I think there's one toe you haven't bruised or broken yet," Aiden grumbled.

"It's not my fault. You have such big feet."

"You know what they say about big feet . . ." Aiden waggled his eyebrows.

"Fuck. Knock it off. Do you really need your hand on my ass?" I complained again, reaching behind me to tug his arm higher.

"Trust me, when you're dancing with Becca, that's where it will end up. Cami likes my hand there, right around the curve of her—"

I stepped back, holding up my hands. "Dude, I am not Cami."

"No shit. Her ass is great, and she's graceful. You need to relax."

"I *can't* relax! You keep telling me what to do and hugging me . . . and feeling me up! It's just not right, Aiden!"

"Me telling you what to do, or the hugging part? Because, seriously—I like the feeling up part." He winked. "You're a little bony, but if I batted for the other team, I'd go for you."

I rolled my eyes. "You are so immature."

He held out his arms, waiting for me to take his hand. "Okay, again. You need a lot of practice."

With a sigh, I stepped into position. "Watch where you put your hands," I growled.

He chuckled. "Whatever, kid. You suck at this, but we're gonna keep trying. Follow my lead."

"That's another thing. How am I supposed to learn if I'm following your lead? Won't Becca expect me to lead? Maybe we should try that?"

He shook his head. "I lead. I'm the guy."

"I want to be the guy."

"Not right now."

"No, let's try it my way."

"No! I'm the guy! I'm too big to be the girl. That's your job!"

"I'm tired of being the girl!"

A voice made us both freeze.

"Is this what happens after hours around here? Maddox, you've been hiding things from me."

Aiden and I separated, then faced the door.

Maddox and Richard VanRyan filled the doorway. They had their arms crossed, amusement written all over their faces.

"How long have you been there?" Aiden demanded.

"Long enough. I think the question is how long have you been at *that*?" Maddox responded.

Aiden glanced at his watch. "An hour or so."

"I was practicing before he got here," I piped up.

Richard's expression said it all. My practicing hadn't helped.

"Um, what are you doing here, Richard?"

He grinned. "I was in Montreal. My flight had a stopover, and there was a mechanical malfunction that grounded us for the night. I called Maddox to see if he wanted to meet for a drink, and he insisted on coming to get me."

"And you're here in the office because . . . ?"

"I heard they were auditioning for *So You Think You Can Dance*. And I wanted to come to see it for myself. By the way, the answer to the question is no. You can't dance, Reid." He started to chuckle. "In fact, both of you suck."

"Hey!" Aiden frowned. "I'm a good dancer. Cami says so."

"Uh-huh."

"She never complains."

Maddox burst out laughing. "Because all you do is crush her to your chest and fling her around. She hangs on for dear life."

"If you think you can do better, be my guest."

Maddox lifted an eyebrow. "You wanna make a little wager?"

"Sure." Aiden put his hands on his hips. "Bring it."

"Hey!" I objected. "I only want to dance with Becca at the wedding. Not be part of some sort of contest."

Richard smirked, ignoring my words. "I'll accept too. Double or nothing."

"That confident, are you?" Maddox returned his smirk.

"When I first knew her, my wife could, and often did, trip over air. She's gotten better, but she still finds being vertical a challenge at times," Richard laughed. "When Katy dances with me, she's grace personified. I think I have a lot to do with that."

Aiden chuckled. "Okay then, I think we have a challenge. You each get a chance with him, and whoever shows him how to dance the best, wins."

"Um." I scratched my head. "I really don't want to dance with anyone else tonight. I think I'm good."

"What's the wager?" Maddox asked, ignoring me as he looked between Aiden and Richard.

"A thousand bucks." Aiden rubbed his hands together. "Whoever teaches him to dance gets the cash."

My eyebrows flew up.

Richard shrugged off his jacket. "You're on."

"What do I get out of it?" I asked.

Richard held out his arms. "The safety of my embrace," he deadpanned. "Now, let's go."

I groaned. This was not how I planned to learn how to dance.

⌒

FORTY-FIVE MINUTES LATER, I shook my head. "Forget it, Richard. Obviously, this is not my thing."

He furrowed his brow. "You literally have no coordination. Or rhythm."

"This doesn't bode well for punching your V-card, Reid," Aiden sang from the desk. "You need lots of rhythm for that." He kicked up his feet on my desk and made a lewd gesture with his hips. "Becca is gonna expect some moves in the bedroom."

Richard's eyes grew round. "You've *never*? Really, I mean, no offense, but how can that even be possible?"

"It just is," I said, feeling defensive. "Becca's good with it. In fact, she finds it hot."

He grimaced. "I don't want to think of Becca and you . . . yeah, never mind." He laid his hand on my shoulder, suddenly serious. "Treat her right, or you'll deal with me."

"Understood."

"Do you need any, ah, pointers, in *that* direction?"

I held up my hands. "No. Just no."

"Okay, simply asking. Back to business." Richard huffed a sigh. "You got any ideas, Mad Dog? The kid has the rhythm of a block of cement."

Maddox stood, draining his beer. He'd gone out, grabbed some pizza and a case of beer, and brought it back. He had returned to the office full time after his accident, and he was almost back to his old self. He and Aiden had been eating, drinking, and critiquing, while Richard did his best to teach me to dance. As with Aiden, it was a total failure.

"One," Maddox drawled, and handed Richard and me each a

beer. "You keep telling him, but does he even know what he's trying to do? What it's supposed to look like? It's Reid, our computer boy. Graphics, games, code. He's all about seeing. He needs a visual." He indicated the monitors behind me. "And not like that. Live."

Richard took a long swallow. "You're right."

Maddox chuckled. "You willing to take one for the team?"

Richard drained his beer and wiped his mouth. "Let's go." He tilted his chin. "Music."

I hit the play button and grabbed my beer. The bottle froze partway to my mouth as Richard and Maddox began to dance. Richard took the lead, with Maddox following his steps. They were loose and relaxed, their bodies swaying, feet moving to the beat. I watched, actually seeing how they simply allowed the music to move them. I studied their feet, wondering how they didn't trip over each other, but neither seemed to have that issue.

"You two look beautiful together," Aiden mocked. "So in sync."

Maddox flipped him the bird and kept going. "Do you see?" he asked me. "Concentrate on your partner, not your feet. Stop thinking. That's not how it works. Feel the music. Guide her by pressing on her back, gently urging her in the right direction."

I frowned.

"Like your game controller." Richard smirked.

A light bulb went on.

"Yes!"

"Okay, you try."

"Can I lead?"

"Yes."

I took Richard's place. I took in a deep breath, blew it out, and concentrated on the music. I ignored the fact that it was Maddox and someone was watching us. I didn't trip. I didn't stumble. I wasn't very graceful, but I stayed upright, earning a round of applause.

"I think that's as good as it's going to get," Richard observed.

I grabbed a piece of pizza and wolfed it down. "As long as I don't maim Becca, I'm good. She's graceful enough for both of us." I sighed. "I think I've had enough lessons for tonight."

"Thank God," Richard muttered.

"What about up-tempo dances?" Aiden asked. "I'm better at those."

I shook my head. "I can barely go slow. I am *not* trying fast. I'll sit those ones out."

Aiden scrolled through my music, pressing play. "No, really. You can do this. Watch me."

Maddox dropped his head with a groan. "Not again."

Aiden started to move.

Grinding, pushing out his chest, and thrusting to the heavy Latin beat. He circled his hips, popped his pelvis, dropped to his knees, and jumped up again. He rolled his shoulders, his pecs, and his hips. It was almost obscene. He grinned the whole time, stroking his chest and making lewd gestures with his hands. He grabbed the back of the chair, grinding against it.

"Usually, I have Cami for this. She loves it—she thinks it's hot."

I gaped, meeting Richard's eyes.

"I can't do *that*."

He began to laugh. Big, loud guffaws that echoed in my office. "And I can't *unsee* that. It will forever be seared into my brain."

"Welcome to my world," Maddox muttered. "He used to practice in the living room at the house we shared. Time hasn't improved it."

Aiden winked, and suddenly we were all laughing. He stopped dancing and turned off the music. "You guys have no appreciation for my talent."

"Is that what you call it?" Richard quipped.

I chuckled. Aiden ignored him.

"I guess you won the bet, Mad Dog. I owe you a thousand bucks."

"Yeah, me too," Richard chuckled. "Worth it, though."

"Promise me you won't ever make me watch you dance like that again, Aiden, and we'll call it even." Maddox waved at Richard. "We can have a guys' night out on you next time you're in town."

"Works for me." Richard lifted his hand for a high five, and Aiden flashed a grin.

"Done."

CHAPTER 11

REID

I FUSSED WITH the sleeves of my shirt, tugged on my suit jacket, and studied my reflection in the mirror. Maddox went with me to help pick out the suit, making sure I had it tailored properly. I wanted to look nice for Becca, so she'd be proud to have me as her date. Although we hadn't made a big thing of being together at the office, and planned to be low-key today at the wedding, it was still a date for us. I was looking forward to spending the evening with her.

The suit was navy with a fine pinstripe. My shirt white, the tie and pocket square Maddox insisted on, red. The suit was the most expensive thing I'd ever purchased, although I knew it was a drop in the bucket compared to what Maddox or Bentley paid for a suit. Still, it looked good, and I had actually enjoyed the shopping trip with Maddox. We kept it between us in case Aiden decided to tag along. After the dance lessons, I wasn't sure I could handle his input on my clothing choice as well.

I slipped on the new shoes Maddox claimed I had to purchase, and my phone buzzed, announcing the arrival of the car service I had hired. I grabbed my keys and hurried out the door, anxious to get to Becca.

~

I KEPT STARING at Becca most of the evening. I couldn't help it. She was always pretty and elegant, but today, she was stunning. Her hair was an intricate weave of curls and small glittery beads, wound together at the base of her neck with some long tendrils around her face and neck. Her dress was red, matching my tie, a simple cut that was off the shoulder and swirled around her knees as she walked. But when she had turned around to get a shawl, I gasped. The back was a deep cowl, showing off the creamy expanse of her skin. Skin that I could touch as I escorted her to the car. That I could stroke as I sat next to her, my arm draped across the back of her chair. Softness that had been driving me crazy all night in anticipation. All of a sudden, dancing had become something I *needed* to do with her.

I had finally told her my concerns. I had even confessed to the dance lessons, albeit a slightly abridged version. After her laughter faded, she had kissed my cheek and assured me we would be fine. I would be fine.

Once the dinner was over, the amusing and mercifully short speeches made by Aiden and Maddox, the dancing began. I watched Bentley and Emmy twirl around the floor, his steps confident and assured. Maddox and Dee were elegant; although they slipped away not long after the music began. Aiden wasn't as smooth as the other two, but Cami made up for it, and he beamed down at her with a look of adoration on his face. Richard had returned to town for the wedding, his wife Katy with him. He pulled her onto the dance floor fast, holding her close as they moved to the music. Each man had his own style and for him, it worked. Now it was my turn to find my style.

I swallowed and caught Becca's gaze. "You want to risk it, BB?"

She smiled and squeezed my hand. "I would love to dance, but not if it makes you uncomfortable."

I stood and offered her my hand. "I apologize in advance for my feet and my lack of skill."

She took my hand with a shake of her head. "We'll do it together. You'll be fine."

She was right.

She slid her arm around my shoulder, letting me wind mine around her waist to draw her close. I spread my fingers wide across the bare, silken skin of her back, caressing the warmth. I relaxed as our clasped hands rested on my chest, over my heart, enjoying having her so close. I grinned at her. "Ready?"

She winked. "I got you."

We began to move. Slowly at first, then it happened. I felt the music, felt Becca against me. She fit under my chin perfectly, and I laid my cheek on her fragrant hair. She hummed with the music, letting me lead her. I wasn't Bentley or Richard, who covered the dance floor with intricate steps, but we shuffled and rocked, and not once did I step on her feet. That was my style.

She squeezed my shoulder. "See, not so bad."

I chuckled. "We're not moving much."

She nestled against me. "I don't mind."

The music transitioned into another song, and we stayed on the dance floor, moving and swaying to the dulcet sound. Becca glanced toward our table and giggled.

"What?"

"You really need to look."

I turned us so I was facing our group. Richard, Aiden, and Maddox all held up pieces of paper, grinning widely. I got an eight from Richard, eight point five from Maddox and Aiden gave me a nine. He thumped his chest when I met his eye.

"Look how well I taught him!" he stated to Richard and Maddox. They both rolled their eyes and gave me a thumbs-up. I had to laugh at their antics.

We danced for several songs, each flowing into another. I grew more confident, moving more fluidly, tucking Becca tight, and gliding my fingers in long strokes along her back. I decided I loved dancing.

It meant Becca was close.

She tilted back her head. "I don't think you gave yourself enough credit. You're doing so well, Reid. I love dancing with you."

I chuckled. "Trust me, I wasn't like this with the guys. Although, I think I figured out why now."

"Tell me."

"I haven't been touched a lot, Becca. No hugs as a kid and all that. I don't really like being close to many people—except you. Having you in my arms, close, relaxes me. I like touching you. The dancing part comes easy with you." My long exhale of air ruffled her hair. "Everything comes easy when I'm with you."

Her eyes shone. "There you go again with your words."

I chuckled.

"I like touching you too," she added.

Our eyes locked, the heat that always pulsated just below the surface beginning to bubble between us.

My steps faltered. Becca's gaze grew intense.

"I want to touch you everywhere, Reid."

I dropped my head to her hair. "I want that too."

She tucked herself tighter to my chest. "Soon?"

I wanted to grab her hand and drag her out of there now. Glancing toward our table, I saw people watching us intently, and I knew it wasn't the right time. Being together in every sense of the word was private. I didn't want people gossiping about us or specifically about Becca. Today was about Bentley and Emmy. Enjoying our first real date. Spending time with our friends. Letting her dance as much as she wanted. I didn't want to rush her out of here and have sex. I wanted to take my time and discover her. Have her all to myself for hours. We already had plans for the morning tomorrow with Richard and Katy, and I knew if I took her home tonight, those wouldn't happen.

I pressed a kiss to her crown.

"Soon," I promised.

THE WEEK PASSED quickly. The office was quiet with Bentley gone on his honeymoon. It had a pace and heartbeat when he was there, the atmosphere electric and charged with his energy. It dimmed in his absence.

Richard stayed for a couple of days, and we had dinner with him and Katy. It was obvious how fond of Becca they both were, and I was glad he seemed to like me since his opinion meant a great deal to Becca. I hoped it would help sway her father when the time came.

Katy and Becca went to the ladies' room, leaving us alone at the table.

"You two look pretty close," Richard observed, sipping his scotch.

"We're getting there."

"This might seem like a forward question, but is she a means to an end for you?" He paused. "Because I would hate to have to beat your ass if you hurt her, and believe me, I would. Contract or no contract."

His directness didn't bother me. I was glad Becca had someone who cared about her that much.

I scrubbed my face. "I know I don't have a lot of experience with women, but Becca is more than a way to lose my virginity. I like her a lot. She likes me."

He nodded. "She does. More than I have ever seen her like anyone."

"I don't plan on hurting her."

"Okay. Just so we're clear."

"Yep."

"Now—" he cleared his throat and looked uncomfortable as he shifted in his chair "—are you covered?"

I frowned. "Covered?"

He waved his hand. "Safe. You know about being safe, right?" He waved his hand. "Condoms?"

I gaped at him. "I am not having this conversation with you, Richard."

"Yes, you are. Do we need to take a trip to the drugstore? Or have Aiden and Maddox already done that with you?"

"I'm not fifteen," I hissed, leaning forward and keeping my voice low. "I know all about safe sex, condoms, and making my partner feel good. I'm a virgin, not an idiot. Just because I haven't had sex doesn't mean I haven't

paid attention to the world around me."

"So I don't need to talk to the guys?"

The image of a trip to the drugstore with Aiden, Maddox, and Richard came to my mind. They would discuss condoms, listing off the pluses and minuses of the different brands. Aiden would ask loudly if I needed a small or medium. He would probably offer to show me how to use one with a banana. There would be a great deal of teasing and laughter for them—and embarrassment for me.

"Definitely not."

"I could take you."

"I'm good."

He began to laugh. "The look on your face is priceless. Katy told me I had to ask and make sure you were protecting Becca." He clapped my shoulder. "You're good, Reid."

I was grateful to see Katy and Becca return to the table.

"I never want to discuss this with you again."

He winked. "Noted."

Becca sat beside me. "Are you okay, Reid? You look a little flushed."

"Yep. I'm fine."

Richard chuckled, pressing a kiss to Katy's cheek.

"My work is done," he stated.

He deserved the sharp kick to his ankle I gave him.

Becca and I had lunch daily. When I saw her in the evenings, I often stopped for coffee and to pick up whatever flowers caught my eye that day. Eleanor, the old woman at the corner store, always had a bright smile and a small, perfect bunch or stem ready to hand me. I loved seeing the look of delight when I would hand Becca the flowers. She insisted her apartment was looking like a flower shop, but she never asked me to stop. I was happy knowing she had fresh flowers all the time and that she thought of me when she saw them.

Every time we were together, I grew more comfortable. With myself. With her. With us. I felt as if I were right where I belonged. Something I had never experienced in my life.

I arranged with Becca to take her out on Saturday. We spent

the afternoon exploring St. Lawrence Market and walking around Chinatown. I took her to my favorite dim sum place for lunch, and we stuffed ourselves on dumplings and sipped fragrant tea in the busy, boisterous restaurant. After taking all our purchases to her apartment, we went to an early movie and had a casual dinner at a local tapas bistro.

We walked to her place, stopping to get ice cream. We paused every few feet and traded cones, and I'd brush a kiss to her lips. Then we continued, our fingers entwined, enjoying the night.

I had never known the contentment I felt spending time with Becca. Everything in me eased, and the world around me seemed brighter. I realized it was the first time in my life I wasn't lonely. The power of those words made me tuck her closer and press a kiss to her head in silent gratitude. She responded by squeezing my hip, knowing that sometimes we didn't need words. She always understood.

We reached her apartment building, and I hesitated. Becca wasn't a night owl like me. She preferred to be in bed early, and it was already ten and we'd been together almost all day. I knew she had to be tired. Maybe she wanted me to get the bags I had left earlier and leave. I stopped on the steps, peering down at her.

She grinned at me, tugging on my hand. "It's early, Reid. Come upstairs."

"Are you sure?"

She tugged again. "Come on. I baked cookies this morning. I was saving them for tonight."

I raced ahead of her. She made the best cookies.

In her apartment, I sat on the sofa. She sat beside me, grinning as I munched on the peanut butter cookies.

"Best ever," I mumbled around a mouthful.

"I tried a new recipe."

"It's a keeper."

"You want to watch another movie?"

"Are you sure you're not too tired?"

"I'm a bit sleepy, but I want you to stay."

That was all I needed to hear. "Okay."

She had purchased a TV, and I had set everything up for her. Smiling, she handed me the remote.

"You pick."

I scanned Netflix, choosing a film I knew she would like. I didn't really care what we watched. As long as I was there with her, I wasn't alone in my apartment. I settled back on the sofa and put a cushion on my lap, patting it in invitation.

She eyed me skeptically. "I'll fall asleep for sure."

"I don't mind."

She curled up, resting her head on my knee. Awkwardly, I tried to pull her hair loose, but I gave up before I hurt her. With a laugh, she pulled out the clip, letting the long, dark waves fall around her shoulders. I ran my fingers through her hair, loving how silky it felt.

Becca sighed, contented. "That feels so good."

I kept stroking her head, and I knew when she fell asleep; her body relaxed and her breathing became deep and even. I let her rest, changing the channel to the news and watching the TV for a while. She shifted, stretched, and curled back up, rolling onto her back. The action caused her shirt to pull tightly over her breasts. The material was thin, almost translucent in the light. The top few buttons had come undone and the lace trim of her camisole peeked out. Fascinated, I stared at the rounded flesh of her breasts—creamy and inviting. My fingers itched to touch them, but I knew I couldn't. She shifted, her brow furrowed, and she huffed out a long breath, then murmured my name.

"Reid."

The sound was plaintive, almost pleading.

Was she dreaming of me?

I leaned down, running my fingers along her collarbone. "I'm here, Becca."

She grasped my fingers, pulled my arm across her chest, and laid her hand on top of mine, resting them on her breast.

Her warm, full breast fit into my hand as if it were made to be there. I tried to remain still, not to flex my fingers, and to tell my cock to stop getting hard.

I failed.

Her breast felt fantastic in my hand. I wondered what it would feel like in my mouth. Becca made a noise low in her throat, making my cock twitch and my fingers flex. It was all I could do not to whimper when I realized her nipple was now a hard bud under my palm.

God, I wanted her.

I shifted, hunching over her. She was so pretty with her dark hair and creamy skin. When she slept, her mouth opened, the edge of her pink tongue resting on her bottom lip. The urge to kiss her was driving me crazy. I didn't know how I had existed before Becca. Kissing her was a drug to me. I wanted it. I craved it.

Her eyes fluttered open and met mine. She glanced down to where my hand rested. I waited for her to get angry and tell me off. Instead, she lifted her eyebrow.

"Did I do that?"

"Yes."

She bit her lip, her voice becoming lower, breathy. "Did you like it?"

"Jesus, yes."

I didn't know who moved first. One minute she was lying down, the next, I was on top of her on the sofa. Our mouths fused together in messy, passionate kisses. Our teeth clashed, tongues dueled, and we moaned and clung to each other. I was desperate to feel her, needing her as close as possible. I pulled her tight, shouting as the sofa disappeared and I thudded to the floor, Becca on top of me.

She stared, her eyes wide.

"We fell off."

Chuckling, I moved her hair off her face and cupped her cheeks. "Yes, we did."

She pushed up on her arms, her chest molded to me. The action brought her hips flush with mine, making me hiss as my erection became trapped between us.

Her face lifted, and she met my eyes.

"Is that for me?"

"Always."

She shifted, rubbing against me. "Are you often this way?"

"Only every time I see you."

She sat up, straddling me.

Without thinking, I gripped her hips. "Becca," I warned, the sensation overwhelming.

She rolled her hips. "You like how that feels, Reid?"

All I could do was moan.

She lowered herself to my mouth, her warm breath washing over my face. "Maybe we need to explore this."

Explore.

Yes. I wanted to explore her. Everywhere.

In one fluid move, she was on her feet. She extended her hand, and I took it, pulling myself up. We stood, our eyes locked.

"Do you want this?" she whispered. "You want me?"

Bravely, I grabbed her hand and cupped my erection. "What do you think?"

Her fingers spread wide, teasing my length. "I think we need to go to my bedroom."

I ran my hand over her head and rested it on her neck, feeling her rapid pulse.

"I-I've never . . . I'm not sure . . ."

She lifted up on her toes, her mouth light on mine. "I know, baby. Let me show you."

I followed her to her room, nerves overtaking me. Regardless of how I quipped or made fun of myself, I wanted to be good for her. Making love with Becca was significant—for each of us.

In her room, she turned on the small, bedside lamp to a dim glow. She turned to me, lacing our fingers together.

"Are you sure?"

I pulled a hand through my hair. "This is all wrong, isn't it? It should be me asking you. I should know what I'm doing."

She grabbed my hand, pulling it to her chest. "No, Reid, this is perfect."

She inched closer, ran her hand up my neck, and pulled my face to hers. "I want to be your first." She kissed my cheek. "I want you to use me, to learn." She ran her lips to my ear, tugging on the lobe, and making me shudder.

"I want you to be more than my first," I admitted.

"Oh yes, Reid." She laughed, the sound low and sultry in the room. "I'll be your first, your last, and everything in between. Count on it."

Then she kissed me, and I let her take control. It was no longer messy or frantic. It was deep, emotional, and sexy as hell. She explored my mouth, the taste of her filling my head. I yanked her tight to my chest, letting her consume me. Our tongues danced, sliding sensuously together. She licked and nipped at my lips. I teased the roof of her mouth and tilted my head to give her access to mine. Anything she wanted, she could have.

She bunched my shirt in her fist, tugging on the material. With a groan, I broke away, yanking it over my head and sending it flying behind me. I fingered the bottom of her T-shirt, and when she nodded, I tugged it off. Her rapid breathing made her breasts move, and I reached out, cupping them in my hand. She stepped back, took off her camisole, and pulled down her jeans, kicking them to the side. She stood before me in nothing but a thong.

A tiny, pink thong.

My cock jerked. My mouth watered. My hands clenched into fists. My breathing became gasps as she reached for my belt, unzipped me, and pushed off my jeans.

Her eyes widened. "You're commando."

I found my voice. "I usually am."

"Your cock . . ." Her voice trailed off.

"What?" I asked in a strangled voice. Did she not like what she saw?

Her hand wrapped around me, stroking gently. "So big," she

whispered, moving closer. "So beautiful." She added her other hand, twisting her fingers slightly, making me groan. "So, so big."

She lifted her face, brushing her mouth on mine. "Tell me what you want, Reid."

"You," I growled. "Naked on your bed."

"What do you want to do to me?"

"Everything."

She stepped back, perching on the mattress. Her hands slid to her hips, but I shook my head. "No. I want to do that. I want to get you naked."

She eased herself to the middle of the mattress, opening her arms.

"You can have whatever you want. Do whatever you want to do."

I slid my fingers into the lace by her hips, drawing the pink satin down her legs. She lay before me, naked and perfect. She drew up her knees, smiling coquettishly. "Ask me, Reid."

I swallowed the dryness in my throat. "Open your legs, Becca."

I almost fell to my knees as her legs opened and I saw her fully for the first time.

"Exquisite."

Her position was relaxed, her expression playful, except she was anything but. Her breasts heaved as she drew in deep breaths, her hands curled into fists on the blankets, and I saw the slight tremor to her body.

Somehow knowing she was nervous as well helped settle my own nerves. I crawled onto the mattress, sliding between her thighs. "You are the most beautiful woman I have ever seen."

"Touch me, Reid."

I lowered my head, kissing her skin. I never lingered in one place, my mouth gliding over the satin of her, exploring and tasting. I wanted to feast on her. Lay claim to every inch of her.

The nape of her neck was warm and salty, and her shoulders tasted like honey. Her nipples tautened into hard buds under my tongue, the feel of them an aphrodisiac. I sucked and licked, playing with one breast then the other, listening to her reactions, learning her noises. She loved it when I scraped my teeth on the peak and sucked it into my mouth, swirling my tongue over the bud to ease the sting. She was ticklish when I trailed my tongue down her arm, giggling when I nipped at the soft skin of her inner elbow and wrist.

She arched and writhed the lower I went. Her hips filled my hands, and I licked a path between them. I sat back, pushing open her thighs, my focus entirely on her pussy. She was bare, pink, wet, and glistening.

"I want to touch you," I whispered.

"Yes. I want you to."

I met her lust-filled gaze. "Not only with my fingers."

Her eyes widened. "Yes."

"I've never done this."

"I know."

"I want this to be good for you."

She sat up, placing her hand over my heart. "It will be, because it's you. It's us."

"I'm a fast learner," I assured her.

She smiled. "I have to learn you as well."

Her words only made me harder. I wanted her to learn me. All of me.

Covering her mouth with mine, I eased her back to the mattress, kissing her until we were breathless.

"Tell me if I do something wrong."

CHAPTER 12

BECCA

HE LOOKED SO nervous. So intense. So sexy. His hair was disheveled, lips swollen, and cheeks flushed. He was lean but muscular, his arms toned from his workouts, and his chest scattered with dark hairs. His waist was narrow, his V, sharp and defined.

And his cock.

Thick and heavy. Hard and erect. Huge. The head glistened with his excitement, almost purple with the massive size of his uncut erection. I was desperate to touch and taste, to feel how he would fill me, but I knew how important the first time was to him. How much he wanted it to be good for me, so I had to let him set the pace. We had already discussed birth control. I was covered, and since he had never been with anyone, he was clean. I had bought condoms and had them in my nightstand, but I didn't care if we used them. I wanted to feel him—all of him.

Never had anyone looked at me the way Reid did. Desperate and wanting. Filled with need and longing. His hazel eyes glittered in the dim light, his full mouth pursed as he slid down my body. Knowing he was that close to my most intimate place, that he was finally going to touch me, made me wetter than I had been. Ever.

He looked at me, then lowered his gaze. I felt the gentle, tentative touch of his finger. I was already so turned on that I inhaled hard at the sensation. He touched again, gliding over my hard bud. My hips flew up of their own accord and I whimpered his name.

He chuckled, quiet but raspy. "Oh, Becca. I love how you feel. So soft." His voice dropped. "Wet."

One finger became two, and he became braver—exploring, feeling, touching.

"So beautiful," he murmured. "Do you have any idea how beautiful you are?"

He met my eyes. "You are every fantasy I've ever had come true, right here. If there was nothing else, I'd be happy for life."

"We have all night. You can have everything."

He closed his eyes and sighed. He lowered his head, and I felt the first light touch of his mouth on me.

I gasped.

He groaned.

He pushed forward, covering me with his lips. Moments later, Reid Fucking Matthews proved how fast a learner he was. His mouth was wicked, his tongue talented. Pleasure racked my body as he sucked and teased. Slid his long finger inside me, then added another. Strummed my clit, humming against the sensitive nub, making me quiver.

He was a natural at it.

He began to consume me, everywhere he touched on fire. Sparks shot through my body, shivers sweeping over me.

I began to stiffen, my orgasm bearing down on me. I cried out his name, gripped the back of his head, pleading and begging. For what, I had no idea, but Reid did. He pressed harder, his fingers stroking me exactly where I needed them.

I exploded, crying, gasping, spasming around his mouth. Calling his name, I arched my back as I gripped the comforter, needing something to anchor myself to the bed.

Reid gentled his mouth, turning his head to the side, kissing my thigh. He caressed my torso with his hands, soothing and soft. Laying his head on my stomach, he kissed my skin, then slid his hands under me, holding me close, letting me recover. He glanced up, pleased, arching one eyebrow.

"Okay, then?"

I grinned. "Epic." Then I surprised him. Sitting up, I pushed him back to the mattress. His erection stood straight and proud.

"I think it's my turn."

"Fuck," he muttered, lifting up on his elbows. "I don't know if that's a good idea."

I trailed a finger up his shaft, teasing the crown. "You don't want my mouth on you?"

"I'm not sure I'll last." He swallowed. "I want to be inside you the first time I come."

"You will be." I hovered over him. "Just a taste." I wrapped my hand around the steel of him. "You wouldn't deny me one taste of your cock, would you?"

"Jesus," he said and panted. "That's the hottest thing I've ever heard."

I opened my mouth and slid him in. He was musky, salty, and perfect. I licked and teased, taking in as much of him as I could. Our eyes locked, his gaze riveted on the way his cock looked gliding in and out of my mouth.

"You look so sexy." He trailed a finger over my cheek. "My cock in your mouth. The way your tongue feels . . ." His head fell back with a long moan. "Becca, please, baby. You need to stop."

I released his cock with a final lick.

I crawled up his legs, straddling him. "Like this?"

He nodded, his brow furrowed. "Are you, ah, ready for me?"

I leaned forward, my lips at his ear. "I have never been wetter or readier, Reid Matthews. I want you so much I'm aching for you."

"I should wear a condom. I want you to feel safe."

"I do feel safe. I want to feel you. Just you."

"Oh God," he hissed. "Are you sure?"

I slid over him. "Yes."

His hands settled on my hips. "I want to be inside you. Now."

I rubbed his cock along my folds, his blunt head hot and wet. Gripping his shaft, I guided him inside, slowly sinking down, steel inch by steel inch until I was full, and our skin flush.

He felt magnificent inside me.

"Fuck, Becca, I can't . . . I've never felt anything like this. Oh *God*."

I began to move. Up, down. Slow and steady, pumping him. He gripped my hips, beginning to move, matching my rhythm. Beads of sweat spotted his forehead. My back felt damp. His grip tightened, his movements picking up. He began to mumble, the words too low for me to hear.

Then, once again, Reid Matthews went to the head of the class.

With a quiet roar, he sat up, shocking me as we fell back, him on top. He grabbed my leg, lifting it over his shoulder. His hips slammed into mine, pushing his cock in deeper, making me cry out. He anchored his hand to the headboard, hovering over me, his eyes wild.

"I'm gonna . . . *Jesus* . . . Becca . . . *I can't* . . ."

His head fell into my neck and his body spasmed. I clamped down on him as another orgasm tore through me. A long, loud groan filled the room as his cock jerked and he came, every muscle in his body tightening, his frame shuddering as he rode out his orgasm.

Then he collapsed on top of me.

Boneless.

I wrapped my arms around him, welcoming the weight.

I touched my lips to his ear.

"Okay, then?"

He chuckled, his chest vibrating against me. When he lifted his head, wonder filled his eyes.

He pressed his mouth to mine.

"Epic."

"IS IT NORMAL to be hungry after sex?" Reid mumbled against my shoulder.

I stretched, feeling seldom-used muscles protesting. I grimaced, turning my head to meet his gaze.

"I think when you've had sex three times in a row, it's probably normal."

He tugged me closer, trailing his lips down my neck. "Did I hurt you?"

"No."

"You winced."

I chuckled at the worry in his voice, rolling over so I could see his face. He hovered over me, frowning.

"Reid, I haven't been with anyone in a long time. Almost two years. And you're, ah . . ."

"I'm what?"

"You're big, okay? Your penis is large."

His lips quirked. "My *penis*? So proper. Ten minutes ago, you were calling it my cock and begging me to fuck you with it." He bent and nipped at my neck playfully. "My dirty-talking Becca."

I laughed.

"Fine. Your cock is huge, Reid. I just need to get used to it."

He was over me in a second, his cock pressing against my hip. It seemed he was making up for the lost years. All it took was a few words, and he was hard and ready to go.

"I'm happy to help you get used to it. They say practice makes perfect."

I pushed against his shoulder. "They say too much of a good thing is bad as well."

He stilled. "Too much? Am I pushing too hard?"

I cupped his face. "Don't look so worried. I'm fine, but I need a bit of a breather." I glanced at the clock. "It's two a.m. You've had me three times in as many hours. Maybe pizza first, then you can, ah, resume your practice?"

"Pizza, then practice. I'm good with that."

"Maybe a little sleep?"

A look of tenderness crossed his face. He lifted a stray curl off my face, tucked it behind my ear, and rubbed his nose against mine in an affectionate gesture.

"Becca Baby, if all I could do was sleep with you the rest of the weekend, I'd be happy. Being with you like this is more than I ever hoped for." He softened his voice almost to a hum. "You're all I ever hoped for."

My chest constricted at his tender words. He could turn from teasing to serious in a second. Melt me with his thoughts he had no problem sharing. Reid didn't play games or hide his feelings. I didn't know if it was because of his past, or if that was simply the way he was built, but I loved it.

"Just a little sleep." I grinned.

A mischievous smile lit his face. "Thank God."

I pushed him away and slid out of bed. I lifted my arms over my head, stretching out my back. Reid watched me, his gaze following my every move. I moved leisurely, letting his eyes roam over me, feeling the heat of his stare. Lust, hungry and rampant, filled his gaze. His cock swelled, tenting the blanket that covered him. He bit his lip, leaning back on the pillows, slowly dragging his hand down his chest. It disappeared under the blanket.

"See what you do to me, Becca?" he asked, his voice gruff. "You are so beautiful, and I want you again. I want to feel your hot, wet pussy wrapped around my cock. I want to hear you moan my name. I want to make you forget about everyone before me. I only want you to remember me. My touch. My mouth. My cock."

His words. His sexy, need-filled words. Suddenly, I needed him with the same intensity.

"There *is* only you, Reid." I stepped forward, placing one knee on the bed. I tugged the blanket away. His fist was around his cock, the head already weeping. "Show me. Show me how much you want me again."

In a second, I was under him, his mouth hard on mine, and his cock stroking my center. I wrapped my legs around his hips, arching my back to bring him closer.

Pizza could wait.

⌒

"YOU HAVE THE prettiest pussy I've ever seen."

I tried to close my legs, but he was wedged between them, refusing to move.

"Reid, until last night, you were a virgin. I don't think you've seen that many."

He didn't look up, his fingers tracing small circles on my thighs. "Not true. In prison, there's tons of porn available. On the net, I can click a hundred different sites and see as much pussy as I want." He glanced at me with a firm nod. "Trust me, yours is the prettiest."

I gaped at him, and his smile fell.

"Shit. I shouldn't have said that part about the porn, should I?"

I began to giggle, trying to hold them in, but I failed. The giggles grew into chuckles, which turned into laughter. He tried to keep a straight face, then gave in and joined me. He turned his head, pressing a kiss to my thigh.

"I say the stupidest things sometimes."

"No," I insisted. "I love your honesty and how you say what you're thinking. It catches me off guard at times, though."

"I don't really look at a lot of porn."

I lifted one eyebrow. "Right. You figured out all your moves on your own."

A sly grin lit his face. "My moves? Are you saying I got it going on, Becca?"

"I'll say your mattress dancing is a lot smoother than your floor dancing."

It was his turn to gape. Then he laughed. He huffed out a long sigh, reaching for my hand and threading our fingers together. "I can't remember the last time I felt this way, Becca. In fact, I never have."

"How do you feel?"

"Easier, happier." He shrugged. "It's hard to explain."

"Losing about ten pounds of sperm in one night will do that for you." I grinned. "I, myself, am feeling a bit . . . full."

Instantly, he was on me, his hands pinning down my arms, his eyes wild.

"I'll show you full."

"Oh yeah?"

He leaned down, skimming his lips over my collarbone, licking his way up my neck to my ear.

"I want you full of me. So full, you feel me every time you move tomorrow. Every time you shift in your chair, you feel a bit of me between your legs."

I stared at him, his words catching me off guard.

He frowned. "Did I freak you out?"

"No," I responded. "You surprised me a little. You're, ah, a bit of a dirty boy when you get going, Reid Matthews."

"Want me to show you how dirty?"

"Yes."

And he did. Boy, how he did.

⌒

REID

I LOOKED AROUND, fascinated at the scope of the building site. Bentley had returned from his honeymoon, relaxed and happy. Richard was once again in town, and we were on-site at the Ridge Towers property. I had seen pictures, the concept model, but I never had visited the site until now. As Bentley talked, and the architect described the position of the buildings and the amenities, I was impressed by the extent and depth of the vision. The place was going to rock.

I turned and stared at the water. The land was a rare find here, and Bentley and the vision he had were going to take full advantage of it.

Maddox stood beside me, taking it all in. "This is going to be an amazing venture."

"It is. Are you still thinking of buying one?"

He chuckled. "Past the point of thinking. I'm buying a place here. The penthouse unit—four bedrooms with the terrace. The biggest one. Bentley blocked it off the list, along with a few others we know people want."

"Wow. That's three thousand square feet. A lot of space for one person."

He faced me, his expression one of happiness. "I won't be alone. We're keeping it private, but since I already told Bent and Aiden, this seems the right time to share. I asked Dee to marry me, and she said yes."

I grasped his hand, shaking it hard. "Congrats, Mad Dog. That's awesome!"

His smile was wide. "Yeah, it is. We know it's fast, but when you know, you know. Dee is it for me, and we want to start our life together."

"I'm happy for you."

"We're getting married in a few weeks, once the campaign starts and we can step back and relax. A small wedding, friends only. You and Becca are, of course, invited."

"I wouldn't miss it."

"I'm flying everyone to the Bahamas. I've rented two villas, and Jen is arranging the wedding for us. No gifts, no pressure. A weekend away with our friends, and our vows on the beach, followed by a late dinner and dancing." He clapped my shoulder. "You can put those dance lessons to good use again."

I swallowed heavily. "The Bahamas?"

"Yep. That's what we want. It's all on me, Reid. Our wedding, our way. No worries on your part."

"Um . . . I don't know if I can go."

Aiden joined us, hearing the last part of the conversation.

"Why the hell not? It's going to be awesome!"

I huffed out an embarrassed sigh. "I don't have a passport."

"There's time. We can put a rush on it."

I couldn't meet Maddox's eyes. "I don't know if I can get one with my prison record, or if their travel restrictions allow me to go to that country."

Maddox was quiet for a moment. "Then we'll go somewhere that does allow it so you can be with us."

I shook my head. "No, you have your plans set. You can't change them. I'll Skype myself in or something. Becca can hold up a laptop for me," I joked, trying to lighten the serious tone the conversation had taken. "I'll wear a Hawaiian shirt, and it'll be as if I'm there."

Maddox frowned but didn't push the subject, for which I was grateful. Instead, he changed topic.

He jerked his chin toward the area the building would occupy. "What about you? You ready to leave your shoebox for something bigger, Reid? Great chance to get in before it goes through the roof, plus you get to choose your layout."

He was right. Their concept was unique. Aside from the placement of the kitchen and bathrooms, you could tweak the floorplan of every unit to suit your taste. All with a price, of course, but still a huge selling feature. Richard was confident when the marketing campaign kicked off in a few days, it would sell out before they broke ground. Given his brilliant strategy, and the uniqueness of the concept, everyone was certain he was correct.

But once again, my past loomed over me.

I met Maddox's curious gaze with a shrug. "I have been thinking about it. But I don't know if I can afford it."

Aiden and Maddox exchanged a look.

"We pay you well, Reid," Maddox pointed out. "You can amortize over a longer period and afford the payments. I can help you figure that out."

I shuffled my feet as I looked at the ground. "I'm not disputing my salary."

"What are you saying?" Aiden asked.

I tugged my hand through my hair in vexation. "God, the two of you are hitting all my weaknesses today, aren't you? I'm not sure I would qualify for a mortgage, Aiden. My credit history has been difficult to build since I got out of prison. It took me two years to get a no-frills credit card, and even now, my limit is low. Given the price tags here, even if I had the minimum deposit saved, I'm not sure a bank would give me the money." I shook my head. "Can we stop busting my chops now?"

Aiden held up his hands. "We're only having a conversation, Reid. We aren't trying to stir up anything, only understand your hesitancy."

My anger deflated at his words. "I know that." I groaned. "It's-it's difficult at times. I know this might be hard to understand, but I still have trouble believing or hoping for things. Sometimes, it's easier not to even admit to wanting them. That way the letdown isn't as hurtful, you know?"

"I get that," Aiden said quietly. "Sometimes it's hard to believe when things go well."

"Yeah."

Maddox was silent, tapping his cheek the way he did when in deep thought. Another glance passed between the two men.

"If you think you're interested, let me give it some thought—numbers are sort of my thing," Maddox offered. "I might have an idea or two we could look at."

I glanced behind me, imagining the building in place and thinking about living there. "Yeah," I confessed. "I would be really interested."

I pushed my glasses onto my head and rubbed my eyes, suddenly exhausted. I glanced toward Becca, who was talking to Richard and Bentley, her expression excited as she gestured and spoke. Seeing her made me smile. Right now, it was the only thing that could.

Maddox cleared his throat. "Which is your favorite unit?"

"The two-bedroom one Liv showed us the sketches for. With the corner den? I loved that."

He nodded. "Nice size."

"Nice price, even if I went standard. That's my dream one, but I would be happy with a one-bedroom, I suppose."

He clapped my shoulder. "Dreams are always a good thing to have, Reid. Sometimes you have to reach out and try."

Richard and Becca joined us. She stood beside me, not touching, but close. Every minute apart from her seemed forever. Leaving her on Sunday was one of the hardest things I could remember having to do. I wanted to stay with her in her bed for days—to have my fill of making love to her—if that were possible. To discover every intimate detail of her body and mind. Walking away felt as if I had left something important behind me. I hated it. I had no experience with those sorts of emotions, so I didn't know if it was normal or if I was simply needy. I gave up trying to hide it, and most of the remainder of the day was spent either texting or talking to her. Luckily, she seemed to want the connection as much as I did.

Since we had become intimate, I found it difficult to stay away from her, and the office was a challenge. I had to fight the urge to seek her out a dozen times a day. To restrain myself from kissing her when we passed in the hall or bumped into each other while getting coffee. But we had agreed to keep it professional at the office. It didn't stop me from stealing a kiss on occasion, wrapping her in my arms behind my closed office door, or taking advantage of private corners if we went out to lunch. The fact that she informed me she also found it difficult at times made me feel somewhat better. It didn't make it any easier, but it was something.

Aiden and Maddox knew that Becca and I had slept together. There had been fist bumps, and Aiden had wiped his cheeks in an overdramatic fashion when I shared the information.

"My boy is all grown-up now," he pretended to sob. "He doesn't need me anymore."

I flipped him the bird, joining in Maddox's laughter.

Maddox eyed me steadily, always the more serious one. "Was it what you expected?"

I shook my head. "No, it was more."

"More than three seconds?" Aiden quipped.

I sat straighter and met his eyes. "Way more. Becca had no complaints, although her neighbor might not have been pleased with all the moaning. She certainly knew who Becca was with, though, since she yelled my name a lot."

He grinned and slapped my shoulder. "That's what I want to hear."

I was certain they had shared with Bentley, but he would never comment on anything that personal.

At least, not directly to me.

Maddox glanced past me. "What about you, Becca? Could you see yourself living here?"

Fuck.

I held my breath waiting for her to answer. I had never thought to ask her that question.

"It's a great spot, and I think it'll be amazing once it's complete. If I were looking, it would be on the top of my list."

Richard crossed his arms. "I loved my condo. If I lived here, a place like this would appeal to me."

"Any chance of that, Richard?" Aiden asked. "You moving here?"

He chuckled with a shake of his head. "No. I'm happy in BC. I love my job and the city. Katy's settled and content. It's a great place for my girls to grow up. That's all that matters to me. Besides," he drawled, "I enjoy my trips to see you guys. If I lived here, you'd be sick of me. And you'd have to fire poor Becca since I would ruthlessly snatch up her job in a heartbeat."

Everyone laughed, including Becca. Aiden leaned forward, shaking his head. "Sorry, dude. She bakes cookies. You can't top that."

"Damn it, foiled by baked goods."

"She's way cuter than you are, and she smells good," I said without thinking.

Richard laughed even as Maddox and Aiden shook their heads. "Is that your professional or personal opinion, Reid?"

I shut my eyes with a groan. When I looked toward Becca, expecting anger, she met my eyes with her warm blue ones filled with amusement. I relaxed and grinned.

"Both."

"Maybe I can add that to my resume."

Bentley joined us with a frown. "Resume? You aren't going to need one of those, Becca. You say the word, and you're part of BAM. Forget The Gavin Group."

Richard grabbed at his chest. "I loaned her to you. And now you're stealing her? Where is the loyalty?"

Bentley chuckled. "All is fair in love and war . . . and business. You trained her too well, Richard. She is already invaluable to us."

Becca threw up her hands. "*She* is right here, gentlemen. I think I have a say in the matter."

Maddox threw a wink in my direction, tilting his head. "What say you, Becca? Here with us, or back to BC with them?"

I expected her to roll her eyes and refuse to answer. Her reply made my day.

"Toronto has some unexpected, added benefits," she murmured. "So, at this point, I'd have to stay." She met my eyes, quirking her eyebrows and making me grin.

I was the added benefit.

Richard groaned. "I give up. I can't compete with love."

Everyone laughed and looked at me.

I froze to the spot, locked in shock.

Love?

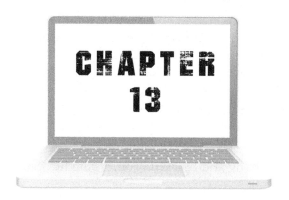

CHAPTER 13

REID

GETTING MARRIED. PASSPORT. Mortgage. Added benefit. Love.
Added Benefit.
Love.

The words kept swirling around in my head. I couldn't dislodge them.

I stood, locked in place, until Aiden turned and called to me. "Quit staring at the view, kid! We got plans to make!"

Shaking my head, I joined them and acted as natural as I could. Becca knew something was wrong. She kept looking at me, trying to get close, but it was impossible. Bentley had a list he wanted made. Maddox kept throwing out numbers. Aiden was talking about protocols. Richard was all over the place, making notes about the campaign, instructing Becca on items he wanted covered. It was all either of us could do to keep up with them.

In the SUV, Aiden sat beside me in the back, his questions endless. I heard the constant murmur of Richard's and Becca's voices as they talked. Bentley was paying close attention to something Maddox was telling him, both of them serious.

We separated when we got to the office, everyone dispersing to handle the tasks they needed to do.

I sat at my desk, making my way through my list. My phone buzzed with a message from Becca.

Are you okay?

I replied quickly.

I'm fine.

My phone rang and I picked it up, seeing her extension on the display panel.

"Hey."

"Fine usually means not fine." Becca's worried voice hummed in my ear.

"I have a shit-ton of stuff to get done. I'm okay, really."

"You looked as if you'd been hit by a Mack truck. When I came over, what were you discussing that was so serious?"

I wasn't sure whether it was okay to say anything about Maddox and Dee, and I decided to check before I told her the news. As for the rest, I wasn't in the mood to share all the snags my former life was currently throwing in my direction. I had no one to blame but myself. Whining about it would do me no good and would only remind Becca I wasn't good enough for her.

"Ah, just a bunch of things they want done. Don't worry."

She sighed. "I know you're stressing over things, and what Richard said—about love? He likes to tease, and it was a general statement." She dropped her voice. "Please don't think any more about it."

The question was out of my mouth before I could stop it. "*Am I the added benefit?*"

My office door shut, and I looked toward the sound. Becca stood there, her phone to her ear. She lowered it, then spoke directly to me.

"You're the best benefit I have ever had. You're my favorite part of this job and this city." She looked at me beseechingly. "I don't expect anything more than you want to give, Reid."

Tossing my phone onto my desk, I was out of my chair in a second and crossing the room. She moved, meeting me partway, both of us reaching for the other. I yanked her close, covering her mouth with mine, needing her on so many levels. The taste of her mouth. The feel of her body pressed close. The silk of her hair under my fingers. It didn't matter that we were at work or that we were crossing a line we had drawn. I needed her. I needed all of her to ground me.

I pulled back, leaning my forehead to hers. "BB, you're my favorite everything. Don't doubt that."

"Don't be upset with me."

"Oh God, I'm not. I promise. His words just hit me." I cupped her face, looking down at her. "I don't know how to love, Becca. No one has ever shown me."

She started to speak, but I shook my head to silence her.

"I feel something for you, more than only physical, and I want to see where it goes. But I can't put a name to it."

"You don't have to," she whispered, laying her hands over mine. "We're just starting, Reid. And this is new for me too. We have so much to discover about each other. About being us."

I brushed my mouth over hers. "I like being part of an us."

"I like being part of your us."

"Yeah?"

"Yes."

I kissed her again and stepped back. "Tonight, Becca. I need to be with you tonight. I know we have dinner and more plans, but when we're done, I need you and me alone."

"Me too."

"Okay." Wanting to lighten the air, I winked. "Now out of my office before I call HR and report you."

"For?" she asked, raising her eyebrow.

Shocking her, I grabbed her and pulled her close. I kissed her hard, long, and deep.

"For making me ridiculously happy." I spun her around and urged her to the door. "Please go before I show you exactly *how* happy and really give Richard something to talk about."

She was laughing as she left.

I adjusted myself and returned to my desk. I hadn't lied—I had a ton of work to do for all three partners, and I needed to concentrate.

Still, the words swirled and the dark thoughts kept pricking at the edges of my mind. I tossed my glasses onto my desk and hung my head as the thoughts became too loud to ignore.

No passport meant no travel. Becca wanted to travel. Even if I was able to get one, there could still be places that would restrict my entry. I wouldn't be able to be part of that aspect of her life.

Bad credit and a prison record meant trouble getting a mortgage. It had taken me a long time to find a place willing to rent to me. The thought of having to go through that process for a different apartment was daunting, never mind the almost certainty of being turned down for a mortgage.

Unless . . .

I dismissed the thought before I had even finished it. Using my skills to beat the system and push through an approval would only prove that Becca's father was right and convicts never changed. I couldn't allow myself to do that. If Becca ever found out, if the guys ever found out, I would lose the trust of the people I cared about the most.

Owning my own place might not be something I could hope to do for a long time.

And as for love . . .

The more my past blocked me from moving forward, the fewer the chances of Becca and me working out. I wouldn't allow her to give up her dreams because of me. In the end, she would hate me for it, and I couldn't stand the idea of that happening. Travel, a home, kids, and marriage—I knew those were all part of her hopes and dreams.

The bottom line was I wasn't good enough for her.

A small part of my heart broke as I realized that perhaps I wasn't the one who was going to share in those dreams.

Locking my feelings and thoughts aside, I turned back to my computer. At least there, I was in control and could do exactly what they expected of me.

It was the only place I knew well and wasn't a failure.

⌒

WE DIDN'T GET dinner out or to see each other privately that night, or any other night that week. The office was chaos, all geared toward the campaign kick-off and the reveal of Ridge Towers.

In another stroke of genius, Bentley went with an unconventional real estate company for the Ridge Towers project. He opted for a family-oriented business rather than one of the larger, well-known groups. The older parents brought a wealth of knowledge of the city and the real estate market, while their two adult children expounded on the technical merits and unique design, which appealed to the younger buyers, both single and family-driven. They covered the bases of all generations, making them the right choice for the project. They had impressed him with their enthusiasm and the family aspect. Families selling to families.

I worked late every night, often deep into the morning hours. The office hummed all day and night, and I wasn't the only one crashing on the sofa to grab a few hours of sleep before starting over again. Becca and I spoke about business, passed in the hall, smiled blearily at each other at meetings, but aside from the occasional brush of our hands, fast text, or meaningful glance, that was our meager interaction. Richard was with her almost constantly, and they worked with the partners directly. My office felt as if it had a revolving door with the number of people in and out of it all day.

Thursday, they launched the campaign. The market was flooded with print, radio, TV, and social media spots. Ridge Towers was everywhere. Bentley was interviewed on-site, where he talked about the venture and his vision. Both Aiden and Maddox accompanied him, but preferred to stay in the background. He was eloquent and passionate; using all the keywords Richard and Becca provided him, hitting all the right notes between the features of the concept and the family angle.

They nailed it.

When the expansive sales office opened on the weekend, complete with 3D videos, computer-generated models, and a full complement of staff to answer questions, the line-ups were out the door. By the end of the weekend, over half the units had sold, with no sign of sales slowing down. Interest was already buzzing for phase two of the project.

Later Sunday night, I brought up the report I had created that linked all sales to the inventory of the building. I was alone in the office. My job was behind the scenes, making sure everything technical ran without a glitch in the sales office, our online presence, and website. Everyone in the IT department had been on hand all weekend, and it had gone well. Any small errors were controlled, fixed, and not seen by the end user to any significant degree. The people at the sales office had nothing but praise for everything we had put in for their use. Overall, I'd done my job well, and because I was grateful to my staff, I had sent them all home for a well-deserved rest.

I scanned the sales, trying not to gape at the substantial dollar figures. They were staggering, and while BAM was used to dealing in large sums, I wasn't sure I would ever get used to them. The penthouses and end units—all the most expensive—were spoken for, including the one I had secretly wanted. Maddox's huge condo, which took up the entire top floor of the third tower, aptly named "M," was the largest of them all. He would live there with Dee and, I assumed, their family. I felt an odd swell of jealousy toward him, but it wasn't for the expensive condo, or his ability to afford it. It was the fact that he was able to do so without his past interfering. He had been able to move on from his mistakes, whereas mine kept haunting me.

I had been grateful to be so busy the past week. It distracted me from the dark thoughts in my head. The trip I might not be able to take. The condo I might not be able to purchase. The life I might not be able to have with Becca. Normally not one to dwell on the negative, I couldn't seem to get past the defeat I was feeling.

Footsteps in the hall distracted my dark thoughts. Aiden sauntered in, sitting down heavily in the chair.

"Hey." Despite his smile, his voice was deep with weariness.

"Hi."

"I was looking for you earlier. We all were."

I frowned. "I was here, working in the server room."

"I sent you a message. Two in fact."

"Sorry." I glanced at my phone. "Shit. I put it on silent somehow. I missed a few messages. Was it important?"

He was fast to reassure me. "No. I wanted to invite you for dinner. When you didn't respond, I was checking to make sure you were okay since it was out of character for you. I saw the lights as I was heading home and came in to see if you were still really working or had crashed on the sofa again. I was going to drive you home if that were the case."

"I'll be crashing soon enough. I wanted to make sure everything was good with the reports and systems before I left. I think I'm more tired than I thought, and I missed the fact that I had the phone off and that there were messages. Sorry about that. Once I'm done, I'll head out and get some sleep."

He waved off my apologies. "You did a great job this week. I know it's been crazy, and I appreciate the effort you put in to make sure everything went smoothly. You've clocked a lot of long hours."

I shrugged. "It's what you pay me for. I'm glad the launch was successful."

He snorted. "Successful? We blew past Maddox's projected numbers. We sold more units in a day than we estimated to sell in a week. Even Richard was blown away. If we keep going, phase one will be sold out in a matter of weeks, not months."

"When will you open phase two?" Although still amazing, the second building wasn't as unique as the first one, and the price would reflect that. Given it wouldn't be available for a few years, I might be able to get a place in that building.

"We're going to hash that out this week. The plans are complete, and the interest is already there. The building will go up fast since the units are more standard, aside from a few on the top floor." He rubbed his face. "To be honest, we didn't think we'd move ahead with phase two so fast. Richard and Becca are on it, though. She came up with some great concepts. Have you seen them?"

"No."

He frowned. "I would have thought she'd have shown you."

"We've been so crazy this week, Aiden, I've barely seen her. I haven't had a real conversation with her since Monday."

"It has been wild, hasn't it?" He grinned. "Things will settle down this week. The sales team will handle it now, Becca will do her thing, and we'll get back to planning."

He stood, studying me. "Are you okay, Reid? You've been . . . withdrawn all week."

"I'm fine. I've been concentrating on making sure everything went off without a hitch."

"It did. You should be proud."

I shrugged. "I simply did my job."

He frowned, narrowing his eyes. "No. You did more than your job. Your program and the features were a huge part of our success. The cool factor of what you and your team did in the sales office put us ahead of everyone else out there." He paused. "I'm proud of you, Reid." He held out his hand. "On behalf of BAM, and personally, thank you."

I stared at his large palm, then accepted his firm handshake.

"We're going to talk later this week once things are back to normal around here. Bentley, Maddox, and I have some ideas we want to look into with you."

My neck prickled, a sense of worry settling in my mind. "All right."

"Don't look so worried. It's a good thing." He tilted his head in assurance. "Your life is moving beyond all the bad shit, kid. You're part of our team, our family. We've got your back."

My throat felt thick, and I could only nod.

"Go home and get some rest. It's still going to be a crazy week."

"Yeah, I will," I managed to get out.

"Okay, I'm heading home. See you tomorrow."

⌒

BECCA WAS WALKING into the building as I was walking out. I stopped in the lobby as she entered, Richard beside her. Despite the smile on her face, she looked exhausted. Richard was talking on his phone and raised his hand in a silent hello, strolling away to continue his conversation. From the tone of his voice, I assumed he was talking to his daughter, Gracie. It was after eleven here, which made it about bedtime for her in BC. Becca told me he hated being away from his family, even for short trips, and he stayed in close touch all the time.

"Hi." I smiled at her. "You're just getting back from the site?"

"No," she replied with a frown. "We had dinner with Bentley, Aiden, and Maddox, going over some things. Did you not get my message?"

"No, I missed one from Aiden too. I had my phone on silent. Sorry."

"You were working?"

"Yeah. Crazy week."

She edged closer, her fingers brushing my hand. "Yes, it has been. I've-I've missed you."

I wrapped my fingers around hers and squeezed. "Me too. But it was a great week, right?"

She nodded enthusiastically. "Amazing. I was going through all the stats with Richard and Bentley. Those cross-channel reports you created for me, Reid, are so useful! I can see the predictive analytics, and I'm able to fine-tune the targeted PII. This is the first time I have reliable touchpoints to prove the effectiveness of our MRM."

"Right," I said with a shake of my head. I knew the data she wanted, but some of her terms were unfamiliar.

She laughed and tried to explain. "Predictive analytics predicts where the user will click next. PII identifies the consumer, which forms a consumer segment to target, and MRM is Marketing Resource Management, which helps manage content. It can be set up to templatize the look and feel of content, along with appropriate messages to deliver to customers."

I blinked. "That was my plan, I think."

She shook her head with a smile. "Sorry, I get excited when someone lets me speak marketing geek. The reports tell me we're on the right track with our ads." She brushed a kiss to my cheek. "You helped me do all that."

The need to have her closer was strong, and I caught her around the waist, pulling her to me. "I have to tell you that listening to your marketing geek is seriously turning me on, BB. It makes me want to interface with your software."

Becca giggled, the sound making me smile.

Behind me, a throat cleared. "Ugh. I really didn't need to hear that."

I didn't even bother turning around. "Go upstairs, Richard. Give me five minutes with my girl. You've had her all week."

"We need to talk if all you need is five minutes, Reid."

Releasing Becca, I turned and glared at him. "I only wanted to wish her a good night."

He laughed, clapping my shoulder. "I know. I wanted to second Becca's thanks. That report is brilliant. I told Bentley I was stealing it and you."

"I see."

"He told me to talk to you about the report since you created it, but I was informed by all three partners you were off-limits." He huffed an exaggerated sigh. "No Becca, no Reid—the least you could do is give me a fair price on getting a licensed copy of that report. I could use that with all of my clients."

"It belongs to BAM, not me. If Bentley says okay, I'll make sure you have it."

"He felt it was yours. I'll talk to him again, because I really want it. Plus any upgrades you add to it later."

"Becca told me what she needed. I just wrote it."

"Well, you make one hell of a team." He winked. "I'm going to give you those five minutes. I'll meet you upstairs, Becca. Then we can call it a night."

He left with a wave, and I turned to Becca.

"He's right, you know," she whispered. "We make a good team."

"You think so?"

"Yes." She stepped closer, linking her arms around my waist. "Why do I feel you're putting up roadblocks, Reid? I know it's been crazy for both of us, but I feel as if you're pulling away. As if there's something you're not saying. Something big."

I pressed a kiss to her forehead. We were both exhausted, our plates full, and under stress. I wasn't going to add to hers by telling her what I was thinking—at least, not right now. Instead, I cupped her face and kissed her. It wasn't deep and passionate, but it was filled with the words I couldn't say, the fears I couldn't express, and the thoughts that haunted my mind. It was soft, gentle, and intimate. It was hard to stop, and even harder to let go.

When I drew back, I dropped another kiss on her head. "Please don't stay too long. You look so tired, BB."

"You look haunted."

I ran my knuckles down her cheek. She already knew me too well. "We'll talk."

"Are you breaking up with me?"

"No." I didn't want to lose her, but once I told her everything, she might choose to break it off with me and I wouldn't stand in her way. She deserved only the best.

I knew after I laid out the facts that she might realize the best wasn't Reid Matthews.

She shook her head. "That feels like a lie," she said sadly, then walked away and didn't look back.

I watched her, wondering if she was right.

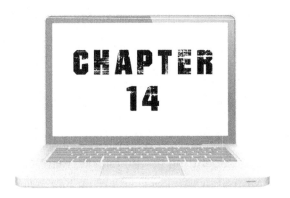

CHAPTER 14

REID

DESPITE THE FACT that we had all worked crazy hours and were tired, everyone was at the meeting Monday morning. The room buzzed with electricity and the excitement of success, and cheerful faces filled the room. Becca sat on one side of me, Richard the other. He was staying another few days before heading home. Becca offered me a smile, but she was quiet, staying busy on her phone. I wasn't sure if it was business or an excuse not to engage, but I let it go. It wasn't the place to ask her.

Aiden and Maddox sat in their usual spots, both relaxed and smiling. Bentley walked in, and everyone sat up straighter. He had a presence about him that made you want to pay attention. Sandy followed him, sitting beside Aiden, ready to take notes or aid him in any way needed. He remained standing and set down his coffee, his gaze sweeping the room. Aiden and Maddox stood, joining him at the head of the table.

"Ridge Towers began as a different vision, and we went through a tremendous amount of difficulty, both personally and professionally, to get to this stage." Bentley paused, clearing his throat. I knew more than anyone what the project had cost him.

"This past weekend was considered a success by some. To us—Aiden, Maddox, and me—it was more than a success. It was a triumph. Each of you in this room helped to make that happen. And for that, we owe you a tremendous thank you."

He began to clap, Maddox and Aiden joining in. Richard rose to his feet, adding to the noise, and soon the entire room rang out with enthusiastic applause.

When we settled, and Bentley sat, he grinned. "Sales are through the roof—pardon the pun—and we're ahead of schedule. Thanks to the brilliance of Richard and Becca and their campaign, Ridge Towers, phase one, should be sold out within weeks." He indicated Richard. "We are thrilled to have joined forces with The Gavin Group and look forward to a long relationship."

Richard smiled. "We're equally as elated with the success and the partnership. If I could, I wanted to add that Becca and I were impressed by the teamwork we saw this past while. We have never worked on a campaign that was handled with so much finesse."

I was startled when his hand fell on my shoulder heavily. "Your technical people, Reid especially, are, without a doubt, the best I have ever worked with. Everything he promised, he delivered—and more. Not one person saw an error or glitch. If there were any, your people were on it so fast, it was as if it didn't happen. You should be very proud of your team."

There was another round of applause, the loudest coming from my three bosses. My ears burned at Richard's words and the clapping. I hated to be the center of attention.

Becca's hand slipped into mine under the table, giving it a quick squeeze. Before she could pull back, I grabbed her hand, holding it tight to my leg, needing her touch.

Bentley spoke more about the project and the future. Aiden and Maddox each had something to say, then Bentley stood for a final address to the table as a whole. "I know you've all put in long hours.

See Sandy today, and she will assign you paid time off as a thank you. You can choose your days to make long weekends and enjoy some time with your family and friends. Lunch today is being catered and is for everyone as another thank you."

Everyone dispersed, and the good mood lingered. Regretfully, I released Becca's hand and walked to my office. I hadn't even sat down when Maddox and Aiden came in. I tensed when Bentley followed, shutting my door. It was rare Bentley joined them, so I knew something was up. Maddox and Aiden sat in the chairs, but Bentley remained standing. It was his way of controlling the room.

I waited for them to speak, unsure what was happening.

Bentley met my curious gaze. "First off, you did an outstanding job. What Richard said was correct. I have never seen anything so smooth in my life."

"Good," I responded. "That was my goal."

"He tells me the report you created gave him information it would have taken him hours to collect. He is beyond impressed."

"Great."

"As part of our partnership, I'm going to let him have access to that report to use. License it to him and The Gavin Group."

"Okay, I'll make the arrangements."

He reached into his jacket pocket and withdrew an envelope, sliding it toward me. "This is for you, with our thanks."

I didn't touch it.

He pushed it farther. "You earned it, Reid. It's yours."

I picked it up, feeling the weight of the heavy stationery. The envelope was thick, my name written in black in Bentley's neat cursive on the front.

I met their gazes steadily. "Thank you. I didn't expect anything. I was only doing my job."

Aiden snorted. "Reid, you go above and beyond your job daily. We're all aware of what you do around here. You deserve it and more."

Something prickled at my eyes, and I blinked to clear them. "Thanks," I mumbled again.

Maddox chuckled. "Okay, we'll leave it there. We have one more thing to discuss with you."

I slid the envelope into my desk drawer. I would look at it later in private. Grabbing a pen, I pulled my notebook close. "Okay, what do you need me to do?"

"You won't need notes," Maddox assured me. "I spoke with Bentley and Bill in the legal department about your passport."

"Oh." My embarrassment reappeared, my ears burning with heat.

He tapped the desk. "You're coming to the wedding, Reid. You *can* apply for a passport, and you should be able to get one. There are no travel restrictions where we're going, if you have a record. Bill is going to work with you on it, and he'll also help you apply to clear your criminal record."

Bentley spoke up. "I'm surprised you haven't done that. Your lawyer should have advised you."

I snorted. "I had a string of public defenders, Bentley. I never had a lawyer who cared."

"You didn't check into it?"

I tossed my glasses onto the desk and scrubbed my face. "To be honest, no. When I got out of jail, I just tried to survive. I did everything I was supposed to do. I stayed within the law. I followed my probation to the letter. When that ended, all I wanted was to move away from it." I met Bentley's gaze. "I never thought about the future. Travel, a job . . . other things—all of it seemed unattainable."

He shook his head. "It's not, Reid. You have a job, a new life, and people who care. A future. You have proven yourself worthy of it to us." He cocked his head, studying me. "When will you believe you're worthy of it yourself?"

His words hit me, and I stared at him.

He leaned on the desk, his voice low. "We're your family, and we take care of family. This company will help with your passport issue and stand behind you to get your record cleared. Whatever you need, we're here for you." He reached out and squeezed my shoulder. "Stop letting your past get in the way, Reid. Grab life and live it."

I gaped at him, only able to nod in reply. Bentley rarely got personal. Aiden and Maddox were the ones I spoke to the most.

He straightened up and tugged on his sleeves. "Okay. I'll leave you to figure it out. Bill has already started the paperwork. You need a picture and two guarantors. Any of us will sign for you."

He strode from my office, leaving me with Maddox and Aiden.

I met Maddox's gaze. "Thank you."

He rose from the chair. "Bentley was right. We're family. You helped me, and I'm returning the favor. That's how we work here at BAM. We have one another's backs."

I extended my hand. "You don't know how much that means to me."

He shook my hand, hard and fast, and winked. "Yeah, I think I do." He left with a wave.

"You okay, kid?" Aiden asked.

"Yeah."

He stood. "The day I hired you, I told you not to let me down."

"I remember." I looked at him, incredulous. "I didn't expect any of this."

"You've earned your place here, Reid. You've held true to your word and made me proud. You made all of us proud." He indicated the drawer. "That is our thanks for a job well done, and the rest is because, as Bentley said, we're family."

His smack on the back was much harder than Bentley's was.

But I was grinning as he left my office.

⌒

AFTER LUNCH, I stopped by Sandy's desk. She finished typing on her keyboard and looked up with a smile.

"Reid."

"Sandy." I winked.

"Coming to schedule your days off?"

I shook my head, laughing. "I don't need time off."

"Yes, you do. Aiden is insisting on it. You have so much overtime, it is frightening."

"Overtime?"

She sighed, pulling up a file on her screen. "Aiden figures we owe you about a month in extra time. Last week alone you worked the equivalent of two weeks. Add in the weekend, and it's even more."

"Can I see that?" I indicated her laptop.

She handed it to me, and I scanned the file. Aiden had been keeping better track of my hours than I thought. With a couple of taps, I erased everything and handed it back. She glared at me.

"Put that back, young man."

I shook my head. "No one asked me to work all those other hours, Sandy. I did it because I love my job. I am not taking time off for it." I chuckled. "I'd only come in here anyway, so why bother?"

She huffed in frustration. "I told Aiden you would say that. They want you to take some time off and enjoy yourself."

"I enjoy work."

"Maybe you could spend some extra time with Becca?" she asked with a wink. "Bentley is giving her a few days off as well."

I frowned and shrugged.

She pursed her lips. Standing, she came around to the front of the desk. "What is going on, Reid?"

Before I could answer, her phone rang. She glanced at the screen with a frown and held up her finger. "Excuse me. I need to take this call."

She lifted the phone to her ear. "Hello?"

Her face turned ghostly white, and tears sprang to her eyes as she listened to a voice on the other end. She made a choking sound, and her trembling hand reached out, gripping my arm.

"No," she whispered. "God, no!"

Her phone hit the floor, and she buried her face in her hands, falling hard into my chest as her legs gave out. Panicking, I shouted her name, trying to hold her upright.

Chaos broke out at my yell. Aiden came running down the hall, his eyes wide when he saw me.

"What the hell?" he shouted, scooping her up. Maddox followed him, Bentley close at his heels. They all gathered around her, concerned.

Maddox grabbed her phone, speaking fast into the mouthpiece, demanding to know who it was on the line. His eyes grew round and he turned his back, lowering his voice. Aiden carried an incoherent Sandy to Bentley's office.

Maddox followed with a grave face.

"What is it?" Bentley demanded.

"It's Max. He had a heart attack."

Sandy's sobs grew louder.

"He didn't survive."

⌒

I TUGGED ON the collar of my shirt, uncomfortable and tense. I had never been to a funeral before, and I found it overwhelming. The flowers, the music, the people, and the sadness.

Jesus, the sadness.

I stood close to Sandy. We all did. Since Max had passed, one of us had been with Sandy all the time. Even when her stepson, Aaron, arrived and Colin was around, we stayed nearby. Colin's sister, Jennifer, arrived last night and we had shaken hands when I offered my condolences, but I hadn't spoken to her otherwise.

I didn't know what to say.

I didn't know what to say to anyone. I recalled the feeling of sadness when Mrs. Reid was gone, the pain of losing Rodney, and the anger of not being able to grieve his passing with anyone. I felt the loss of Max, saddened by his death, yet in the face of the devastation of his family's grief, it seemed insignificant. I didn't want to take away from their pain by expressing mine.

The first time Sandy had brought me to her house, Max was accepting and kind. Our conversations were always spirited and interesting. The affection between them was obvious, and he teased her about her adopting yet another "misfit," as he called us. The term made me laugh, given he was including Bentley, Aiden, and Maddox in the description. I enjoyed spending time with him. Diagnosed with late-onset MS, Max struggled with his failing body, since his mind remained razor-sharp. They'd had their home refitted to accommodate his needs, and I developed some cool voice-activated systems to augment what he already had in place. I knew the disease took its toll on both of them in different ways, but Sandy was devoted to him.

Now, she was lost. It hurt to watch her. Always vibrant and filled with light, she was a pale shadow of herself. The shock of the massive heart attack that struck Max had taken some of her life as well. Colin rarely left her side, and Bentley, Aiden, or Maddox, often all three, stood behind her, carefully monitoring her needs. They were worried over her lack of tears. She hadn't wept since receiving the call. Not once.

She did all the right things. Shook hands, kissed cheeks, accepted murmured words of condolence, and offered platitudes of thanks. She was dressed in a black suit, her hair swept into its usual chignon, but everything was off. Her suit jacket gaped open, her hair not as perfect as usual. Her expression was empty, her smile forced and sad, her posture defeated and closed off with her grief.

Somehow, that hurt more than Max's death.

Van appeared beside me, his gigantic frame poured into a suit. Used to seeing him in T-shirts, jeans, or overalls, I had barely recognized him. He had his jacket pulled tight across his shoulders, the sleeves taut around his biceps, and he looked as uncomfortable as I felt in my suit—as if we were pretending to be someone that we were not.

"How you holding up?" he asked, shaking my hand.

"Fine."

"I see you boys are keeping a close watch on Sandy."

"Yeah." I cleared my throat. "Did you know Max?"

"I did," he stated. "I've done a lot of work at Sandy's place. She is constantly changing things, and Max let her do whatever she wanted.

We had some great conversations. He liked to watch me work." He shook his head. "He worshiped her."

"She felt the same for him."

"I know. I liked being around them. It was always a lesson in how a relationship should work, you know?"

Since I was failing at my first attempt at a relationship, I couldn't offer him an opinion. "She's going to miss him."

Van nodded, draining the cup of coffee he was carrying. "She will. And as sad as that is, it's a testament to the love they shared. We should all be lucky enough to have someone miss us when we're gone."

Then, as if he said too much, he turned and walked away, his long stride carrying him fast.

Becca stepped beside me. "Are you all right, Reid?"

I glanced down at her, offering her a tight smile. "I'm fine. It's Sandy who needs our help."

She frowned, edging closer. "I know you spent a lot of time with him. Sandy said Max was very fond of you." She indicated the guys behind Sandy, watching over her. "She said he was fond of all of her adopted boys."

"He was very kind. He never judged me. I appreciated his company."

She slipped her hand into mine. "It's okay for you to grieve, Reid."

I swallowed and looked away. "I'm fine."

She sighed. "You keep saying that. *You're* fine. *We're* fine. Everything is *fine*. I think I hate that word."

I was at a loss how to respond to Becca. Another week had gone by without being alone with her. Without touching her. I missed her easy company and gentle spirit. I missed her body and the deep sense of belonging I had when we were together intimately. I wanted hours to be with her. To talk and laugh. To make love to her. To be *us*. But Sandy took priority, and Becca understood that.

At least, I thought she did.

"Now isn't the time to talk about it," I murmured.

Her hand dropped from mine. "Will there ever be a good time for you?"

I faced her, keeping my voice low. "What does that mean?"

Our gazes locked. Her eyes filled with sadness and confusion. "I know something is going on in your head, Reid. It's been messing with you since the launch, and now you're burying it along with your grief. You're using it to push me away."

I shook my head. "No. I'm trying to help Sandy. She needs me."

"Of course she does. She needs all of you. But Bentley, Aiden, and Maddox are still going home to their partners and talking to them. You've completely shut me out. Your door is closed at the office, you don't respond to my texts, and you walk right past my building when you leave Sandy's at night."

I frowned. "What?"

"I saw you twice. You went right past me. You could have stopped. Even if all you wanted to do was talk, I would have been there for you." She cupped my cheek. "I wanted to be there for you, but you refuse to let me."

I stared at her, silent and tongue-tied, my emotions and fears at war in my head.

She shook her head and stepped back. "You're right. It's not the place. But Reid, you need to find the place and the words." A tear slid down her cheek. "Or I might not keep waiting."

She slipped through the crowd, walking away from me without a backward glance.

And I let her.

⌒〜

I HANDED SANDY a cup of tea, the steam carrying the scent of bergamot into the air. She accepted it with an absent smile of thanks. I sat across from her, sipping my cup. I wasn't big on tea, but I didn't mind the occasional cup, and Sandy preferred it to coffee.

Glancing around, I grimaced at all the arrangements in the room. Despite the fact that the obituary asked for donations to the MS Society in lieu of flowers, they had arrived daily. The funeral home sent a vast amount of them to various nursing homes and hospitals to add some brightness to those places.

Aaron had left to return to Ottawa, with plans to come back next week. Jennifer had only stayed for the funeral, leaving for Europe the same day, anxious to return to her life. Colin was back at work in the busy ER, having taken most of the week off to be with Sandy.

Bentley, Aiden, and Maddox were at home, after spending the bulk of the day with Sandy. I worked then came to spend the evening with Sandy. Neither of us had eaten much of the casserole someone had brought for dinner, but at least I got her to eat a little.

"This is the hard part," she mused.

"What?"

She set down her tea, pulling a shawl around her shoulders. With her hair down and free of makeup, she looked younger than her years, despite the exhaustion on her face.

"We had a long time to prepare for this, but I still wasn't ready. Max always thought the MS would kill him before anything else." She sighed. "In many ways, he would have preferred it happen this way. He dreaded thinking his body would wither away, leaving him trapped."

I shifted in my chair, my throat tight.

"People gather when someone dies. They hover and check, make sure the spouse or child is being taken care of, then after the funeral, they go back to their lives, and that person has to learn to live again." She pulled her legs to her chest, linking her arms around them.

I cleared my throat. "You're not alone, Sandy. We won't let you be."

She shook her head. "No, Reid. You can't babysit me all the time. It's part of the process. I have to learn to live again. It will take me a while, but I will do it."

"I'm here. We all are—anything you need."

"I know, and I'm fortunate. I never had kids of my own, but I have you boys, and my grandkids—especially Colin. You all bring me so much joy. I consider myself fortunate." She was silent for a minute, playing with the fringe on her shawl. "I have been very lucky. I have a job I love, people I care about. My marriage was the greatest blessing.

I loved Max so much, and he was crazy about me. Right from the moment we met—it was instant. We had a wonderful life together. Not perfect, but no one's life is. I have so many amazing memories."

She leaned her cheek on her hands, studying me. "That's what life is, Reid. Building memories. One sweet moment at a time. You build and store them. They help bolster you when you need them."

All I could do was nod. I had no words to offer.

"Right before I got the call, I asked you something."

"We don't have to talk about that right now."

"Yes, we do. I know you're struggling, Reid."

"It's not important, Sandy. You're the one I'm worried about."

She smiled sadly. "I'm grieving for the life I have lost. For the love that I will miss every day. What you're doing is far more painful to watch."

"What I'm doing? I'm n-not doing anything," I sputtered.

"You're shutting down. You're throwing away the chance of a lifetime. You're letting your doubts and worries dictate your actions."

My body froze. "What?"

She unfurled her legs and leaned forward. "I know you, Reid. I see you pulling away from Becca. I know why."

"How?" I choked out.

She chuckled, the sound actually real and amused. "You forget who I am. I see everything that happens in the office. Bentley, Aiden, even Maddox, tell me what's going on. I know about your passport, your record, even your worries about buying a home." She threw up her hands. "Those are *problems,* Reid. Issues. Problems can be solved. Issues overcome. You have friends who will help you. But letting them become bigger than they are, and deciding *they* dictate your life instead of dealing with them?" She shook her head. "That's what you're doing."

"I—"

She interrupted me. "Do you think Max and I had an easy time of it? Everyone shunned us. Mocked us. Treated him like shit at the hospital for the longest time. People called me every name in the book—all because he was older and divorced. But we loved each other. That was all that mattered. We had each other. We made our life together."

I remained silent.

"Becca is the perfect girl for you. You're already in love with her. You're simply too scared to admit it."

"I don't want to limit her life because of my past."

"You don't want to risk your pride in case she says no," Sandy informed me, sat back, and crossed her arms. "Love is worth the risk, Reid. With the right person, it's worth everything."

"Maybe I'm not the right person for her. She deserves so much better than me."

"Right. She deserves someone who isn't kind, thoughtful, smart, and would adore her for the rest of her life? Who would put her first?" She snorted. "Get over yourself, Reid. For someone as smart as you, you are being shortsighted. Nothing is insurmountable. Ask for help. Let people in." She drew in a deep breath. "Allow yourself to feel, Reid. The good and the bad."

Emotion choked my throat and filled my eyes. I stood so fast, my chair tilted, hitting the floor with a dull thud. "I should go. You're tired."

She stood and faced me, challenging. "You haven't cried for Max."

"Neither have you," I shot back. Horrified at my words, I grabbed her hand. "Sandy, I'm sorry—I didn't mean . . ."

"You're right, I haven't."

"Why?"

"Because to cry means it's real. Max is gone. He won't kiss me goodnight anymore and call me darling. He won't tease me about my boys or wake me with sweet kisses." Her voice wavered. "He won't be here to hold my hand when there's a storm and tell me everything is fine. He won't love me endlessly, because he has ended. The life we shared has ended."

I could only stare.

"Max's biggest regret was that we never had children. He'd had a vasectomy because his first wife didn't want any more children. He tried to have it reversed, but it didn't work. We tried to adopt, but because of his age, we weren't approved." She tilted her head, studying me. "I wish they had given me you, Reid. I would have surrounded you with love no matter how much you cried and screamed." A tear slid down her face. "I would have shown you how much you deserved to be loved then. Just like you do now."

That broke me. I wrapped her in my arms and wept. She cried with me, both of us sharing pain no one else would understand. Her tears soaked into my shirt, and mine ran down her neck. Somehow, they helped relieve the ache I hadn't been able to get rid of for days.

She kissed my head. "I found my kids with you boys. All of you. Bentley, Aiden, and Maddox filled a place in my heart that was empty." She kissed me again. "And you completed it, Reid."

I lifted my head, and she wiped my face, her expression gentle. "Don't let love pass you by because you're scared or because of the what-ifs, Reid. Grab it. Live it. Life is too short for that sort of regret."

"I don't know what to do, Sandy."

"Yes, you do, my boy. What you have done since I met you. Be honest. Talk to Becca. Tell her your fears and what is holding you back. Let her be part of the decision. Part of loving someone is letting her see you. All of you."

She shook my shoulders. "Before it's too late, Reid. Tomorrow is not a guarantee. All we have is now. Remember that."

I lifted her hand to my mouth and kissed the knuckles. "I'm supposed to be looking after you. Not the other way around."

She shook her head. "No, you've done enough. You all have. In fact, I need some time alone to think. To remember. To figure out my next step."

"You're not leaving BAM, are you?" I asked. The thought made me anxious.

"And leave the four of you on your own?" She smirked. "The place would shut down in a month."

I had to laugh. She was right. A week without her and we were all floundering.

"No. I'll be back next week. I need something other than these walls around me. I need to find my new reality, but BAM is still a part of it. A big part." She winked. "Don't tell Bentley, but I'd be lost without them too."

"Your secret is safe with me."

She held out her arms. "Give me a hug, and go home, Reid. Or even better, go see Becca. Let her in."

I hugged her tight, feeling both grateful and sad. "I don't want to leave you alone."

"You have to," she replied, still hugging me. "It's what I want."

"Is there anything I can do?"

She pulled back, cupping my face. "Yes. Be brave. Cherish what you have. Be happy."

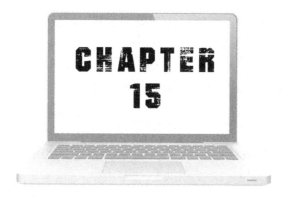

CHAPTER 15

BECCA

THE CONSTANT SOUND of the rain hitting my window would normally soothe me, but tonight, there was no soothing.

I had never met Max, but yesterday at the funeral, it was obvious many held him in high regard. Seeing Sandy so broken and vulnerable had shaken me. She was always in control—fearless and direct. All the men of BAM had hovered over her, worried and desperate to help, but unable to give her what she needed because her husband was gone.

I blinked away the tears forming in my eyes. All I could see was Reid. His stark loneliness that was so evident in a room full of people. Bentley, Aiden, and Maddox all sought out and stayed by their respective partners. Reaching out to clasp their hands or tucking them close as they watched over Sandy—drawing strength from their presence, allowing them to share in their grief.

Reid stood apart, not talking, not showing emotion, and not knowing what to do. He added more bricks to the wall he was recreating around himself, shutting out his friends, his emotions, and me.

Especially me.

Whatever had occurred—whatever words flipped that switch in his head, I couldn't fight. The rare moments he would allow himself to relax, to smile and murmur something sweet or funny had ceased totally since the weekend of the launch.

It felt as if he was as lost to me as Max was to Sandy.

I tried to talk to him at the funeral and again today in the office. But my texts went unanswered, and his door remained closed, even when I knocked. I left early, dejected, unsure, and wondering if I had made the biggest mistake of my life coming to Toronto and becoming involved with Reid.

Richard and Katy had warned me of the downfalls of having a relationship in the office. I hadn't listened to them—instead, only hearing my heart, which told me they were wrong. Reid was different. *We* were different.

I hadn't expected his withdrawal when faced with a difficult situation. I knew his past figured in all of this, but how, I didn't know, and he refused to say.

With a sigh, I went to the kitchen and poured a glass of wine. My dinner sat, untouched, on the stove, the pasta not temping my appetite in the slightest.

A sharp knock at my door startled me. I reached for my phone, grateful for the security system Reid had installed. I had a neighbor down the hall who loved to "drop in" for a chat and stay for hours, and tonight I was in no mood to deal with her babble. I tapped the screen, expecting to see her face, shocked when, instead, I saw Reid. He stood, head bowed, hands clutching the doorframe as if it were the only thing holding him up. His jacket was wet, his hair plastered to his head. I set down the phone and made my way to the door, opening it.

Reid lifted his head, his expression devastated—pain, fear, and need rolled off him like a tidal wave.

He swallowed, and his voice was rough when he spoke. "I-I didn't know if you would answer your door."

"Why are you here, Reid?"

"I-I need you, Becca."

My heart shattered as I spoke. "I can't just be the girl you turn to when you need something. It hurts too much."

"That's not what you are."

"What am I?"

Water ran down his face. I didn't know if it was the rain or tears. His eyes blinked, cleared, and became glossy again.

"My future."

I GRABBED A towel and blanket from the linen closet, and returned to the living room. After his one-word-changed-my-life statement, I had led Reid to the sofa and made him pull off his wet jacket and sneakers. I removed his socks and wrapped his feet in a blanket. His toes were almost blue from the cold, leading me to wonder how long he'd been walking in the rain.

He sat on the sofa, perched on the edge, his hands clasped and head bent. Briskly, I toweled his wet hair.

"You need another trim."

He looked up, his hazel eyes filled with a new emotion. "Would you cut it?"

"If you want."

"I want."

"Okay. Now lose your shirt and pants."

A glimmer of a smirk tugged his lips. "Shouldn't we talk first, BB?"

I shook my head. "You're soaking wet, Reid. You need to take off your clothes before you catch cold. You can wrap this blanket around you, and I'll toss them in the dryer." I cupped his face. "We are going to talk. By that, I mean you are going to talk, and I'm going to listen. Understand me?"

His large hands covered mine, and he turned his head, kissing one palm, then the other. "Yes."

He stood and removed his wet clothes.

I watched him, appreciating his build. He was lean and strong, his skin stretched taut over his muscles, sexy and appealing. His big hands made short work of the buttons and zippers, his long fingers nimble. Thinking about the way he used his body and those fingers to bring me pleasure, I had to avert my eyes before I made the mistake of tackling him to the sofa and fucking him before we talked.

I hoped that would happen afterward.

I threw the wet bundle into the dryer and carried a hot cup of coffee to Reid. He wrapped his hands around the mug and sipped the steaming liquid. A shiver ran through his body.

"Thank you. I needed that."

I sipped my wine, letting him warm. "How long were you walking in the rain?"

He ran a hand over his face. "What time is it?"

"Almost nine thirty."

"A little over an hour, I guess." He met my gaze and shrugged. "I needed to find my courage to come and see you."

"Well, here you are."

Tentatively, he reached for my hand, playing with my fingers. He lifted it to his mouth, kissed the palm, and pressed it to his face. "Yes, I am. And you're here." His voice sounded thick. "God, I needed you to be here."

"Tell me why."

He drained his coffee and set down his mug, then turned to me. "I've been struggling."

"I know that. What I don't understand is why."

He exhaled long and hard, picking up my hand again.

"I thought I was moving forward in my life. Moving away from my past. Sandy let me know, without a doubt, I was doing anything but that. I was drowning in my past and letting it swamp me."

"Tell me, Reid."

I listened as he told me about his conversation with Sandy. I couldn't help the tears that flowed down my cheeks as he told me about her statement of wishing she'd had the chance to be his mother.

"She would have been a wonderful mother to you."

"She would have, but as weird as it sounds, I wouldn't trade my life until now for that to have happened."

"Why?"

"If she'd been busy being a mother, she might not have met Bentley and the guys. She wouldn't be a part of BAM. Neither would I."

"You would rather have that job than erase a lifetime of painful memories?"

He edged nearer to me so our knees were touching.

"My job brought me to you. I would rather have you in my future than good memories of my past. I want the memories you and I create to be the ones I think of when I'm old and gray."

My breath caught at his powerful words.

"What brought this on, Reid? Tell me, please."

He sighed. "It was a combination, Becca. The fact that Maddox was getting married and I realized I might not be able to go because I didn't have a passport and I wasn't sure I could get one because of my record. The idea of buying a place for us at some point—I don't know if I can get a mortgage with my past. I mean, what bank wants to back someone who went to prison for stealing from another bank?" He dropped his head. "All I could think of was I wasn't good enough for you. That you deserved someone who could give you everything you wanted."

I took in a deep breath and forced myself to remain calm.

"How do you know what I want, Reid? You never asked. This isn't the first time you've made a decision, based on what you think is best for me, without asking, you know."

His gaze flew to mine. "I know you want to travel. You've said so. You said you'd like to buy a condo in Ridge Towers if you were staying here."

"Yes, I have said that. I've also said I want to bungee-jump and try parasailing, but if it doesn't happen, my life won't come to an end."

He furrowed his brow. "I don't understand."

I smiled. "You need to stop deciding what I need, Reid. What would be best for me. You aren't my parent. I want you to be my partner. I want to discuss things with you. Make decisions together." I tilted my head. "You know, I somehow managed to make it twenty-five years on my own. I went to school, held down a job, moved three times, and I was part of one of the most successful launches in the history of BAM. All without someone second-guessing if I should be doing those things." I smirked. "Even my father knows better than to question me when I make a decision in regard to living my life."

"I don't want to hold you back."

I flung up my hands. "There you go again. Who says you're going to hold me back?"

"If I can't—"

I shook my head in anger. "Reid, one of the things that drew me to you was your optimism. Your zest for life. The way you tackled every project with a 'Let's do this!' attitude. It was as if nothing was going to stop you. What changed? Why are you letting these doubts overwhelm you?"

His response was immediate. "Because I never had so much at stake until now. Until you."

"Reid—" I whispered.

"I want to make your life better, Becca, not to cause you worries and issues you shouldn't have to deal with."

"Shouldn't I be allowed to decide what I do and do not want to deal with?"

This time, he remained quiet, thinking over my words. Finally, he spoke.

"Yes, you should."

"We'll deal with it together. Stop with these unilateral decisions when it comes to our future!"

"Do we have a future, Becca? Or have I messed this up so badly, you're done with me?"

"You have messed up, yes. But not to the point of being done with you. Not by a long shot."

He closed his eyes, his shoulders sagging with relief.

I leaned forward, my voice firm. "Listen to me, Reid. What did Sandy tell you? You aren't alone anymore. We can take your problems and break them down, one by one, and solve them. The same way you do with an IT problem. You never tackle it as a whole. You break it into manageable steps, and you work at it until you solve it. Until *we* solve it. But you have to let me in. Talk to me. Talk to your friends. We all love you and want to help."

His eyes flew open. "You-you love me?"

I hadn't meant to say those words to him. I didn't think he was ready to hear them. I didn't think I was ready to say them. Yet, there they were—hanging between us like a shining spotlight. I knew I could tell him I loved him as a friend and that he meant a great deal to me, but not the way it came out.

But tonight was about the truth.

"Yes, Reid Matthews. I'm falling in love with you. That's why this hurts so much."

"I don't want to hurt you."

"Stop shutting me out. Let me share your life."

Our gazes locked. His was filled with emotion and worry.

He blew out a long breath. "I can't tell you I'm falling in love with you, Becca."

My breath faltered. "Oh."

He cupped my face. "Because I'm already there. I love you, Becca Holden. I don't know what I'm doing, but I love you so much and I want you in my life."

I wasn't sure who moved first, but I was under him on the sofa, his mouth on mine.

Hard and deep.

Possessive and claiming.

Filled with want and passion.

Repeating with his body, the words he had said out loud.

I love you.

His firm, rough chest pressed into mine, his body pushing me deep into the cushions of the sofa. I slipped my hands under the blanket surrounding him, caressing the warm, damp skin on his back. He groaned into my mouth, kissing me deeper, overwhelming me until all I could think about was him. His taste. His scent. How he reacted to my touch. The way I felt his desire.

How much I wanted him in return.

He pulled back, his breathing erratic. "I'm squishing you."

"What a way to go," I teased.

"I need to be with you, BB. Will you let me?"

"You never have to ask." I trailed my fingers down his cheek, feeling the coarseness of his stubble and the dampness of his tears. "I'm yours, Reid."

"Say it," he pleaded. "I need to hear it."

"I love you."

"I never thought I would hear those words from anyone."

"I'll say them every day."

One more tear ran down his cheek, then he stood and scooped me up, holding me close to his chest. He walked swiftly to my room, his arms keeping me tight to his body.

"I'm going to work to be the man you deserve, Becca."

I smiled at him.

"You already are, Reid. You already are."

⌒

I EXPECTED REID to toss me on my bed and be all over me in an instant. I knew he was ready. I had felt how ready he was. But he surprised me when he laid me down tenderly, kneeling beside me, only looking, not touching. I felt his gaze everywhere, warming my skin, making me long for his touch.

"Reid," I whispered. "I need you closer."

"I need you to know how much you mean to me."

I opened my arms. "Show me."

He crawled up the mattress, nestled between my legs. His mouth covered mine, the stroke of his tongue long and sensuous. Piece by piece, he pulled off my clothes, and let me push away his boxers so we were skin-to-skin. Rough rolling over soft. Hard muscles sculpting and fitting into my rounded curves. His hands never stopped—they touched and stroked. Caressed and teased. Plucked and rubbed. All done with gentle sweeps, tender arcs, and the lightest of pressure. He touched me everywhere until I was nothing but a mass of desire, wanting him more than I had ever wanted another man. The whole time, he whispered to me, words filled with devotion and love.

"You are so beautiful."

"Always, Becca. I will want you this way always."

"You are home. You're *my* home."

"I love you."

Finally, I begged, "Please, Reid."

He hovered over me, the blunt head of his thick, hard cock rubbing against my center. Our eyes locked, our gaze never wavering as he slid in, inch by inch, until we were flush. I groaned at the sensation of having him inside me. He began to move, his thrusts slow, even, and deep—his movements meant to draw out my pleasure. He kissed me, his tongue mimicking his cock, drugging my senses.

All that existed was Reid. His body. His cock. His love.

"More, please." I arched, wrapping my legs around his hips to bring him closer. "I need more of you. Faster."

"No," he groaned. "I want to savor you. Savor this. Just feel me, baby. Feel how we fit together. Know we're going to be this way every time." He slid his hand under my ass, lifting me, pushing deeper. His forehead pressed to mine, his breath hot on my face. "Every single time I make you mine."

He sped up, still gentle, but hitting me exactly where I needed. I tumbled over the edge, crying out his name.

He stilled, his body taut, groaning my name as he rode out his orgasm. He buried his face in my neck, murmuring words I couldn't understand. I didn't need to—his tone said all I had to know.

He was with me, and he wasn't going anywhere.

Reid was back. And he belonged to me.

CHAPTER 16

REID

THE LAZY FEELING of serenity drifted through me. The rain had picked up, and unlike the cold wet that had beat against me outside, now the sound was soothing as it hit the window. Becca was nestled beside me, her warmth and scent wrapped around me like a blanket. Turning my head, I pressed a kiss to her crown, gently sliding my hand up and down her arm.

She lifted her head, smiling at me, languid and sated. "Hey."

I lowered my head and kissed her plump lips. "Hey, BB."

"You okay?"

I grinned. "More than okay. You?"

She snuggled closer, draping her arm over my waist. "Perfect." She chuckled softly. "You wore me out, though."

I tucked her head under my chin. I had made love to her twice, the second time nowhere near as sweet as the first. That had been to show her my feelings—how much she meant to me.

A short time later, watching her slumber, seeing her breasts rise and fall, the nipples still rosy and peaked from my mouth, my cock had stirred. I tugged down the blanket, revealing more of her naked perfection to me. Her body was a work of art. The swell of her breasts, the curve of her waistline, the roundness of her hips. Her skin was silky and smelled of vanilla and sugar. She was delicate yet strong, her limbs and muscles toned and flexible. Compact, but powerful. I loved how she felt against me, our bodies meshing, aligning so well despite our differences.

She mumbled in her sleep, rolling to her side. I traced the ridges of her spine with my finger, marveling at the simple beauty of her back. Her ass was rounded, and I couldn't resist cupping one cheek, the firm muscle twitching in my grip. Two beauty marks rested side by side on her shoulder blade, and I kissed them, my tongue lingering on her skin. I dragged my mouth down her back, desire taking over. Easing her onto her back, I closed my mouth around her nipple, sucking and licking as she began to stir. I glided my fingers to her core, still wet from our earlier lovemaking, teasing and stroking as she woke, groaning my name.

Her eyes still closed, she arched, driving my fingers deeper. My cock was desperate to replace them, but I wanted her ready and awake. She shook, her body already close, opening her eyes to meet mine. Desire swam in her blue depths.

"Oh God, Reid."

"I need to fuck you, Becca. Now."

"Yes," she whimpered. "Now."

In seconds, I was nestled between her legs, sliding my cock into her heat. She wrapped her legs around my waist, and I took her. My need was rampant as I drove into her hard and fast—mindless and aching. I felt her everywhere as my orgasm built like wildfire in my veins, burning and twisting so hot I was certain all that would remain was ash when I climaxed. She was right there with me, her back bowing off the bed, gripping my arms, tightening her legs and making the sexiest sounds as I had her.

Her orgasm hit, her neck straining as she stiffened, milking my cock, her muscles fluttering and urging me to join her. I braced myself on her headboard, thrusting as my balls tightened. Pleasure took over, and I came, shaking, gasping, calling her name, the intensity so great for a minute it was as if I was lost in a sea of sensation.

I collapsed on her chest, unable to speak.

"Are you sore?" I asked, trying not to be turned on thinking of what we had done.

"You have to ask?" She laughed. "That was amazing." She kissed my chest. "We're amazing together."

"Yeah, we are."

My stomach grumbled loudly in the room.

She lifted her head. "Did you not eat dinner? Or did you build up an appetite?"

"Both."

"I made pasta but never ate it," she confessed. "I can heat it up if you wanted."

Suddenly, I was ravenous. "I want."

WRAPPED IN A blanket, sitting at her counter, I inhaled the pasta she had made. Two huge bowls were gone before I felt replete. As usual, Becca ate slower, watching me eat with a small grin.

"What?" I wiped my mouth, draining the glass of milk she had placed in front of me.

She shrugged. "I love to watch you eat. Especially if I've made it. Your enjoyment makes me smile."

"Food in prison is pretty bland. It's supposed to be nutritional, but there's no flavor." I sighed, playing with my fork. "I'm sure the fact that you're in prison has something to do with it."

"That makes sense."

"When I got out, I went for a cheeseburger. I had been craving one for years." I shut my eyes, remembering the flavor. "I thought I was going to cry over it. It tasted like freedom. Every time I eat something delicious now, I appreciate it more than ever."

I glanced at her. She was watching me with a tender look on her face. Leaning forward, I kissed her. "Your cooking is such a treat. Thank you."

She hummed.

Not wanting to get into another deep discussion, I changed the subject.

"So what is on the agenda this week, now that the campaign is up and running?"

She sipped her water, setting down the glass. "I'll maintain it, adjust the ads and placement. Sales are still so strong, we want to keep it visible. Once Bentley is happy, we'll wind it down and move on to phase two. Plus, he had me working on a few other things. He wasn't kidding when he told Richard he could keep me busy full time. I'm amazed at the number of projects BAM is involved in."

"I know. The company is so diversified."

"I have to get to the bank and deposit my bonus," Becca said, excited.

"Bonus?"

She frowned. "Oh, um, maybe I wasn't supposed to say anything?"

"No, that's great. They gave you a bonus?"

She nodded. "When we went to dinner on that Sunday night. Bentley gave me an envelope and said it was for going above and beyond. I know Richard refused the one he was offered the next day and told Bentley he wanted access to your report instead."

"That makes sense. Bentley told me to license it to The Gavin Group." I squeezed her hand. "I'm glad they rewarded you, BB. You deserve it."

She bent low, as if telling me a secret. "It was five thousand dollars, Reid. I was shocked how generous they were."

"I'm not. They believe in rewarding their staff, and they make sure to take good care of us. Bentley appreciates loyalty."

She hesitated, then asked, "You didn't get one?"

"Yeah, I think I did. They came to see me after the meeting and gave me an envelope. I put it in my drawer, meaning to open it later. When Sandy got the call about Max, I forgot."

"You should open it tomorrow and say thank you."

Chuckling, I kissed her nose. "I will." I sat back. "Any big plans for the money?" I knew if Becca received five thousand, mine would be equal, perhaps even a little higher. Some was going into the bank toward my future. Our future. The one I needed to talk to her about some more. But I wanted to splurge a little as well.

"I-I'm going to surprise my dad and go see him. Sandy arranged my days off around a long weekend so I could have more time. I'm going to go for five days."

"Oh." It made sense she would want to do that. Still, I was disappointed. I had thought maybe we could go away together, but I knew she missed her father. "He'll be thrilled, I'm sure."

She inhaled, squaring her shoulders. "Would you come with me, Reid? Meet my dad?"

"Is that a good idea, Becca?"

"I love you," she replied.

Her words made me smile and reach for her hand.

"You're part of my life. He knows I've been seeing someone."

"Does he know about my past?"

She swallowed, looking away.

"Becca, we can't hide it. He'll find out eventually, and he'll be angry we weren't truthful."

"I thought he could meet you, get to know you, then I would tell him."

I shook my head. "No. You tell him when you talk to him this week. Once he knows, if you still want me to come, I will."

"Really?"

"I love you." I repeated her words. "I want to be part of your life. That includes your father. So, if he is willing to give me a chance, I'll give him one too."

She launched herself at me, almost knocking me off my stool. I encircled her with my arms, holding her close.

"I'll call him later today."

I kissed her head. "Okay. We can book flights next week."

She pulled back. "My treat."

I began to shake my head, and she frowned. "I want to pay for the trip with my bonus."

"I'll make you a deal. You pay for the flights; I'll pay for the hotel. I know you said your dad is in a small place."

"Yes. If I were going alone, I'd stay with Richard and Katy, but I'd like to stay in a hotel with you, Mr. Matthews."

I cupped her ass, bringing her body flush with mine. "Oh yeah?"

She grinned. "Hotel sex is awesome."

Hotel sex. Another first.

I stood, lifted her, and headed to the bedroom. "I think we need more practice to build up to the hotel sex."

Her mouth was hot against my neck.

"Lots more."

SANDY WAS AT the staff meeting Monday morning. Her blouse was crisp, her hair perfect, but there was a sadness to her expression that had never been there before. I wondered if it was something that would ever fully leave her. I was glad to see her back—everyone was glad. We'd all missed her.

After, I was busy at my desk. Reaching into my drawer to grab a new pencil, I lifted out the envelope Bentley had handed me. I had forgotten about it again, but I knew I should open it and take the contents to the bank. I also had to thank the guys properly.

I tore open the seal, and withdrew a folded document containing several pages of what appeared to be legal wording. There was no bonus payment.

Instead, there was something so unexpected I stared at the document for long, stunned moments, reading and rereading the words, certain I was mistaken.

I lurched to my feet and hurried down the hall. Sandy looked up as I stumbled to her desk. I knew the guys were in their usual Monday morning partners' meeting, and there was no way I was getting past her without their allowing it.

"I need to see them."

She shook her head. "You finally opened it."

"You knew?"

"What did I tell you, Reid? I know everything that goes on in this place." She picked up her phone, speaking into the receiver. "Reid needs some time with all of you. I suggest you let him in before he falls down in front of my desk."

She hung up and indicated Bentley's door. "In you go."

Before I could move, she lifted her hand. "You deserve this, Reid. But remember your manners."

I met her eyes, seeing the smile they contained.

"I can do that," I croaked.

Three sets of eyes watched me stagger into Bentley's office. Three wide grins lit their faces as I sank into the sofa beside Aiden, lifting the pages. "I don't understand."

Bentley leaned back. "I think I'll let Maddox explain, being our numbers man and all."

Maddox observed me, tapping his cheek thoughtfully.

"Reid, since you joined BAM, you have proven to be more than an employee. You've put yourself on the line for us more than once, and you've shown us loyalty and commitment. You have become our friend—part of our family. You know how we feel about family."

"You take care of them," I mumbled.

"Good. You pay attention." Maddox grinned. "The other day you told me you wanted to live in Ridge Towers. You also confessed to your worry about getting a mortgage, and were concerned if you would be able to save enough for the deposit."

I swallowed, my throat thick. "Yeah," I rasped out. "But—"

Maddox held up his hand. "I spoke to Bentley and Aiden. We already knew we were going to give bonuses for this project. The results have been nothing less than amazing, and we like to reward our staff well."

I shook my head. "This isn't a bonus. It's . . ." I struggled to find the words. "I was expecting . . ." I hesitated. "Not this. I wasn't expecting this."

Bentley stood and rounded the desk, leaning on the edge. He crossed his arms. "We're aware it's unorthodox, but frankly, Reid, the things you have done for us have been unorthodox. You helped find Emmy. You eliminated a huge problem for Maddox. You've proven to Aiden, repeatedly, that there is nothing you can't do. Nothing you won't do for us. That deserves more than a bonus."

I lifted the papers. "But it's a condo. You've given me a *condo*."

Maddox chuckled. "It's the smaller one in my building. We're going to use the one Dee lived in briefly as our corporate place. The other one is sitting empty. It's one-plus bedroom, but the size is generous, so there's lots of space for all your equipment. This transaction does two things. You get to move in to a great, secure building right away. You'll pay the monthly condo fees and taxes, the same as everyone else, and you'll be building equity, which you can use toward a place in Ridge Towers. The value is currently about four hundred thousand for this place."

I almost choked. Aiden patted me on the back.

"Stay with us, kid. Things are just getting good."

Maddox laughed. "We had planned to do some renos to the place, but we've decided you can look after that. Get with Van, and he'll make sure it happens. I suggest an overhaul of the kitchen and bath to maximize your investment." He winked. "You'll get the company rate."

They gave Becca a bonus of five thousand dollars. They gave me a condo.

"I can't accept this—it's too much."

"You can and you will. It's all bound and legal. Bill has the papers drawn up. You can move in right away and make yourself a home. Your life is changing, Reid," Bentley stated firmly. "You can't sleep on the floor of your office all the time now. You need a place where you're settled. Where Becca can be with you."

His words made sense. Still, it was a lot to take in.

"When Ridge Towers is closer to completion, you can decide if you want to move." Maddox smirked. "And if you'll be moving alone. If my suspicions are right, you'll need a two-bedroom with room to grow."

Aiden leaned forward, earnest. "We could have simply handed you a condo in the Towers, but we felt this was better. You can move right away and get out of that little place you hate. You can do some renos and increase the value. Then sell it and move on. On your terms."

"Only because of your charity."

"No." Bentley's voice was steely. "This isn't charity. This is our way of thanking you. If you don't want to move later, you don't have to. Or you can move elsewhere. We're simply giving you the tools to start." He sighed. "We all think you deserve that, Reid. A fresh start and a leg up. We did that for each other. Now, we're doing it for you."

"It's so much."

"It's what we feel you deserve."

I closed my eyes, so many feelings exploding in my head. There was only one thing I could say. "Thank you."

"Do you still want to live in Ridge Towers one day?"

"If I can. Maybe phase two."

Bentley cocked his head, studying me. "Why phase two?"

"The unit I really wanted is off the list," I admitted. "Most of the two-bedrooms are taken now."

Aiden flipped through a list he was holding. "B-8A? That one?"

"Yeah, I thought the views would be amazing on that corner, and I liked the layout."

He nudged my shoulder, showing me the list. Beside that unit number, was my name, typed in bold letters.

"Wh-what? How?"

"Mad Dog told us, and we removed it from inventory. We'll discuss pricing closer to the time."

"But—"

Maddox interrupted me. "We'll help you with a mortgage, Reid. You can sell the condo, which will more than meet your deposit requirement. Whatever financing you need, any of us—in fact, all of us—will co-sign for you. You *will* have a mortgage and you *will* own a place in Ridge Towers. This is our bonus to you for everything you have done and we know you will do in the future."

My mouth opened, but no words came out. To my horror, the room swam in front of me, and I struggled to contain my feelings, quickly ducking my head. I was about to break down and cry in front of my bosses. I couldn't allow that to happen, yet even as I tried to stop it, a tear splashed on my knee. Followed by another. I couldn't contain the swell of emotions. They were too vast and deep.

Aiden's big arm came around my shoulder. "It's okay, kid. We make a lot of grown men cry. It's sort of what we do."

I barked out a laugh and lifted my head. I was shocked to see all three men grinning at me, their eyes damp. In that moment, they weren't my bosses. They were my friends. My brothers. They had given me the gift of a fresh start. A place to call my own—something I longed for but could never put into words.

Jumping to my feet, I lunged first for Bentley, hugging him hard. He chuckled and gave me a brief slap on the back. Maddox was ready for me, letting me pounce on him, laughing as he hugged me in return. I turned to Aiden, the man who had risked a lot to give me a second chance.

He opened his massive arms. "Come to Papa, kid." His hug almost broke my ribs, but it was worth it.

All of what they did for me made everything worth it.

Because of them, I had a new path and a future. Something to offer.

I couldn't wait to tell Becca.

CHAPTER 17

REID

BECCA AND I wandered through the condo. I was still in shock over the extravagant gesture. When I'd told Becca, her eyes had grown round, and she'd flung her arms around my neck, excited and pleased for me. I insisted she come with me to see the place that evening.

Sliding the key into the lock and stepping into what was now my home was surreal. It was a great layout with a kitchen to the left and a good-sized living/dining area on the right. To one side was a small space—what Maddox referred to as the *plus*. It would be an excellent area for my desk and equipment. The bedroom and bathroom were generous in size. Compared to where I lived currently, it was a palace.

Becca laughed at my excitement over the air conditioning. I had none and the windows were old with no screens, so at times, with the sweltering summers in Toronto, I often had to escape to the cool interior of the office to sleep there. It would be amazing to have a place that was cool during the heat of the summer.

To me, it all appeared perfect, although both Becca and Van nodded knowingly as they looked around.

I'd sat with Maddox in the afternoon to run through numbers. He showed me how, if I used the money I had saved now, the investment would pay off more than the meager interest I earned each month. He helped me set a budget for the renovations, almost as excited as I was about the project.

Van made notes, returning to the kitchen where Becca was looking into the cupboards. "Well, it's an awesome place, but the guys are right. Some upgrades and it would be even better."

Becca agreed with him. "The kitchen and bath."

"Yep. I suggest the floors too. Some paint and a little trim work would make the place feel modern and updated."

"It all looks fine to me. But if you think it needs it, then we'll go ahead."

Van laughed, crossing his arms and leaning on the counter. He was almost as big as Aiden, taking up a vast amount of space. His hands were calloused, and usually, there was paint or dust on his jeans. However, his dark navy eyes were kind, his voice low, and he was knowledgeable and approachable. I helped him a lot with various programs, and I knew Bentley relied on him and trusted his judgment.

"The place will be empty by the weekend. We can pull out whatever we decide to reno and get started. You can pick what you want in the way of cupboards, floors, counters, fixtures. Bentley told me to make it a priority."

"I have no idea what I want."

He chuckled. "Liv can help you with that. You can tell her your budget, what your preferences are, and she'll go from there."

I looked at Becca, helpless. "Maybe you can come with me?"

"Oh, I'd love to!"

"I could call Liv. She lives not far from here. If she's home, she could come over and have a look."

"That would be awesome."

He pulled out his phone, walking out of the kitchen.

I shook my head. "This is too much."

Becca hugged my arm. "It will be great."

"I prefer things simple."

"I know."

I stepped toward her, sliding my hand over hers. "But make it the way you want it, Becca. I want you here with me a lot, so make sure you like it."

She lifted up on her toes and kissed me. "Okay."

⌒

LIV SNAPPED CLOSED her laptop. She had come over after Van called her. Professional and quiet, she had walked around, talked to Van, made notes, and asked me some questions.

"Okay, here're my thoughts. You don't want a major overhaul or walls moved."

"No."

"And you want simple."

"Yes."

"We'll do the same flooring throughout except the bath. One of the engineered wood floors. Wide planks. Easy to clean and maintain. In the kitchen, new cupboards, counters, and backsplash. The already-upgraded appliances look good. We'll do clean lines. Modern. In the bathroom, we'll update the fixtures and put in a cool multi-head shower. You said your favorite colors are blue and gray, so I'll keep that in mind. We'll go with a nice earthy tone with some pops of color. I have your budget, so I'll work it through with Van and have ideas to you in a couple of days."

"Wow. Okay."

"Bentley's instructions," she informed me with a wink. Then she smiled, the action transforming her face. She was pretty, but her smile was killer. She had soft tawny-colored hair which she wore in a long braid and had luminous, golden-colored eyes. She was expressive, always using her hands, and her voice was soft but direct.

She was the same in the office. Pleasant and helpful, always willing to go the extra mile—and another person Bentley relied on. Like Van, she carried traces of her work with her. Paint flecks in her hair or telltale signs of colored marker on her hands from her designs. They were an interesting duo. Professional and friendly, yet Van watched her closely, and I also noticed how often she deferred to him, as if seeking his approval.

"Becca is going to help me pick stuff."

"All right."

"I want to choose the furnishings gradually, myself." I wanted to do that with Becca. Have her with me trying out sofas and chairs. Testing out beds.

That was going to be my first purchase.

Liv nodded in understanding. "Sure. We'll do the reno, and you can complete it when you're ready."

She and Van left, and I walked around again. The condo had simple furnishings in it already since they'd used it as a guest suite, but we'd take those out right away. Maddox told me I could keep anything I wanted, but the idea of picking out my own furniture suddenly appealed. It would be my first real home.

Becca stood beside me, sliding her arm around my waist. "Happy?"

I dropped a kiss on her head. "Yeah, I am."

"You deserve this, Reid."

I sighed. "Everyone keeps saying that. I'm trying to come to terms with it."

She squeezed my hip. "You do. You deserve all good things."

I gazed down at her. Her blue eyes held me captive and I smiled. "Do I deserve you?"

"Yes. And you have me, Reid."

I pulled her close, my mouth hovering over hers. "That's all I need."

⌒

BECCA GRINNED AT me across the desk. "Are you excited?"

I shook my head. "I think so."

She laughed. "Liv is amazing!"

I perused the conceptual drawings of the condo Liv had left me. When she'd arrived earlier, she'd pulled cupboard, counter, paint chip, even floor samples from her large bag. She had limited the choices, though, so it wasn't as overwhelming as I feared. She'd explained her ideas, and with Becca's help, guided me toward the items I preferred. All her designs were as she promised. Clean, simple, and modern. She'd even created a built-in set of shelves in the small room where my desk would be to hold my collections. She explained she could reconfigure my steel shelves to fit underneath the new ones for the equipment I kept on hand.

"Form and function, Reid," she said, showing me a picture. *"I have a great desk in storage that would work well. If you want it, it's yours."*

I liked it. Thick and solid, the metal would suit the room and be sturdy enough I could leave the makeshift one of cinder blocks and wood behind. In fact, I was leaving it all behind me, except my personal things and the one set of shelves I had built. I had given notice, and looked forward to being out of that place as soon as possible.

I grinned at Becca. "I noticed she added furniture to her drawings. Do you think that's her subtle way of telling me what to look for?"

Becca chuckled. "Maybe. I think it's simply how she works, but the style does suit you."

"It does."

"We'll go shopping when we return from BC."

I leaned back in my chair. "You booked some flights?"

"I have dates. I wanted to make sure they're okay for you."

I studied her. "Did you talk to your father?"

She met my gaze. "Yes."

"Did you tell him about me?"

"Yes, Reid, I did."

"What did you tell him exactly?"

"That you were wonderful and kind. Thoughtful and sweet." She lowered her voice. "That I loved you and I wanted him to meet you."

"What else?"

She sighed and pushed away her sandwich. "I told him what you did for a living and how we met. And yes, I told him about your past."

"And?"

She rubbed her forehead. "He wasn't pleased, Reid. I didn't expect him to be. I told you he's black and white with his views. He said what he thought, I told him why he was wrong, and we agreed to disagree."

"In other words, he doesn't approve."

"In other words," she countered, "he needs to meet you and make up his mind after that happens. I want you to spend some time with him. Let him get to know you. I'm sure he'll realize the kind of person you are once he does."

I contemplated her words. "What if he doesn't, Becca?"

She shook her head. "That won't happen. Once he sees how happy you make me, and he talks to you, it will be fine. I know it."

She desperately wanted to believe her words. I had a feeling it was going to take more than a few days and some conversations to get him to like me. But for her, I was willing to try.

"I've never been on a plane before," I told her, wanting to stop her worry and make her smile. "Another first with you, BB."

"The list keeps growing."

I held up my hand and counted. "Yep. My first real crush, first meaningful kiss." I winked. "You got my virginity, my first trip in a plane, or even staying in a hotel. All of them—yours."

"Anything else?" She looked into my eyes.

"My love. You are my first and only love, Becca."

Her smile appeared. The gentle one only I saw. Shy, tremulous, and sweet. She leaned over my desk. "You still say the best things, Reid Matthews."

I met her halfway with a long kiss.

"All for you, BB. All for you."

I FOUND THE airport fascinating. I wandered around, looking at the monitors and systems, marveling at the scope of it all. The flight was long and uneventful—though the take-off was unlike anything I had ever experienced before now. Becca napped while I did some work on my computer, and we watched a movie together to pass the time.

After we landed, I turned to her. "I preferred the take-off to landing."

She smirked. It was sexy and cute on her.

"I know."

"You too?"

"Yes, but the death grip on my hand was sort of the indicator."

Looking down I realized how tight I was holding her palm, and I released it with a quick kiss to her knuckles.

I had arranged a rental car for us. I didn't know how to drive, but Becca did, and it would make it easier to get around. Luckily, the hotel was quiet and our room was ready. I made sure to book a nice suite with a sitting area and a big tub in the bathroom for her. She enjoyed soaking in the tub and I hoped she would be able to relax while we were there.

I stored away my clothes and stood on the small balcony of our suite, looking at the pretty city. The air was warm and filled with the scent of the many flowering trees around the hotel. I inhaled deeply as my nerves began to tighten. Becca wanted to go see her father this afternoon, and I was beginning to get anxious about meeting him. Richard had called and told me to make sure to stand up to him and not to take any of his bullshit.

"He's a hard man until he accepts you," he cautioned me. "Very protective of Becca. We certainly had a rough start, even though we get along fine now. I'm sure you'll be okay, but if you need backup, give me a call."

Becca's arms wrapped around my waist, and she hugged me tightly. "Did you want to stay here while I go see my dad?"

I reached behind me and pulled her to my side. "No. I came to meet him, so I will."

She smiled, although I saw the tension in her eyes.

"Don't worry, BB. You said he was a big sports fan. We can talk football or baseball. We'll find our common ground."

"He's blunt."

Thinking of Rodney, I smiled. "I'm okay with blunt."

She sighed. "I warned him to be nice. I told him how much you meant to me. Sometimes, he, well, he says rude things."

"The way he did with Richard?"

"He told you about that?"

"Yeah. I can handle him, Becca. I'll be respectful."

She sighed and leaned her head on my shoulder. "I hope he reciprocates."

I had to chuckle. He was Becca's father. How bad could the man be?

A FEW HOURS later, I knew the answer to that question—and it wasn't positive.

Gerald Holden had already decided to hate me, and he had no issues letting me know. We had stopped and bought some things for him Becca knew he liked. I had added a bottle of his preferred rye, hoping to make a good impression. I failed.

He was a tall man, his once-broad shoulders stooped over his cane. His hair was salt-and-pepper, his eyes the same color blue as Becca's. It was the only resemblance I could see between them. His expression was dour, except for the smile he had for Becca.

"Dad!" she exclaimed, throwing her arms around his neck. "You look good!"

"Ah, Rebecca," he replied. "You're just buttering me up."

"Never," she teased and stepped back. "Dad, this is Reid Matthews. Reid, this is my dad, Gerald."

I extended my hand. "Mr. Holden, sir. I've heard so much about you. It's a pleasure to meet you."

He eyed my hand as though it would bite before accepting it.

"Reid," he stated shortly. "I don't think I've heard enough about you."

"Dad," Becca murmured with a warning tone in her voice.

"It's fine, Becca." I smiled, even though I felt the cool dismissiveness of his greeting. "Your dad and I need to get to know each other." I held out the bottle of rye. "Becca tells me this is your favorite."

He took the bottle, lifting one eyebrow. "Booze as a hello? What's next—you have some weed in your pockets to share?"

"Dad!"

He laughed dryly. "Just teasing the boy, Rebecca. Come in and sit down."

I followed them into his place. Small and neat, it contained a love seat and chair, plus a little table and kitchen setup. A bedroom and bath were right off the living area. Becca had explained he had his meals in the main dining room and used his kitchen area for snacks.

"He was never much of a cook," she said. "So he took one of the suites with the meal plan. I don't have to worry about him eating, and he enjoys the social aspect."

Becca busied herself putting away the few things she had brought him. He placed the rye on the table and addressed me "Was the trip all right? The drive here okay? I know there is construction on Maple Avenue. Did Rebecca tell you to avoid that?"

I cleared my throat. "The trip was good, Mr. Holden. Becca went around the construction, so the drive over was fast."

"Becca drove?"

I noticed he didn't tell me to call him Gerald.

"Yes, sir. I don't drive."

"You don't drive?"

"No, sir, I don't. In Toronto, I walk or take the subway. Traffic is horrendous, and I never bothered to learn."

He leaned back, eyeing me speculatively. "Hard to learn in prison, I imagine."

Somehow, I wasn't shocked how quickly he brought up my past. I met his cool gaze.

"No, pretty near impossible. I haven't been in prison for some time, though. But there hasn't been a need to learn, and I have no intention of buying a car for myself, so I haven't bothered."

"You haven't *bothered*," he repeated. "I assume you have no problem letting my daughter play chauffeur." His tone said it all.

You're a lazy, good-for-nothing loser.

Becca joined us. "I like to drive, Dad. You know that. Reid's right—in Toronto, it's easier to walk or take the subway. That's why I sold my car. Parking alone would break me," she informed him, trying to lighten the air. "If I could even find a place to park the car, that is."

It didn't work, and things went from bad to worse. Every chance he got, he took a dig at me. He'd ask snide questions about my upbringing. My record. The work I did "playing with computers." Becca jumped in and defended me every time, but it did no good. By the end of the afternoon, I'd been on the defensive nonstop, and my head ached from being so tense. All I wanted was to go back to the hotel and get away from her father. Luckily, we were having dinner with Richard and his family, so we had an excuse not to be there for the entire evening.

Before we could leave, he shifted in his chair. "Becca, I forgot. I need some cream for my coffee later. Could you run to the shop downstairs and get me a small container? Have them charge it to my account."

She glanced my way, nervous. I tilted my chin, letting her know I was fine. I knew what was about to happen, and I figured we might as well get it over with.

I wasn't wrong.

As soon as she was out the door, he turned to me.

"I don't like your kind, boy."

"My kind?" I asked, despite knowing exactly what he was saying.

"I checked you out. You stole millions of dollars. You're nothing but a thief. A liar and a thief. I don't know how you hoodwinked the people you're working for, but they'll figure it out soon enough."

I remained calm. "Is that right?"

"Yes. I'm sure you're somehow ripping them off too. They'll

get wise to you." He narrowed his eyes. "Do they know about your background?"

"Every sordid detail."

That seemed to shock him. I leaned forward, keeping my voice level. "Listen, Mr. Holden, I get it. You don't think I'm good enough for your daughter. You hate ex-cons. Becca told me your feelings on that subject. But, sir, you're wrong. I was a kid. I made a stupid mistake, and I paid the price. I learned my lesson."

"Really." His retort was dry and filled with contempt. "In my experience, that is rare."

"Maybe. But for me, it's true. I have a new life. Good people in it. The best one is your daughter. I love her, and I wouldn't do anything to jeopardize that or the opportunities I've been given."

He grunted.

"Maybe if you gave me a chance, let me tell you my story, you'd see I wasn't the lowlife you've decided I must be." I met his baleful glare. "Do you really think your daughter would fall in love with someone as undeserving as you seem to think I am?"

"I think you've fooled her and a lot of other people. Leopards don't change their spots, boy. I've seen it too often. It's only a matter of time before you fall back on your old habits."

I barked out a laugh, fed up. "Listen to yourself. You sound like some bad TV cop. I'm not a criminal."

"Your record says different."

"My record shows I made a mistake, went to prison, served my time, and have lived within the law since then. It doesn't tell you the why or the person I am now. I have a good job and a future. One which contains your daughter, I might add. I'd wanted us to get along for her sake, but you're making it difficult."

"I have no desire to get along with you. You're a phase. She'll get over you soon enough, boy."

I stood, tired of the conversation and knowing we were only going to go around in circles. I refused to let him know how his words rankled, that they struck a chord of worry within me. I was apprehensive Becca would find someone better, more worthy of her. But right now, I was tired of his disparaging attitude and lack of compassion. Given the kind person I knew Becca to be, I found it difficult to believe the man in front of me had raised her.

"My name is Reid, not boy. I'm sorry you feel that way." I shook my head. "Becca wanted us to find some common ground and maybe be friends."

"We have nothing in common."

I stared at him, upset at his arrogance and knowing there was nothing I could do to change it. At least, not today.

"Yes, Mr. Holden, we do. We both love Becca. I came here because she wanted me to meet you. It's important to her. You may want to think about that."

I turned and left the room.

⌒

I RAN A hand over my face, taking a long sip of beer. "Jesus, Richard. He's a piece of work. How the hell is he Becca's dad?"

Richard chuckled as he placed the steak on the grill, the delicious smell immediately hitting me. I was starving.

"He's pushing you hard."

"No shit."

"He's testing you."

"Well, I fucking failed. I don't know what to do."

The sound of laughter drifted over, and I looked toward the noise. Becca was in the pool with Gracie, Katy sitting on the edge with Heather, trailing her toes in the cool water. She cooed and giggled while Gracie clapped her hands in delight.

Becca had accepted my explanation that I was heading to the car to give her a few moments alone with her dad when I bumped into her in the hall. She hadn't said anything in the car, even when we stopped for flowers and wine. We already had gifts for the little ones we had brought from Toronto.

Richard and Katy had been welcoming, and I'd had a swim and a couple of beers, so I was more relaxed than I had been all day. I was helping Richard cook dinner—in other words, bitching at him about Gerald Holden and the stick up his ass when it came to me.

Richard shut the lid, letting the steaks cook. He indicated Becca. "If she's as important to you as you say, you keep your mouth shut, and you piss him the fuck off by going back tomorrow. You kill him with kindness."

"And what does that get me besides more insults?"

"It shows Becca you're trying. Gerry is using your prison record to get under your skin. He's terrified of you."

My beer bottle froze on its way to my mouth. "What?"

He shrugged. "He told Katy he had hoped Becca would go to Toronto and decide the big-city life wasn't for her then come back to Victoria. I think that was why he didn't put up a fuss when she decided to go. But it hasn't worked out that way. She loves Toronto, the office—and you. Not much incentive to leave that behind. And he's decided you're the main cause."

I drained my beer and set it on the table. "Becca's decision, not mine."

"I know. And I agree he's being an ass. A total dick. So show him up and go there tomorrow guns blazing. Be funny. Ask him a thousand and one questions. Make him talk."

"And when that doesn't work?"

"You tried. I'll invent some horrible emergency and get Mad Dog to call you, and you can spend the rest of the weekend working."

I laughed. "I might take you up on that." We were spending the day with her father tomorrow and had plans the day after to play tourist around the city so Becca could show me all the places she loved. Sunday, there was a family barbeque at the residence, and Richard, Katy, and the girls were joining us.

"I only have to make it through tomorrow without losing my temper again or being rude," I mused out loud.

Richard flipped the steaks and grinned. "You made it through four years of prison without pissing anyone off enough they shanked you. This should be a walk in the park."

I burst out laughing. "I wasn't in maximum security. No one got *shanked.*"

He lifted one shoulder, teasing. "But the possibility—what street cred it gives you that you survived."

"Not with Mr. Holden."

"Another tip." He smirked. "Stop with the Mr. Holden shit. Call him Gerry. Don't give him the edge. He's *her* father. Not yours. Respectful, not beholden."

"Weid!" Gracie called. "Weid, come in da pool!"

"You're being paged." Richard laughed. "I suggest you join her."

"Do I have time?"

"Yep. I'll add the lobster and shrimp soon. Katy has everything in the pool house, and we're eating out here, casual. You can come to the table in your suit."

"Okay, then." I hurried to the pool and performed a huge cannonball that made Gracie laugh loudly. Thankfully, watching her and Becca together made me forget what I would face tomorrow.

I was good with that.

CHAPTER 18

REID

ON THE WAY back to the hotel, Becca glanced my way. "Feel like some ice cream? My treat."

I grinned at her, feeling lazy. I was relaxed, having enjoyed the evening with Richard and his family. "Sure, BB. Ice cream sounds good."

We pulled into a parking lot. The place was busy, the line long. I stood behind Becca, and wrapped my arms around her waist, pulling her to my chest. "What's good?"

"The triple threat."

I read the sign. "Wow. Caramel, chocolate, and marshmallow with three scoops of ice cream? Are you going to eat that all by yourself?"

She giggled. "No, usually Katy and I would share it. We'd come here sometimes and leave Richard with the girls. Especially if she was pissed with him and needed to vent."

"They seem very happy."

"Oh, they are. But Richard can be a handful. And all couples need time apart. Sometimes it was just an excuse for ice cream."

I kissed her head. "I got it."

When we got to the window, I ordered, and Becca used her debit card. The girl behind the window shook her head. "Sorry, it didn't go through."

Becca frowned. "That's odd."

"Try again." The girl handed her the machine.

"No, it declined."

"I'm sorry. We've had some issues today. A squirrel ate through some wires, and they did a temporary repair, but things haven't worked well all afternoon."

Laughing, I pulled a twenty from my pocket. "Squirrels. Great."

We sat down, and Becca huffed. "I wanted to treat you."

I took a huge bite of the sweet mixture and swallowed it. "God, this is good. You can treat tomorrow. Maybe the wires will be fixed."

She chuckled. "Okay."

We ate, watching people around us, and enjoyed the warm evening.

"You know," Becca began, "I'm not sure if I'm more embarrassed or impressed about what happened today."

I grimaced, swallowing more ice cream. "Sorry?"

She sighed and put down her spoon. Resting her chin on her hand, she studied me. "I'm aware what an ass my father was today, Reid. I can't apologize enough for him."

I didn't deny her statement. "It's not your place to apologize."

"Hardly a fun weekend for you, though. I wanted it to be great."

I finished the ice cream, wiped my hands, then threaded our fingers together. "It is. We're together. We had an awesome evening with your friends, and tomorrow, I'll try really hard to get your dad to approve of me."

She looked wistful. "He's gotten worse. He's so grumpy. And you kept your cool and never rose to the bait."

Remembering Richard's words earlier, I decided to give her dad the benefit of the doubt. "He wants what is best for you, BB. I'm not what he had in mind. Give it a little time."

"That's very generous of you since he rode your ass all day."

"And he might tomorrow. But we'll get through it, and we have a couple of days to have some fun."

"Why are you being so nice about this?"

"Because I love you."

Our eyes locked across the table. Her gaze lowered to my mouth and her tongue peeked out, running over her bottom lip. "Reid?"

"Yeah, BB?"

"I want to go and have some fun right now."

I stood. "Let's go."

~

GERALD WASN'T HAPPY to see me return the next day. Becca had the whole day planned with things she wanted the three of us to do. He wasn't enthused about any of them. I took Richard's advice and kept trying to engage with him. I asked him about Becca as a child. Commented on various pictures he had around the room. Asked to see more of them. I even inquired about his career as a police officer. Anything to make him talk. After lunch, he announced he needed to rest for a while, and I was grateful when he shut his eyes, feigning sleep. I was so exhausted, I needed a nap myself—only I wouldn't be faking. He made being nice damn hard work.

Becca's phone rang, and she looked at the screen. "Oh, it's Maddox."

She answered and spoke quietly. Her face paled, and she asked him to repeat himself. She looked at me, panic written on her face as she listened. "I don't understand, but I'll check into it right away," she said. "I don't know what to say, except I'm sorry. I'll get it cleared up and bring you the money next week."

Money?

She hung up and looked at me, confused. "Maddox says my rent check bounced. He thought it was strange and wanted me to know."

"What?"

Becca tapped on her phone screen, her face even whiter when she looked up. "Reid, my bank account balance shows I'm overdrawn, and my credit card is maxed out! Oh my God, what's going on?"

I dug into my knapsack, and pulled out my laptop. I had her sign in to her banking site, and she scanned her accounts.

"It's all gone," she whispered. "All my bills that I pay at mid-month automatically—they're all being rejected. My checking account is overdrawn, my savings are gone, and my credit card is to the limit."

I held out her phone. "Call them now."

TWO HOURS LATER, Becca hung up from yet another call. "They've put a freeze on everything. They say it will take time, but I should get most of the charges reversed."

"What about your money?" her father asked.

She shrugged. "Someone withdrew it all. Somehow, they got a hold of my information and made a duplicate debit card. They got it to override the daily limit and drained everything." Her watery eyes widened. "Last night—that's why my debit card didn't work."

"Yeah. Someone was stealing your money." I cursed under my breath.

Gerald sniffed. "Sound familiar, Reid?"

I ignored his comment. I knew he was trying to get a rise out of me, and that didn't matter to me right now.

"Okay, Becca. What else did they say?"

She shrugged. "That they're working on it and will be in touch. All my cards have been canceled, and new ones will be issued."

I shook my head. "They can be doing more."

Becca frowned. "He mentioned I should check and make sure my other online profiles hadn't been touched or hacked."

"Okay, I can do that."

Gerald spoke up. "I called a friend in the fraud department. They're going to check into that for me."

Becca sighed. "Thanks, Dad."

"I can do it faster," I insisted.

"Illegally, you mean?" he asked, his tone smug.

"Faster," I retorted.

Becca glanced at me, uncomfortable. "Why don't we see what they come up with and go from there?"

"Because they could be using your information to procure other credit cards and racking up debt in your name. If they got your banking information, they got everything they need, Becca."

"They'll get on it right away. I'm sure they'll call soon, Rebecca," her father insisted.

I shook my head. "We're not talking about some kid who took your card. This can happen in an instant with the technology they have access to. Let me do this, Becca."

She hesitated.

Gerald spoke. "Why don't we let the proper channels handle it? I'm sure Reid here is overreacting." He paused. "Maybe he is looking for any excuse to get back to his old habits." He cocked his head. "Maybe somehow he caused this mess."

Becca pushed away from the table, her hands clenched tightly in fists. "Dad, stop it! Reid had nothing to do with this. He's trying to help, which is more than you're doing with your not-so-subtle digs at his character. Leave it alone!"

He laughed, the sound forced. "Oh, I'm only teasing, Rebecca. Reid can handle it, can't you, boy?"

I swallowed my reply.

"It's not funny," she insisted.

"No, it's not, Rebecca." Her father sighed. "Let's leave it to the law-abiding professionals to handle it. Someone will call me soon."

Becca sat down, not meeting my eyes.

"Okay."

AN HOUR LATER, my patience had reached its limit. There was very little I could do trapped inside her father's place. He didn't own a computer, and the internet was shitty. The link I had was slow and dropped constantly. I had a hot spot from my phone, but I needed a strong connection and some major machinery. Becca had fallen silent, constantly worrying her lip and wringing her hands, then glancing at her phone, only to remember she had turned it off.

The phone rang, and her father listened for several minutes, speaking in a low tone I couldn't hear. He hung up and smiled at Becca.

"They're going to get to the bottom of it, honey."

She sagged in relief.

"First thing after the weekend, they'll be looking into it and doing the right thing. In the meantime, I can give you some cash to tide you over." He glanced my way, distaste on his face. "Do I need to call the hotel and pay the bill?"

"I am paying for the hotel bill, and I don't require your help." I stood, grabbed my laptop, and shoved it into my bag.

"Where are you going?"

"Monday is too late, Becca. I need to work on this now."

I ignored her father's scoff.

"I need to stop them in their tracks before they destroy your name and credit rating."

"How?" she asked.

Gerald spoke up. "Doing what he does best, I imagine. Breaking the law." He met my gaze, his eyes calculating and frosty. "What excuse will you use then, Reid? You did it in the name of love?"

I was done, fed up to the teeth with his holier-than-thou attitude and his snide remarks. I didn't care about his opinion—or Becca's anger over my decision.

"I'm doing it because, whether or not you believe it, I know how to fix it. How to handle it so your daughter isn't stressed and upset. So her privacy and information aren't out there being compromised."

"With your *shortcuts,* no doubt. Circumventing the law."

"With all due respect, sir, *fuck you*. You can sit there and judge me, but I'm not going to stand around and wait for people to do 'the right thing.' Not when I can make it happen faster and stop it now."

He snorted, his eyebrows lifting at my words. "Typical. Taking the easy way out. Bending the rules."

I shrugged. I was done with his attitude and rudeness. "You're entitled to your opinion."

I slung my knapsack over my shoulder and headed for the door, flinging it open. Becca followed, reaching for my arm.

"Reid, please."

I turned, looking down into her pain-filled eyes.

"Don't—" she pleaded, her lip quivering.

I shook my head. "Don't ask me to stay, Becca. I can fix this. And regardless of what your father thinks, what I'm going to do isn't illegal. It's making things right."

Her eyes filled with tears that ran down her cheeks. "I-I don't—"

"Hey," I whispered, cupping her face. "Hush. I'm not angry at you."

Her hands gripped my wrists, her body trembling. "I have to choose now. This is making me choose."

I glanced behind her at her father. He was watching us closely, a self-righteous look on his face, knowing he had won. I refused to give him the satisfaction. I hated him for making her so upset and forcing the issue.

"It's okay, baby. You don't have to choose anything."

Her brow furrowed in confusion.

I leaned my forehead to hers. "I never had a family, Becca. No parents to love me. I longed for that my whole life."

Her voice trembled. "I know."

"Your dad loves you so much he is willing to risk your anger instead of letting you make a mistake."

"You're not a mistake," she whispered.

I kept talking. "I would never ask you to choose, baby. I love you too much. He's your father—your family. That's forever. There is no choice here."

I pressed a kiss to her head and pulled back.

Her eyes were huge, the tears endless. "Wh-What are you saying?"

"You stay here with your dad. I'm going to go and do what I do, get my stuff, and head home."

Her fingers grappled, tugging on my sleeve. "No, Reid—I can fix this. It'll be fine. I'll talk . . ."

"No."

She stared up at me, wordless.

"You have tried. We both have. It's clear nothing we do will change his opinion of me. I love you, Becca. But sometimes, that isn't enough. Because he will never allow it, and I refuse to be part of the reason for your sadness. I won't let you be caught in the middle of a feud for your affection." I kissed her lips softly. "It'll be okay, baby. You'll be okay."

Her mouth opened, but no words came out.

"I'm going to fix your problem. I promise you that. I will make it right for you."

I backed away and pulled the door shut behind me.

I was lying—to her and myself. One thing I knew for sure: I wouldn't ever be okay again.

Not without her.

I HAD TEXTED Richard as I grabbed a cab, and he arrived at The Gavin Group building a few minutes after I did. When I explained what had happened, he let me into their server room, not hesitating for a moment.

"I won't do anything that can be traced back to this place. All I need is the power and some machines."

He waved his hand. "It's yours."

"You don't need to check with Graham?"

"You're good. We trust you."

I pulled out my laptop. "Any of your IT people around, by chance?"

"No, do you need something?"

"An extra pair of eyes and hands. And access to your network room, so we can get to work."

He held up his pass card. "I can do all that."

"Great."

RICHARD STARED AT the screen. "Should I understand what you're doing?"

"No. I'd be surprised if you did."

"Can you explain it in small words?"

I laughed, my eyes never leaving the screen. "I've back-doored into the banking system. It appears the hackers laid a URL to misdirect real users to a phishing site. I found the key logger they placed to get log-in info and passwords from users. They embedded them within an email that was sent as the bank's newsletter. But they left their coding fingerprints behind, and now I'm finding the people who did this."

"For what purpose?"

"I'm taking Becca's money back—and wiping every trace of her from their system. Then I'm going to load a virus into their machines so powerful it will destroy them."

For the first time, he sounded nervous. "They won't know?"

"No. My laptop . . ." My voice trailed off, and I cleared my throat. "Let's just say my laptop is invisible. I'll be rerouted and thoroughly masked, so even if they try, they won't be able to figure it out before they explode."

"Are you sure you can find them?"

I glanced at him. "I already have."

"Holy shit. Maddox told me you had mad skills. I guess he was right."

"I don't use them anymore, but this is an exception."

"Are you really leaving when you're done, Reid? Walking away from Becca?"

"What can I do, Richard? Force her to choose between her father and me? I dislike him, but he is her family."

"She loves you."

"For how long? She'd hate having to hide the fact that she talks to him or goes to see him. I won't make her do that." I snorted. "You can be fucking sure I'm not coming back." I sighed and passed a weary hand over my face. "Besides, if this backfires, I'll be back in jail tomorrow."

"And if it doesn't?"

"Becca's credit will be restored, her money back in her account. The people who did this will be helpless. They'll start again, but they won't have her information or probably hundreds or thousands of others. I've disabled their malware and reinforced the unauthorized access points for the bank. And hopefully, I will have damaged such a huge part of their network, and flooded so many of their machines, it will take them long enough to rebuild their protocols that the police will be on them first."

"Are you going to help with that?"

"If you ever stop talking and let me do what I need to do."

He stood. "Okay. I'm going to call Katy and tell her not to wait up for me." He stopped at the door. "Reid."

Pausing my frantic typing, I looked at him.

"You won't go to jail. I won't allow it, nor will the BAM boys. Somehow, if this goes bad, you have people on your side this time. You hear me?"

I met his intense gaze.

"You're risking your own career and life to protect someone I consider my family. I won't forget that."

I nodded and looked back to the screen. He left, pulling the door shut behind him.

Becca was his family, but she was my world.

Even if I wasn't part of hers anymore.

I RUBBED MY tired, aching eyes. I glanced at my phone to check the time. It was almost four in the morning. I scanned all the files one last time and saved them to an encrypted drive. I had done it. I even had a physical address and had already called in an anonymous tip to the police. I had sent Richard out to buy me a cellphone I used for that purpose and then disabled. My tracks were covered. I had managed to look around their setup, and it was scary. Scary how badly structured it was. I was in, invisible and undetected—searching fast. Downloading evidence. Reversing what they had done, with Becca being my number one priority. Then I planted my seeds and got the fuck out of there.

By now, their system was in shambles, computers frying. Hard drives wiped, and hopefully, police showing up at the door of the well-to-do home they were running their operation from, escorting them out in handcuffs.

The way I was certain Becca's father hoped I would be later today.

I removed all traces of me from The Gavin Group's system, making a mental note to tell Richard they needed to up their security and put some more firewalls in place.

I shoved my laptop into my knapsack and trudged down the hall. Richard was asleep at his desk. He had disappeared for a while, returning to hand me coffee and a sandwich and asking if I needed help. When I said no, he had left again, allowing me to work in peace.

I knocked on the doorframe and walked in, slinging my knapsack onto the other chair, before sitting down and scrubbing my face.

Richard stretched, rotating his neck to relieve his stiff muscles. "Is it done?"

"Yep. Becca's money is back in her account. The same goes for several dozen other people. The rest will have to be handled—" I held up my fingers in quotation marks "—the right way."

He chuckled. "Gerald has been an ass."

I looked past him to the dark sky outside his window. "I'm not arguing."

I risked a glance at him. "Did you, by chance, check on Becca?"

"I did. She went to see Katy and is currently asleep."

"Okay." I blew out a painful breath. Despite what happened, part of me had hoped she would show up here, knowing this was where I would come to work. But she was with her friend, and that was probably for the best. I could go back to the hotel, grab a few hours' sleep, and be at the airport to wait on a standby seat before midmorning.

"What happens now?"

I held up the USB drive. "I'll copy this and send it to the bank president and the police. It will give them everything they need to put these people in jail, and perhaps the information to help get more people their money back."

"You shut them down?"

"Totally."

"Wouldn't the bank already be on it?"

I shrugged. "Probably. They'll follow their protocols and proper procedures. I'm better and faster, though." I chuckled.

He lowered his voice, making it sound like Al Pacino in *Scarface*. "Don't fuck with you, eh?"

I chuckled. "There're lots more where they came from. But if I stop one group, it's at least something. Helping Becca was what mattered. They had all her information. She would have had credit cards in her name piling up the debt and God knows what else. It would have taken years for her to recover from it."

"You risked your freedom to prevent that. Do you know how huge that is, Reid? I told Maddox, and he was furious with you, although he understood."

I wiped my hand over my face, exhaustion setting in. "Yeah, there were a lot of texts. I ignored them. I'll deal with them when I get back."

"I'll drive you to the hotel."

"I'd appreciate that."

We were silent on the drive. He pulled up in front of the building, shifting into park. He looked over at me. "Get some sleep, and we'll talk when you're more coherent."

"I'll call when I get home."

He shook his head. "We'll talk before that. Trust me."

I opened the door, too tired to argue. He drove away, and I trudged inside, leaning heavily against the wall of the elevator.

Silence greeted me when I entered the room. The atmosphere felt as heavy as my footsteps while I stumbled into the bedroom, planning to fall face-first onto the bed. I needed sleep so I could think clearly. Prepare for the next step.

Nothing prepared me for the sight of Becca sitting on the bed, reclined against the headboard.

I gaped at her. "What are you doing here, Becca?"

She raised her chin. "Where else should I be, Reid?"

"With your father or Katy." I closed my weary eyes. "Not with me."

"My father is my family, Reid. Katy is my friend."

I opened my eyes and frowned, not following her train of thought. "Okay?"

She tilted her head. "They're important, but they aren't you, Reid."

"I don't understand."

"You were wrong earlier."

I laughed bitterly. "I was wrong about a lot of things, Becca. Care to enlighten me?"

"You said I didn't have to choose. But you were wrong. I did have to choose."

My heart rate picked up. "And?"

Her voice quivered. "I choose you."

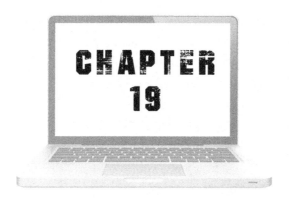

CHAPTER 19

REID

I WOKE, SURROUNDED by the feel of Becca's arms around me, her soft skin under my cheek and her fingers drifting up and down my back. For a moment, I was convinced it was a dream, but I lifted my head and met her tired blue gaze.

"Hi, BB." I sounded sleepy.

"Hey."

"You're here."

"There isn't anywhere else I want to be."

Frowning, I cleared my throat. After Becca had dropped her bombshell, she had insisted I come to bed. I pleaded for five minutes and grabbed a hot shower, needing to loosen the tense muscles in my neck and back. The aching soreness had set in from hours of hunching over the keyboard in the cold temperature of the server room at The Gavin Group.

When I stepped back into our room, Becca was waiting. She lifted the covers, and I slid in beside her. Immediately, she pulled me to her body, encouraging me to lay my head on her chest, then wrapped her arms around

*me. I sank into her warmth, the feel of her against me better than any shower
in the world.*

"I don't understand what's happening," I confessed.

She pressed a kiss to my head. "Sleep. We'll talk when you wake up."

*I could feel the pull of exhaustion hitting me harder than ever. My body
relaxed, and my eyes drifted shut. I struggled to get the words out.*

"I fixed it, Becca. Just the way I promised."

"I know," she whispered. "I know, Reid. Sleep."

"Where is your father?" I asked with a grimace, sitting up and
grabbing a bottle of water from the nightstand, draining it in long
swallows.

She leaned against the headboard. "At his place. No doubt stewing
over our argument and grumbling about what a failure of a father
he is."

"No, he did a great job as a father—you're amazing. It's being
a decent, nonjudgmental human being he's rather shit at," I said
without thinking.

Her eyes grew round, and I grappled to apologize. "Shit, I
shouldn't have said that."

She shook her head. "You're right, though. We had the biggest
fight ever after you left. I didn't hold back, and I told him how ashamed
I was of what he said to you." She reached for my hand. "I owe you
an apology. I never should have listened to him, and I shouldn't have
let you walk away."

I lifted one shoulder. It had hurt, but I understood. "He's your
dad."

"And you're my forever."

I turned slightly, facing her. "Yeah?"

She cupped my cheek, her fingers moving restlessly on my skin.
"Yeah. You walking away made me realize how selfless you were being.
The exact opposite of my dad, who was being self-righteous and rude."

"What happened? I asked.

"We argued. I told him what I thought of his behavior and how
angry I was at myself that I had let you think I doubted you. He

pointed out you had walked away. I informed him you had sacrificed your feelings so I didn't have to make an impossible choice. That, above all else, proved to me how much you really loved me. I told him if he couldn't see that, we had nothing else to talk about." She sighed and ran a hand through her hair, pushing back the messy waves from her face. "It got loud and ugly, and I walked out."

"I'm sorry, BB."

She shook her head. "No, I am, Reid. I should have listened to you right away. I should have told my dad off big-time the first day. I regret bringing you here." She sighed. "If you still want to leave today, we can."

"No. I want you to show me the city. All the places you love. Meet your friends for dinner the way we planned." I took her hand in mine. "I assume Richard knows what happened between you and your dad?"

She sighed, her fingers tightening within mine. "Yes. I was so upset, I called Katy, and she came and got me. We took the girls for a walk and ice cream, then she drove me to the office."

"Wait. You were there?"

"Yes. I watched you for a while, and I got you a sandwich and coffee. I asked Richard to give it to you. He drove me back to the hotel."

"Why didn't you come into the room?"

"I watched you for over an hour, but you never noticed me. You were in the zone. I didn't want to disturb you. I came here to wait, and Richard went to see my dad. He told him off—again."

"Wow."

"So, we need to take a cab to get the car."

"Are you going to go up and see your dad?"

"No. We both need to cool off. We said things—harsh things. Today is only for you and me." She met my eyes, her gaze anxious. "If you want that?"

"I want." I grazed her cheek with my knuckles. "I think we had our first fight, BB."

Her sigh was shaky. "It was a big one."

"But we're here. Together."

"Yeah."

"And you love me."

A tear ran down her face. "So much, Reid. I'm so sorry—"

I laid a finger on her lips, silencing her. "It's okay." I edged closer. "You know what, Becca?"

"What?"

"I have another first for us."

"Our fight?"

I shook my head, quirking my eyebrow. I'd had enough of heavy and the pressure of the last several hours. "Make-up sex. I heard it's epic."

A smile crossed her face. She crawled onto my lap and cupped my cheeks. Her mouth hovered over mine.

"I'll make sure of it."

⌒

"OH GOD, BECCA," I groaned. "You need to stop."

She met my eyes, slowly sliding her mouth off my cock. "Really?" she murmured. "You want me to stop doing this?"

I pressed my head into the softness of the pillow. "I can't even watch you. You look so sexy with my cock in your mouth, I'm going to come right now."

"That's the plan." She slid her mouth down my shaft, her tongue doing that teasing, twisting thing to it, which drove me crazy and brought me back to the edge.

"Jesus," I hissed, unable to keep my hips from propelling upward, trying to get close to the source of pleasure. I fisted my hands in the sheets. "Becca, baby. Let me be inside you, please."

After one long, final lick, she pulled herself over me, straddling my hips. "Like this?"

Her heat was right there. Barely skimming the head of my cock. Tormenting me. "Yes."

She leaned back, bracing her arms on my thighs, and sank down. Slowly. Easing herself onto my cock inch by torturous inch. Until we were flush. Until I was surrounded by her.

"Oh God, Reid. You feel so good inside me." She moaned.

"Becca—"

Her voice dropped, her fingers clutching my skin. "Fuck me, Reid. I want you to fuck me."

I loved hearing her say what she wanted.

And I loved fucking her.

Rising up, I gripped her hips, pushing her back on the bed, sinking farther inside her. She gasped at the feel of me. I groaned at the feel of *her*.

Then I gave her what she wanted. Fast strokes, hard pumps, pounding my hips into hers, making her grip me close, crying out my name. I lifted her legs to my shoulders, driving deeper. Harder. Hitting the spot that would push her over the edge.

She moaned and arched. Met my thrusts, cried my name. Her nails dug into my biceps, the slight pain only driving me higher. Nothing mattered in the moment. Nothing outside this room, this woman, was important.

Only her. Only the sensation of being lost with her.

There was no other place I wanted to be.

My orgasm hit me. Unexpected. Hard. A tsunami of ecstasy that tightened my balls, lit up my nerves, and shook my body. I roared her name, feeling her stiffen around me, her release spurring mine to lengthen and grow until I could barely breathe. Until I collapsed on her chest, spent. Unable to move except to press my lips to her damp skin and murmur her name repeatedly.

Finally, I slipped from her and rolled, keeping her close. Our ragged breathing calmed, the heat of our skin cooled, and I dragged a blanket over us, not wanting her to get cold.

"You," she mumbled, her lips on my throat. "You are a fucking sex god."

I chuckled.

"I had no idea you were going to become like this."

"Like this?" I asked, curious.

"So good," she replied. I could feel her smile on my skin. "You're so good at sex."

"I think you mean we're good." I dropped a kiss to her head. "Together."

"Insatiable."

"I need to make up for lost time. I figure in another five years, I should be good. By then, we can go at it once or twice a day, and I'll be satisfied."

She laughed, kissing my chest and lifting her head. "You're the most amazing lover I've ever had, Reid."

I narrowed my eyes. "I'm the last lover you'll ever have, Becca."

"Okay," she whispered. "I'm good with that."

I cupped her cheek. "I mean it. No matter what. Promise me we'll find our way back to each other."

"Always." She drew in a deep breath. "I'll always choose you, Reid."

I brought her mouth to mine. "I know, BB. I know."

⌒

BECCA WAS FINISHING in the shower when my phone rang with an unknown number. Wary, I answered. "Reid Matthews."

"Reid, it's, ah, it's Gerald. Gerald Holden." He hesitated. "Rebecca's father."

"I know who you are, Gerald," I replied dryly. "How did you get my number?"

"Richard gave it to me."

I reminded myself to kick Richard's ass the next time I saw him—which would be tomorrow.

"What do you want?"

"So much for the niceties, I suppose," he muttered. "Are you still here? In Victoria?"

"Yes."

"I need to ask a favor of you."

Becca walked into the room, a towel wrapped around her body. Water glistened on her skin, her hair a dark mass of waves draped over her shoulders. She walked toward the closet to get some clothes as I listened, my eyes following her movements. She was pretty and graceful. I loved watching her move.

I realized he was waiting for a response. "Well, this should be good. What can I do for you, Gerald?"

At her father's name, Becca's head snapped up. Frowning, she held out her hand as she stomped across the room. I tried not to laugh at her anger, shaking my head and holding up my finger to stop her.

"I would like you to bring my daughter and come see me today." He cleared his throat. "If that isn't asking too much."

"Wouldn't it save us all a lot of time and grief if you just berated me over the phone? Listed my faults and the reasons for your intense dislike while I shaved or something?" I stood and paced the room, frustrated. "That way, you get what you want, and I can feel as though I've accomplished something while being told what a loser I am and how I will never be good enough for your daughter." I barked out a laugh. "The added bonus is I can spare Becca listening to your venom. So, why don't we do that, Gerald? You can start anywhere you want. Maybe alphabetically would be good. A is always a good place to start. I'll even help you. Ass. I'm an ass for speaking to my girl's father this way, but hey, it's exactly what you expect of a bastard like me, right? Look—I already gave you B. You can carry on with C now. I imagine coward will be at the top of your list. Or maybe you have a better word. Go ahead. Hit me."

I sucked in some much-needed oxygen after my diatribe. Becca gaped at me from across the room. There was complete silence on the other end of the phone.

Then he started to laugh. Big, loud guffaws. I pulled the phone from my ear, wondering what the hell was going on. Finally, his laughter died and he spoke.

"Reid, I'm asking. I'll beg if you want. Give me fifteen minutes."

I looked across to Becca. Her brow was furrowed, her eyes fixed on the bundle of clothing in her hands. She wasn't going to ask me to do anything I didn't want to do, even though she was torn. I could see that from her body language.

"Fine. You get your fifteen minutes. Unless I get fed up and walk out."

"Thank you."

"And I'll be taking Becca with me this time."

"Understood."

I hung up and tossed my phone on the bed. "We're going to see your dad before we go sight-seeing."

Becca's eyes glowed in the room. "I love you, Reid Matthews. You're a good man."

I stomped across the room. "Whatever. I want breakfast first. I prefer to have my character torn apart on a full stomach."

I stopped at the door, turning.

"And that includes pancakes. A huge stack of them."

She nodded, a soft smile lighting her face. "Okay."

⌒

I SHIFTED UNCOMFORTABLY in my chair. The pancakes, bacon, and eggs I had wolfed down were weighing heavily on me, and I wondered if perhaps we should have held off eating until after her father spoke his mind. Again.

Beside me, Becca sighed. The grip she had on my hand tightened. She leaned forward. "You asked us here, Dad. What did you want to say to Reid?"

If it were possible, Gerald Holden looked more uncomfortable than I did. His shoulders were stooped, and he looked older than yesterday. Not so intimidating.

Or maybe he looked that way because I no longer gave a shit.

He cleared his throat. "I owe you an apology, Reid."

"You owe your daughter one as well."

He frowned but nodded. "I was out of line yesterday."

"Which part?" I snorted. "There were so many insults; I don't know which was worse."

Becca squeezed my hand, and I scrubbed my face with my free hand. "Sorry. I guess I'm angrier than I thought I was."

Gerald leaned back. "You have every right to be. I apologize for all of it. The insults and innuendos, even the outright hostility."

"Why?"

"I beg your pardon?" he asked.

"Why are you apologizing? Do you mean it, or is it simply to get back into Becca's good books?"

Our eyes locked; mine challenging and defiant, his wary and sad. He shook his head. "I mean it. I'm an old man, Reid. Stuck in his ways, as Rebecca has pointed out. Cantankerous and pigheaded, as Richard stated." He passed a hand over his head. "I have always been overprotective of Rebecca. I know that. Yesterday, I was—" he paused as if searching for the right word "—wrong. I was wrong to judge you. Becca says I'm too black and white, and she's right. I was that way on the job. I had to be. I've seen so many things, witnessed so much bad stuff—"

I held up my hand, my eyes narrowing in anger. "And I haven't? I was stuck in prison for four years. I saw plenty of things that still haunt my dreams. I've had to handle the rejection my past mistakes cause me time and again. I can't escape it, and I probably never will. Don't use your job as an excuse. You simply decided not to like me." When he didn't deny it, I kept talking. "I will tell you something, though—I was questioned, handcuffed, and put in jail, and those cops still showed me more respect than you did yesterday." I jabbed my finger into my thigh in vexation. "I would never do anything to hurt Becca the way you did. She comes first. She has from the moment I met her."

"He treats me so well, Dad," Becca interjected. "I've never been happier."

"I can see that."

I didn't respond. He'd asked me there, so it was his time to speak.

"I acted appallingly, and I said things I shouldn't have. Made assumptions based on my history, rather than the person standing in front of me." He straightened his shoulders. "I was wrong about you."

"What changed your mind?"

His expression softened. "The blatant love my daughter has for you. She reminded me so much of her mother the way she stood her ground and told me off." A flash of a smile appeared across his face. "She's never done that before."

I waited.

"Richard told me off as well. Plus, he told me what you did, Reid. You put yourself, your career, and your very freedom on the line to make sure Becca's issue was resolved. You didn't allow anything or anyone to stop you. She was your priority."

"She always will be."

"I know that now. I knew it the moment you left last night. You let me off the hook. You could have demanded she go with you, but you didn't. I heard what you said about family and not coming between us." He sighed, the sound long and slow. "I knew I had made a mistake, but I was too stubborn to do anything about it."

I leaned forward, resting my elbows on my knees. "Becca told me once that you trusted her decisions. You never interfered once her mind was made up. To me, that means you trust her judgment."

He nodded, confused.

"Why didn't you extend that trust to me?" I asked. "I was angry you dismissed her feelings for me as if they meant nothing—when, in fact, they are everything. The disrespect you showed for us both is what angered me the most. You should have known she would never believe in someone who was the kind of person you had decided I must be. You never even gave me a chance."

I felt Becca tense beside me, waiting for his response. I lifted her hand, kissed the knuckles, and held it close to my chest.

Gerald met my eyes. "Because I was afraid I would lose her to you."

"Daddy," Becca whispered under her breath.

"And now?" I asked.

He tapped his cane on the floor as he mulled over my words. "Now, I think I was as much of a pigheaded asshole as Richard said I was being. I think you will care for Becca the way I have always wanted her to be cared for. And," he added, "I think you understand the need for family. My worries were simply that. Given what I witnessed yesterday, I can put them aside."

We stared at each other, neither breaking the gaze.

He finally spoke. "The question is, can we move forward, Reid? Can you put aside my behavior, accept my apology, and we go from there?"

I pursed my lips, looking down at my feet. I knew I could insist on a better apology. I could call him on so many of his nasty words and drag it out until I felt the slate was clean. I could refuse his offer of forgiveness and walk away, taking Becca with me, and let him suffer. Except, I thought of Rodney and the pain he felt with the separation from his daughter. His wish they could reunite. The grief and regret he felt daily over the silence between them. I knew what he would say to me. Would I want Becca to regret the last years of her father's life, having to be caught in the middle between us? For Gerald to suffer meant Becca would as well. Regretting that would mean she would regret me, and I didn't want that to happen. Rodney would want me to be the better person.

"I think we can do better than an apology."

Gerald frowned. "Oh?"

I stood and extended my hand. "Hello, Mr. Holden. I'm Reid Matthews, Becca's boyfriend. I've heard so much about you from her. It's good to meet you, sir."

His hand was shaking as he closed his fingers around mine. I could hear Becca's stifled sobs behind me.

"It's good to meet you, Reid. Please, call me Gerald."

I winked at him. "Gerry, it is."

CHAPTER 20

REID

WE LEFT SOON after our talk. Gerald insisted we enjoy the day, the way we had planned. I was grateful since I wanted the day with Becca. We both needed the break. We agreed to come back on Sunday for the family brunch since Richard, Katy, and the girls would attend as well.

Becca showed me around Victoria. She took me past her old school, where she lived, and the place she waitressed on weekends and during the summer. She pointed out various attractions, and we had lunch with some of her friends. They were wonderful people, and I enjoyed hearing their stories about Becca when she was younger. It gave me ammunition to tease her.

We did a boat cruise in the late afternoon, with the sun shining on the water, catching the glints of gold and red in Becca's hair as she leaned into me by the rail. The breeze picked up some strands, tickling my face. I laughed and gathered her hair into my fist, pressing a kiss to her neck.

"Okay, BB?"

She peered up at me, her shy smile in place. "Today was a good day, Reid."

I kissed her again. "Yeah, it was."

Emotion filled her voice and her eyes. "Thank you."

I wiped a tear from her cheek. "You don't have to thank me for anything."

"Yeah, I do. You amaze me, Reid Matthews. Every time I think I can't possibly love you more, you prove me wrong."

"Then I hope to prove you wrong for a very long time, BB."

She smiled even as another tear ran down her face.

"Hey," I murmured, turning her in my arms. "No crying."

"Okay." She sniffled.

I laughed. "Why don't we go back to the hotel? We can order in Chinese food, watch a movie, and snuggle on the sofa for a while. Later, we can go back to that place for another triple threat."

"I'd like that."

"Good."

"Maybe we could get some extra chocolate sauce." She kissed my chin, her fingers fluttering over my skin. "For after."

"Oh yeah!" I grinned. "After. I'd like that."

She snuggled in tight to my chest.

"Good."

⁓

ON SUNDAY, I watched Gerald with Richard's children. Gracie climbed into his lap, patting his face and babbling away to him. I could see why Richard loved her lisp. There was no choice—you smiled listening to her. Heather was asleep on Gerald's shoulder, his hand spread wide across her back. Veins protruded under the thin skin like a dull roadmap, his wedding ring loose on his shrunken finger, but his hold was sure. He was patient and loving, his voice soft and soothing. He listened and played. Teased and laughed. Offered kisses and cuddles to both girls. He was the perfect image of a grandfather.

That was the man I had hoped to meet while here. The caring

man Becca told me stories about.

The man who would be part of my life.

It hit me right then.

My future.

I wanted to marry Becca, knock her up, and have babies together. Lots of babies. Gerald would be an awesome grandfather.

The table fell silent. Richard's fork was partway to his mouth, frozen midair. Katy's eyes were round with shock and Becca gaped at me.

Apparently, I had uttered that shit aloud.

Except, it wasn't shit. It was what I wanted. More than anything. I wanted babies. A family. I wanted them with Becca.

Richard shook his head. "Reid, shut off the not-so-inner monologue. You're digging your own grave, kid."

Gracie bobbed her little head. "Wats notted up, Daddy?"

Richard threw Katy a pleading look. She shrugged as if to say, "You're on your own."

"It's a game, baby girl."

"Tan I pway?"

"No!" he almost shouted. "It's . . . it's like baseball. You *hate* baseball."

"Otay," she lisped with a frown. "Iz it, Mommy?"

"Yep. Just like baseball. Home runs and all. Only with smaller balls." Katy smirked.

It was my turn to gape. I found the courage to peek at Becca, expecting anger. Her head was down, and she wasn't looking at me. I stole a glance at Gerald, who was shaking his head.

"I'd like grandkids, Reid. But even given our friendlier status, I'd prefer to be kept in the dark about your plans to achieve them."

Becca made a strange choking sound. Panicked, I turned in my chair. "Becca? BB? You okay?"

Her head fell back, and she began to laugh. Peal after peal of loud laughter. Katy joined in, and Gracie clapped her hands in delight.

Richard and Gerald exchanged a glance.

"You warned me, Richard. The kid is gonna keep me on my toes. You were right—entertaining as *shit*, though." He mouthed the word shit, but we all got it.

I leaned over. "Becca?"

She cupped my face, still laughing, and kissed me. "I love you."

I grinned against her mouth. "Is that a yes?"

"We'll talk."

I settled back in my chair, letting them all laugh at me.

It wasn't a no. I was good with that.

THE FLIGHT ATTENDANT handed me a bottle of water, that I accepted with a thank you. I sipped as I stared at the screen of my laptop, not really seeing anything. I shut the lid, deciding not to try to work. Maybe I'd watch a movie instead. Becca had fallen asleep almost as soon as we got on the flight, tired from the weekend. As I scrolled through the list of movies, her sleepy voice startled me.

"Given up on work?"

Turning, I pressed a kiss to her head. "Yeah."

"Anything good to watch?"

"Same ones as the way here. Maybe I'll have a nap."

She snuggled close, laying her head on my shoulder. "Okay."

She was silent for a few minutes then tilted her head back up. "Thank you for yesterday."

I grinned. "Your dad and I are buds now."

"You certainly are."

After brunch, Richard took his family home, and we spent the afternoon with Gerald. It turned out that he loved playing cards, so he and I got into a serious game of rummy. He told me how he often passed the time with solitaire, and I asked him if he ever played FreeCell on the computer. When he admitted he only used the computer in the lobby on occasion, I had shown him the game on my laptop. He loved it so much that while he and Becca took a walk around the garden, I slipped out and bought him a tablet, then loaded it with a bunch of games I thought he would enjoy. I showed him the messenger feature so he could keep in closer contact with Becca. I laughed when he asked if I was listed in his contacts, and I added myself.

"Wait until I show everyone this beauty tomorrow!" He grinned. "They're all gonna be so jealous of my technology. Tom is always bragging about his tech-wiz son and all the computer stuff he does, but he doesn't have anything this slick."

"Glad to be of service."

"So I can send Becca a message anytime?"

I met Becca's pleading eyes across the room.

"Ah, no, there's a limit. You can send her five a week, and she can reply."

"Oh, like a phone plan."

"Yes." I nodded seriously. "Just like a phone plan."

"Well, hey, five is good. You too?"

I threw her a grin. "I have a bigger plan. You can send me seven."

"Great." He tapped at the screen awkwardly. "This is going to keep me busy for a long time," he muttered, not looking up. "Thanks, son."

The whole weekend was worth those two words.

Becca squeezed my arm. "You were amazing."

"Your dad is pretty cool when he isn't being such a jerk."

She sighed. "I know."

I nudged her gently. "Kidding."

She smiled, dropping her voice. "And what about you, Reid? Anything you want to say about your revelation you dropped during brunch?"

I feigned forgetfulness. "Which one?"

"About getting me knocked up and marrying me?"

"Ah, the baseball conversation."

She laughed. "Yes, that one."

I turned in my seat to face her. "I didn't know I had said my thoughts out loud, Becca. I meant them, though." I tucked a piece of hair behind her ear, caressing the tender lobe with my fingers. "I want to marry you. Have a family."

"I see."

"Is that something you might want one day?" I paused and looked into her eyes. "With me?"

Her gaze was warm and soft. She slid her hand over mine. "I want everything with you, Reid. But I want us to know each other more. I want you to be sure you want to marry me because you love me, not simply because I was the first girl to give you a blow job." She winked, letting me know she was teasing.

I leaned my forehead to hers, chuckling. "Well, you are pretty stellar at that. That'll keep me interested for at least fifty years. We can figure something out after that is done."

She giggled. "Sounds as if you have it all figured out."

I kissed her fast. "That didn't even make my list of why I want to marry you. There are a hundred and one other reasons."

"Why don't you tell me what they are over the next few months? When you're finished, we can discuss it again."

I lifted her hand and kissed her wrist. "Sounds like a plan. The first and most important is I love you. Every single thing about you."

Her smile lit up her entire face. "That's a great start."

"So we're hedging toward a yes?"

She leaned her head on my shoulder. "So far, so good."

I grinned. "Okay."

⌒〜

I ARRIVED AT work early the next day. I knew Becca had a meeting first thing outside the office, and I was anxious to get into work. I wanted to catch up on what I had missed.

I hadn't heard from Aiden or Maddox again after I had texted them and said I'd handled the situation. I knew they weren't pleased with what occurred, but I was sure once I sat down with them, and they understood why I did what I did, everything would be fine.

A text from Aiden appeared as I was going through emails. It was short and to the point.

Bentley's office. 5 minutes.

I stared at the words, anxiety beginning to tighten my muscles. If Aiden had called me into Bentley's office and hadn't dropped by to tell me, it wasn't going to be good. I groaned as my head hit the back of my chair. Bentley was probably going to give me shit about what I did on the weekend. I knew he had spoken to Richard.

I walked down the hall, stopping at Sandy's desk. She studied me with a serious expression.

"Should I be scared?" I asked, trying to get her to smile. It didn't work.

"You took a big risk."

"It was one I had to take." I drew in a big breath. "How angry is he?"

"Enough you should be prepared."

"Even though it all worked out?"

She shook her head. "That isn't the point, Reid."

"I know." I met her eyes. "I had to, Sandy. I had no choice."

Her gaze softened. "I know. But there are consequences to our actions, even if they are done with good intentions."

"Okay." I squared my shoulders. "I'll go in and take it."

She squeezed my hand. "Good luck."

I knocked before stepping into Bentley's office. All three of them were there, their faces grave. I swallowed at the sudden thickness in my throat, wondering if I was as prepared for this as I thought a few minutes ago.

I sat down in front of Bentley's desk. He studied me for a moment.

"You had a busy weekend." His tone was cold.

I shifted in my chair, uncomfortable. "Yeah."

"If your plan had gone awry and you'd been detected, a multitude of problems would have arisen. The implications of all of them disastrous. If you'd been caught, you'd be back in jail."

"But that didn't happen. I was careful."

He carried on as if I hadn't spoken. "You would have ruined your life, embarrassed the company, and ended up in the one place you swore you would never go back to."

"I had to do it, Bentley. I know how these hackers work. By the time the bank got to it, they'd have sold Becca's information and debts would have been racking up against her. It would have taken years for it to all get sorted! I knew I could shut it down. I had to do it."

"That wasn't your concern."

I reared back, shocked. "What? How the fuck can you say that?"

"Reid," Aiden admonished.

I ignored him.

"Not my concern? Becca *is* my concern!"

"Your concern should have been your prison record and staying clean. What were you thinking? If you'd been caught, Reid, I don't know if we could have helped you!"

"I wasn't caught, and I knew I wouldn't be. I took the necessary precautions—extra, even. Technically, nothing I did was illegal. I didn't touch the bank's site. I only used it for a reference point. I went directly after the people causing the issue. I shut them down. Nothing I did can be traced back to me, BAM, or The Gavin Group."

Bentley ran a hand through his hair and glared at me. "You were still hacking. As for The Gavin Group, that's another thing. Involving a business associate. I'm *not* happy about your doing that."

"Richard gave me permission. He said he spoke to Graham." I huffed, my anger starting to build. "At least *he* trusted me to know I wouldn't do anything I wasn't supposed to."

Bentley leaned on his fists, fury rolling off him. "What you were supposed to do was let the bank and their people handle it. You can't break the law every time it suits you, Reid. This needs to stop."

It hit me. The whole maelstrom of emotions from the weekend. Too much had happened, and I was done with reacting calmly to it. I was furious, the words out before I could stop them, my voice louder and more abrupt than I had ever used when speaking to my boss.

"So, what are the rules, then, Bentley? I can break the law, use my talents, when it suits you? The company? It was fine when you needed my help to find your girlfriend. Or when Maddox needed my skills to stop his past from ruining your company. Let's not forget how thrilled you were when the system I built brought the company accolades, or the reports I created made you all look good with your new business partners." By the end of my speech, I was almost snarling in anger. "So it's fine to bend the law for you or Aiden or Maddox? But not for the woman I love? Not without your permission?"

The room was silent. All of them stared at me in shock.

"Screw that. You're angry with me? Fine. Fire me. But I don't regret it. I will do whatever it takes when it comes to Becca. What I did not only helped her, but some other people who were caught in this fraud ring. The information I sent to the police will help the bank and the fraud squad stop these criminals, and the only thing I feel is relief I was able to help. For your information, I knew the risks and I was prepared for those consequences." I stood so fast my chair toppled over. "But I wasn't prepared for this bullshit. I thought, of all the people who knew about it, you three would understand and support me. Obviously, I was wrong."

I turned toward the door. "I'll be in my office. If you want me out of here, let me know, and I can be gone in an hour. You won't have to worry about me embarrassing your company again."

I stormed down the hall, ignoring Sandy and headed to my office. I shut my door hard enough the hinges rattled and headed to my desk. Dropping into my chair, I held my head, cursing myself.

What had I done?

I'd yelled at my boss who had the right to be angry with me. Basically, I told him to fire me. I pulled on my neck muscles. I had let my temper get the best of me. I reacted instead of thinking, the exact way Rodney used to warn me against doing.

I was an idiot.

I glanced around, sadness and regret replacing the anger. It wouldn't take me long to clean out my office. I knew there were some filing boxes in the cupboard, and I dug around to find them. I set them on the sofa, but I sat down again, unable to start the process of transferring my things into the containers. They had just given me a condo, which I was certain they would take back. Where was

I going to go?

How was I going to explain this to Becca? She would be so disappointed in me. Of everything I could think of, that would be the hardest part to handle.

I wondered if Bentley would allow me to apologize. Thinking about what I had said, I was sure the answer was no. Nobody spoke to him the way I did a short while ago. Not if they wanted to work for him. I had blown it.

Defeated, I hung my head again, not even bothering to lift it when the door opened and I heard heavy footsteps.

"I haven't touched the computer, Aiden. You can take it and change all the passwords while I pack up," I mumbled. "Leave Maddox to watch over me so you know I don't steal anything or touch the system."

"I don't need your computer," Bentley's voice informed me.

I lifted my head. He stood inside my office, his arms crossed. Aiden and Maddox were beside him. This was my only chance, and I wasn't too proud to try.

"I'm sorry," I croaked. "I'm really fucking sorry, Bent."

"For what you did, or for telling me off?"

"Telling you off. But even losing my job, I don't regret what I did."

"Did you quit?"

"No."

"I don't recall firing you."

"I assumed that was why you were here."

"You assumed wrong. I came to apologize."

My mouth opened, but no words came out.

"You're right, Reid. We can't expect you to use your hacking abilities and extreme knowledge when we need you to for our own purposes, then forbid you to use them when you feel it's necessary. That would be unfair to you and extremely selfish of me."

"But?" I asked, sensing there was more to his words.

He shrugged. "Everything you said was right. We have asked you to lay yourself on the line when need has called for it. And you have never refused us. I hope never to ask you again." He stepped forward, loosening his arms. "I hope you never are put in the position of deciding the result is worth risking your freedom." He sighed. "I overreacted, and I shouldn't have. I didn't mean to call your character into question. I know how much BAM means to you. I know everything you do for me—for this company." He shifted on his feet. "I was upset when I heard what happened, Reid, but not for the reasons I stated earlier."

"I don't understand."

"You have become like a younger brother to all of us. The thought that you put yourself out there without our protection upset me. The thought of you going back to jail horrifies me. I can't imagine this place, or our lives, not having you in them."

"I didn't do it to upset anyone. I try, Bent. I stick to the law. I don't look for opportunities to hack. This was an exception. What I did for you guys were exceptions. It's my way of protecting *you*."

Our gazes locked. His was serious and concerned. Mine determined and sincere. But not angry. That emotion had passed for us both.

"No more, Reid. We need you here."

"All I can promise is to try. Maybe you guys need to stay out of trouble too."

They all laughed, breaking the tension.

Bentley held out his hand. "Deal."

I stood, and we shook firmly. "So, I still have a job?"

He rolled his eyes. "As if I'd ever let you go. You know you're too valuable to us."

"Would this be a good time to ask for a bigger budget? I want to expand the server room."

He laughed. "Nice try."

I shrugged. "It's what I do."

He clapped my shoulder. "You do so much more than that, Reid. So much more." He squeezed the muscle tightly. "You're part of the team. Be sure to stay around." He studied me. "You stood up to me. Very few people do that."

"Yeah, I did. I guess I should apologize for my rudeness."

"No, I deserved it, so I'll let you off the hook this time." He smirked. "You've come a long way, Reid."

He turned toward the door, then glanced back with a wink. "Don't make a habit of it, though."

He pulled open the door and left. Maddox clapped me on the back and followed him. Aiden regarded me, shaking his head.

"What?"

"You keep things interesting, kid."

I chuckled.

His hand fell on my shoulder. "Be careful, Reid. We need you here. Becca needs you here."

"I will, Aiden. I swear. I had no choice. Not with that."

He nodded. "I know. But we care."

It was my turn to clap his shoulder.

"I know. You'd be lost without me."

He flexed his shoulders, grinning. "Whatever, kid. I just like having you around to order pizza."

"Should I charge it to Maddox today?"

He opened the door and winked. "I think Bentley."

"I'm putting your name on it."

"Right on," he called, walking down the hall. "I'm good with that."

⌒〜

BECCA CAME INTO my office, holding her laptop. "Reid, this is . . ." Her voice trailed off as she took in the boxes still sitting on my sofa.

"What's going on?"

I waved my hand. "Nothing. It's fine."

She set down her laptop on my desk and looked behind her. "Why are there boxes on your sofa?"

I sighed. "Bentley wasn't overly happy with me, and we had words. I might have yelled and told him off." I shrugged. "Or something to that effect."

"Because of what you did? For me?"

"Yes."

She narrowed her eyes. "Well, I have something to say to him myself." She headed toward the door, determined and angry. I jumped up, catching her around the waist before she made it there, and pulled her back. I closed the door as she tried to wiggle out of my hold.

"Hold up, tiger. We've settled everything."

"You aren't losing your job over this!"

"I won't. I didn't. We had words, and we cleared the air. Everything is fine," I soothed. "You can retract your claws now. No need to go for the kill."

She huffed out a snarl, making me laugh. She flung her arms around me, pressing her lips to mine. Surprised, I yanked her close, kissing her enthusiastically. She was breaking one of her own rules when it came to heavy petting in the workplace.

I was good with that. So good, I decided I needed to shuffle over to the sofa, and get rid of those boxes, then put it to a far better use. Namely, Becca under me, moaning my name. It would ease the tension of the morning.

Becca, however, had other ideas. She eased back, pressing one final kiss to my mouth.

"What was that for?"

"For being you. For putting me first. For being so . . . *manly*." She growled the last word.

I punched my hips into hers. "Why don't I show you how manly I am?" I reached behind me, flicking the lock. "The sofa is very comfortable."

She watched me, her brow furrowed in contemplation. I could feel her indecision.

"I can be fast, baby."

She slid her hands up my arms. "That would be so naughty."

I nodded. "I like naughty."

She rose on her toes, and I lowered my head eagerly just as the door behind me shook with fierce knocking. "Reid! Pizza is here, and Bentley is out for blood. You didn't get him any goat cheese." The door handle rattled. "Come on, dude!"

"I'll be right there!" I bellowed, hoping he would go away. But I knew the moment was broken.

Becca's wide eyes met mine. "I guess I'll have to give you a rain check."

"Yes. You owe me."

A grin curled her lips. "Maybe a private dance later? I learned a new move on the pole I haven't shown you."

I loved watching Becca dance using her pole. She made every fantasy I had come true, and sex was always wild with her after she was done.

If I allowed her to finish a routine. I wasn't sure I had ever seen one in its entirety.

She was too sexy for her own good. Or mine.

I bent down and kissed her.

"Deal."

CHAPTER 21

REID

THE SOUND OF the engine in the plane was a muted hum. For the second time in a month, I was on a trip. I glanced around the interior of the private plane in awe. Leaning over, I grinned at Becca. "Good thing we didn't fly private the first time. Commercial would have been an extreme letdown after this luxury."

She laughed. "Don't get used to it. I don't think we can spring for this ourselves."

"Probably not."

Once again, I pulled my passport from my pocket, still amazed at how a small booklet could make me feel so joyful. I could travel now, and once Bill finished the work needed to expunge my record, I would be free to travel anywhere Becca wanted to go. My past would no longer restrict my life.

I met Sandy's caring gaze. Maddox and Dee had offered to put off their wedding, but she insisted they keep their plans. They agreed as long as she came to the wedding, since it was important to both of them to have her there. After some consideration, she decided to join us. Still grieving, she had sadness about her, although she did better when surrounded by people. I continued to go over a couple of nights every week, with Becca often accompanying me. We knew no matter how happy Sandy was for Maddox, she would find it difficult, and we planned to stay close to her as much as possible. I smiled at Sandy, and she winked, returning to the book she was reading.

I gazed past Becca at the vast, blue sky.

"What kind of wedding do *you* want?" I asked quietly. Marriage was a topic we spoke of frequently in passing. We'd talk and ask questions, and then move on to another subject. It was our way of feeling each other out with no pressure. I wanted to marry Becca. I liked the idea more all the time, and I was certain she felt the same. We had never discussed details, though.

She pursed her lips. "Small, intimate. I'd like my dad there. Friends. A pretty dress and some flowers."

I thought of Bentley's wedding. "Cake?"

She chuckled. "Yes, cake too."

"So, in BC, then?"

"I don't think my dad could travel, so it would have to be."

"Okay."

She peeked up at me. "Yeah?"

"As long as you're my wife at the end of the day, I'm good with that."

She looked confused. "We're just talking, right? You're not asking?"

I kissed her hand. "I can do better than asking en route to another wedding surrounded by people. So, yeah. Just talking." I bent low to her ear. "But 'yes' is looking pretty certain now, isn't it?"

She kissed me. "Yes, yes, it is."

I sat back and relaxed, not hiding my grin. "Good."

⌒

DANCING WITH BECCA on the sandy beach was a little trickier

than dancing on a smooth floor, but somehow, we managed. Maddox and Dee exchanged vows under the bright sun, then we spent the afternoon enjoying the island. Dinner happened at sunset, followed by a short speech by Maddox himself, before the real party started. There was champagne and music. Laughter and stories.

And love. It saturated the entire day.

I look down at Becca, holding her tight in my arms. Luckily, she was content to sway to the music, happy simply to be close. Looking at the moon glimmering on the water, I squeezed her hand lying on my chest. "Wanna take a walk with me?"

With a smile, she agreed, and we slipped away. The air was warm and sultry. We were both barefoot, and we walked along the edge of the water, letting the cool waves brush against our skin. From behind us, we could hear the faint strains of music and the laughter of our friends.

I tucked her into my side, enjoying the island breeze and her closeness. When we came to the outcropping of rocks, Becca stopped and sat on one of the large, flat boulders and patted the space next to her. We watched the waves kick up on the beach, the silence between us easy. I entwined our fingers, lifting her hand to my mouth for a kiss.

"You want children," she stated unexpectedly.

"Yes, I do. I want a family."

"How many?"

"Well, I think it's easier when they come one at a time." I nudged her playfully. "But I would like a couple of them, I think."

She chuckled. "How soon?"

I frowned. "I hadn't thought much about that, to be honest. We're young still, so there isn't any rush. In the next few years, I guess?"

"I want to establish my career, and I want to work after I have kids. I went to school for a long time to get my degree, and I want to learn my craft."

Her words made sense. "I get that."

"You wouldn't mind getting married and waiting a while for kids, then?"

"No. It makes sense in many ways. If we have kids, we'll need a bigger place. We can save and be ready for them." I squeezed her fingers. "We could live in my new place. It would be big enough for the two of us until we're ready to move on."

She stared out at the water, nodding slowly. "Yes, that would work." She slipped from the rock, and I stood to join her. I glanced down and brushed the sand off my pants. Looking up, I expected to see her waiting for me. Instead, she was down on one knee. In her hand was a slim silver band.

My heart rate picked up. "Becca . . . what are you doing?"

She smiled up at me, tears already in her eyes. "Reid Matthews, I love you. We've shared a lot of firsts together, but I wanted to add something you weren't expecting."

"BB . . ." I breathed out her name.

"My mom gave my dad an engagement ring. He wears it with his wedding band. I wanted to offer you one." Her voice quivered. "I want to marry you, Reid. Will you let me be the first for the rest of your life?"

I stared at her, shocked. With a grin, I joined her on the sand, then pulled the ring I had brought for her from my pocket. "I would love to, Becca Holden. As long as you'll be mine."

She laughed as we slid a ring onto each other's finger. "I can't believe we both planned this."

"I can. We're made for each other."

She stared down at her ring. It wasn't huge and wildly expensive like the one Bentley or Aiden purchased. Sandy had taken me to see Darlene, who helped me pick a simple setting and a beautiful diamond. It suited Becca. Becca suited me. It worked.

My hand felt strange with the addition of the thin band. But it felt right.

My entire life finally felt right.

I kissed her. "I love you, Becca Holden, soon to be Becca Matthews." I grinned. "Or since you asked me, am I going to be Reid Holden?"

She laughed. "No, I guess I'm old-fashioned in that sense. I want to be Becca Matthews."

"Nothing would make me prouder."

Her smile lit my world.

"I love you, Reid Matthews. I can't wait to be your wife."

I grinned.

I was good with that.

EPILOGUE

REID ~ FIVE MONTHS LATER

I GLANCED AROUND my desk, making sure everything was in order. All that remained were a few files of things I had been working on over time—nothing that anyone had to take care of while I was gone. The system was in top form, and I knew my staff would maintain it while I was gone for two weeks.

Honeymoon or not, I also planned to check in. Becca knew me too well; she asked that I limit it to once every couple of days, and I do it while she slept. I was still a night owl, and normally, she was out by eleven, so I had no issues with that. I was sure she'd sleep well after days spent on a hot beach and exploring the ruins in Mexico that she wanted to see. Plus, I planned to wear her out by making love to her as often as possible.

Just the thought of sex with *my wife* got me going. I was looking forward to exploring her as often as possible.

A gentle knock on my door brought me from my thoughts, and I looked up. Sandy smiled at me. "The boys want to see you in Bentley's office."

I frowned. "Everything okay?"

"Yes. I think they want a last word before you go."

"Okay. You have everything, right?"

Leaning on the doorframe, she crossed her arms. "Reid Matthews, of course I do. I have all the paperwork, the rings, and everything else you need."

I winked. "That is why you're my best lady."

She laughed. Our wedding was going to be very small, and Becca and I decided against a traditional wedding party. Her dad would give her away, and Sandy would accompany me. They would be our witnesses. It was what we wanted, and it felt right for us. The rest of our friends were guests.

I glanced at my phone. "Do they really need to see me? They'll all be with me on the plane tomorrow." As a surprise, they had chartered a private plane, so I knew the journey would be a comfortable one with lots of time for talking.

She lifted one shoulder. "They're waiting."

"Okay. I'll be right there."

I shut down the laptop and made my way to Bentley's office. Emmy walked toward me, slowly trudging down the hall, one hand resting on her rounded stomach. Bentley was leaning against his doorway, trying to look nonchalant and failing miserably. He watched over her zealously.

Stopping, I grinned at Emmy. "How you doing?" I winked. "Need some help?"

She rolled her eyes. "Is he watching?"

I cut my gaze to Bentley. "He's pretending to be busy on his phone, but we both know he's crap at typing without his eyes on the screen, so unless it's hieroglyphics he's sending, I would say yes."

"What does he think is going to happen in the hall?" She huffed.

"Well, you are rather top-heavy now. Maybe he's worried you'll topple." Emmy was petite, and her "baby belly," as she called it, was rather prominent. She had begun wobbling around four months, and now it was a pronounced waddle. She complained constantly about not remembering what her feet looked like anymore, and she still had weeks to go before the due date. We had made sure to schedule the wedding date so she could join the celebration.

"He is driving me crazy." A mischievous look crossed her face. "I can make him run down the hall fast by making one noise. Wanna see?"

I chuckled. "I think he heard your plans."

"Not funny, Freddy," he called.

She looked over her shoulder. "Whatever, Rigid. You can stop stalking me now."

"I'm observing. Carefully," he corrected her.

She muttered something under her breath about overly protective CEOs and blew him a kiss. She disappeared into her office, and I hurried down the hall to Bentley's office, following him inside.

They all greeted me with a smile, but the atmosphere felt serious. I sat down. "What's going on?"

Bentley smiled. "Ready for the next step in your life? Big changes."

"I think so," I replied with a small shrug. "Becca's been living with me the last couple of months. I don't expect a piece of paper will change my life that much."

All three of them laughed, making me wary. Something was going on.

Bentley slid a folder my way. "Maybe this piece of paper will change your mind."

Curious, I pulled the folder close and opened the flap. It was fat with legal documents, and I scanned the first several pages, unsure if I was reading the documents properly.

"I-I don't understand."

"This is our wedding gift to you, Reid," Maddox spoke. "We've each given you a share in the company. You are now a part owner of BAM."

I blinked, shock rendering me speechless.

Maddox grinned. "Your share, albeit small, is worth a fair bit of money." He threw out a figure that almost made me fall out of my chair. "It is a valuable asset for you."

Bentley cleared his throat. "The documents say it all, but I'll give you the fast version. These are non-voting shares. If, at any time, you chose to leave BAM, they revert to the original owner at the price they are valued at today. Namely, the three of us. But until that time, which we hope is never, you have a stake here."

I shook my head to clear it. "Why?" I managed to get out.

Maddox laughed. "You've earned it, Reid. We wanted to give you something tangible, something for your future." He pointed to the folder. "Check out the second set of papers."

My hand shook as I flipped to the second set of documents. It was a pre-approved mortgage for the condo in Ridge Towers. My gaze flew to Bentley's.

"It's yours, if you want it. If you prefer a house or another place, the mortgage is transferrable. Your shares make you wealthy enough that you can afford to live wherever you want. A mortgage is no longer an issue." He sat back with a smile. "Your past is no longer an issue. This gives you the ability to move forward once and for all."

"Becca loves Ridge Towers," I said, still in shock.

"Then it will be yours."

"I don't-I don't know what to say. I can't believe you guys are doing this for me," I mumbled, unable make my voice louder. "I never expected . . . Not in a million years . . ." My throat was thick with emotion. Gratitude filled my heart. Exhilaration hummed below my skin, making my hands shake. I stared down at the papers, the words becoming wavy as my emotions began to overtake me. It was too much to process all at once, and I didn't know how to handle it.

Becca's hands slid over my shoulders and the press of her lips on my cheek calmed me. In a second I was on my feet, pulling her into my arms, needing her close. I buried my face into her neck, letting the feel of her calm me.

"Did you know?" I asked quietly.

"They told me this morning."

"Becca, this changes so many things. I can give you *everything*."

She cupped my face. "I have everything. I have you." Her eyes glimmered in the light. "This changes nothing, Reid, except to show you how much you are loved. You belong here, with the people you care the most about." She smiled. "Your brothers."

Aiden stood and crossed the room, gripping my shoulder. "She's right. You came to us a broken kid, Reid. Eager to learn and grow. You helped us in ways we can never repay. You've grown into a responsible man with a bright future. You've become a friend and brother to each one of us, and we want you to be a part of our future. This gift was a no-brainer for us." His hand was heavy on my shoulder. "We're proud of you."

I looked at Bentley and Maddox. They were grinning in agreement. Sandy had slipped in with Emmy, her smile wide. Emmy gave me a thumbs-up.

"You three are my family. This place was the first home I ever had. Somewhere I was safe and welcome. Because of you, I met Becca." I cleared my throat. "I can't imagine not being here with you guys. I would be proud to be part of this company." My gaze swept the room. "I love all of you."

I extended my hand to Aiden. "Thank you."

He laughed, yanking me in for a hug. His massive arms squeezed the air out of me. When he was finished, Maddox and Bentley stepped in, exchanging hugs, backslaps, and laughter. I never let go of Becca's hand.

I met Aiden's eyes. He had taken a chance on me, and I would never forget it. "I won't let you down."

"I know, kid. I know."

THREE YEARS LATER

THE OFFICE WAS quiet, the afternoon sun beaming into the room. Files, lists, and equipment covered my desk. I ignored it all, my focus on the small bundle in my lap.

I watched my son, his tiny fingers as they gripped mine, his wide blue gaze flitting around the room.

"New space, eh, buddy?" I whispered. My heart so filled with love for the small person I'd created with Becca, I could barely be away from him. "Today is our first baby and dad meeting. I get to have my own sidekick!"

Theodore Rodney Matthews greeted my exciting news with a wide yawn, clearly not as thrilled as I was about being at work.

Becca and I were married surrounded by our friends in BC, and we honeymooned in Mexico. Bill helped me, and with his hard work, I had my record expunged. For the next two years, we used every day of vacation and satisfied her desire for travel—visiting England, Greece, and exploring Canada.

We moved in to Ridge Towers and settled down, deciding we were ready for our family. Neither of us expected it to happen as soon as it did. Becca came off birth control, and her doctor told us it could take months to conceive. We were fine with that. Practicing making a baby was high on my list of fun things to do with Becca.

Even after three years, not much had changed between us. My Becca was still smart and funny, and her smile sweet and shy. There were moments I was still dumbstruck, unable to formulate the right words to say to her; although her kisses usually freed them up for me. I still stopped by the corner store and picked up flowers for her from Eleanor, who'd kiss my cheek and call me a good boy.

After I arrived home one such night, Becca was busy on her laptop. I kissed the top of her head, laid the flowers on the table, and sat down across from her.

"I didn't see you all day."

"I had a meeting outside the office. Then I worked from home." She shut her laptop and shifted on the sofa. She picked up her flowers, inhaled the fragrance, and looked nervous. "I got you something today too."

"Oh yeah?"

"It's in the kitchen."

Curious, I got up and went to investigate. On the counter was a teddy bear, holding a card on thick stock. Inscribed were the words

Can't wait to meet you, Daddy. See you soon!

I pivoted, finding Becca behind me, tears in her eyes. I had her in my arms in seconds, kissing every inch of her beautiful face. "Becca, BB," I whispered adoringly. "Say it."

"I'm pregnant, Reid. We're going to have a baby."

Until Theo, or Teddy, as Becca called him, was born, it was the greatest moment of my life.

Now, gazing down at my son, I knew what it was to be complete. The fierce protectiveness I felt for him was all-consuming.

My son would never wonder about his parents. He would never be abandoned or struggle to find his place in the world. He would never know the pain or fear of loneliness. His well-being and happiness were paramount to me.

My alarm went off, and with a grin, I stood. "Let's go, Theo. Your uncles are waiting."

⁓

THE NEW NURSERY took up an entire floor of the building. It was open to all the staff, and the people who ran it were capable, warm, and loving. It was busy and vibrant with bright colors, and it was filled with laughter. Bentley and Maddox were already waiting in our favorite corner, Addi playing with Brayden, the two of them fast friends. Bentley's second daughter, Chloe, was in front of him, clutching his fingers as he encouraged her to stand. Maddox chuckled, watching his daughter, Shelby, asleep in his arms, her pudgy hands outstretched. I sat down, holding Theo close.

Bentley grinned at me. "Hey, Reid. How's Becca?"

"Good. She's only checked in on me four times since I left the condo with Theo."

Maddox chuckled. "Dee texted me hourly the first time I left with Brayden. She's gotten better with Shelby."

"We miss Becca around here."

"She misses everyone, but she'll be back soon." With the nursery on-site, Becca planned to return to work in a few months. We could both be close to our son.

Aiden came in, Ava wrapped in one massive arm. He sat down, releasing her. She immediately scrambled over to Theo, cooing and clapping her little hands. Ava loved babies, and she especially loved Theo. She sat beside me, leaning close, talking fast to him. He watched her, his face serious, as if he understood whatever gibberish she was saying to him.

Maddox looked at Aiden. "You okay?"

He groaned. "Cami is ready for this baby to be born. So am I. She can't sleep, she can't get comfortable, the little guy is pushing at her all the time and using her bladder as a soccer ball." He shook his head. "Pretty sure I'm to blame for basically everything."

"You are," we all chimed in at once.

"How did I forget this part?"

Maddox laughed, shifting Shelby to his other arm. "Because they're worth it. You doing okay, Reid? Need anything?"

"Aside from a little more sleep, nope. We're good. Great, in fact."

Bentley settled Chloe into his arms, sliding the nipple of her bottle into her mouth. "Then I think the weekly meeting should commence. Everyone has their baby and is ready?"

I peered down at Theo. His eyes had drifted shut. Safe, peaceful, and loved in my arms. He'd sleep there the whole time.

I was good with that.

I grinned. "Ready."

Coming soon
Van—Vested Interest #5

Vince Morrison, known to his friends and coworkers as Van.

Good with his hands, be it crafting a piece of wood, playing his guitar, or pleasing a lover—he excels at them all.

Friendly, flirty, and talented, he's cool under pressure . . . and hot everywhere else.

But he keeps his heart closed, even as his interest and emotions are tested.

Olivia Rourke works alongside him at BAM.

Talented, private, and intriguing, she touches something inside him he can't deny.

He wants to know her. In every possible way.

He wants her to know him.

Her past cautions her to stay clear. Van is everything that she wants and exactly what she cannot have. She has someone else to think of who is more important.

Can either of them risk their hearts?

A NOTE FROM THE AUTHOR

Multiple Sclerosis touches so many families. There is much left to do for research to help those affected by this debilitating disease.

When I wrote the scenes that touched Sandy and Max so strongly, I couldn't have done it without the assistance of the lovely and caring Darlene Avery Ward. Thank you my friend.

Please support the Nations MS Society and the work they provide to MS patients in advocating and organizing events to raise awareness and funds for research.

https://www.nationalmssociety.org/

A WORD OF THANKS

AS ALWAYS, I have some people to thank. The ones behind the words that encourage and support. The people who make these books possible for so many reasons.

To my readers—thank you for taking a chance on this series. Your love of BAM makes me so happy!

Deb, thank you for all your hard work. As usual you make my words flow. Love you, my friend.

Lisa, thank you for your expertise and help. You rock it.

Beth, Shelly, Denise, Janett, Darlene, Carrie, Suzanne, Trina, Mae, Jeanne, Eli—I love you and am honored to call you friends. You humble me.

Caroline and Peggy, thank you for your support and keen eyes.

Flavia, thank you for your efforts and belief in my work. You made my world a brighter place.

Karen, my wonderful PA and friend. You hold my hand, keep me sane (okay, as sane as possible!), and encourage. You talk me off the ledge and yell at me when needed. It's not an easy job, but I appreciate all you do. There are not enough thanks, but there is a ton of love.

To all the bloggers, readers, and especially my review team. Thank you for everything you do. Shouting your love of books, posting, sharing—your recommendations keep my TBR list full, and the support you have shown me is so appreciated.

To my fellow authors who have shown me such kindness, thank you. I will follow your example and pay it forward.

To Christine—thank you for making my words look pretty!

Melissa—your covers make my books shine. Your teasers and banners are epic. Thank you!

My reader group, Melanie's Minions—love you all.

And, as always, My Matthew. My everything. Love you forever.

BOOKS BY
MELANIE MORELAND

Into the Storm
Beneath the Scars
Over the Fence
It Started with a Kiss
My Image of You

The Contract
The Baby Clause (Contract #2)

Bentley (Vested Interest #1)
Aiden (Vested Interest #2)
Maddox (Vested Interest #3)
Reid (Vested Interest #4)
Van (Vested Interest #5) ~ Coming Soon

ABOUT THE AUTHOR

NEW YORK TIMES/USA Today bestselling author Melanie Moreland, lives a happy and content life in a quiet area of Ontario with her beloved husband of twenty-nine-plus years and their rescue cat, Amber. Nothing means more to her than her friends and family, and she cherishes every moment spent with them.

While seriously addicted to coffee, and highly challenged with all things computer-related and technical, she relishes baking, cooking, and trying new recipes for people to sample. She loves to throw dinner parties, and enjoys travelling, here and abroad, but finds coming home is always the best part of any trip.

Melanie loves stories, especially paired with a good wine, and enjoys skydiving (free falling over a fleck of dust) extreme snowboarding (falling down stairs) and piloting her own helicopter (tripping over her own feet). She's learned happily ever afters, even bumpy ones, are all in how you tell the story.

Melanie is represented by Flavia Viotti at Bookcase Literary Agency. For any questions regarding subsidiary or translation rights please contact her at *flavia@bookcaseagency.com*

www.melaniemoreland.com

Made in the USA
Monee, IL
12 January 2022

88778632R00148